THE RED WITCH

ROBERT SANBORN

vinci
BOOKS

BY ROBERT SANBORN

League of the Moon

In Your Dreams

The Red Witch

Blood, Magic & Mercy

Black Magick & Envy

Soul of the Witch

This one's for my mother, Geraldine L. Crombie.
Because you love everyone unconditionally.

Vinci Books

vinci-books.com

Published by Vinci Books Ltd in 2025

1

Copyright © Robert Sanborn - 2022

The author has asserted their moral right to be identified as the author of this work in accordance with the Copyright, Designs and Patents Act 1988. This work is a work of fiction. Names, characters, places and incidents are the product of the author's imagination or are used fictitiously. Any resemblance to actual persons, living or dead, places and incidents is entirely coincidental.

All rights reserved. No part of this publication may be copied, reproduced, distributed, stored in any retrieval system, or transmitted in any form or by any means, including photocopying, recording, or other electronic or mechanical methods, nor used as a source for any form of machine learning including AI datasets, without the prior written permission of the publisher.

The publisher and the author have made every effort to obtain permissions for any third party material used in this book and to comply with copyright law. Any queries in this respect should be brought to the attention of the publisher and any omissions will be corrected in future editions.

A CIP catalogue record for this book is available from the British Library.

Paperback ISBN: 9781036705428

Printed and bound in Great Britain by Clays Ltd, Elcograf S.p.A.

"By the pricking of my thumbs, something wicked this way comes."

— A witch from *Macbeth* by William Shakespeare

CHAPTER 1
HOMECOMING

Henry watched the moon rise full and bright above the Atlantic Ocean from the seventh-floor hospital room. Its silvery trail danced atop the lazy waves of the dark water. Sunset had arrived only thirty minutes before and now he, Joanne, and little Delilah made their way down through the Salem Hospital, across the parking lot, and into the sultry August night. They were ecstatic. Delilah was healthy, happy, and amazingly *quiet* for a newborn. Both were thinking the same thing at the same time—*probably won't last.*

The trip from the hospital to their apartment on Lafayette Street took five minutes. It was a Sunday night in August in Salem, after all. Not like it would be when the calendar hit October in a couple of months. Salem is the Halloween capital of the world. Every year, thousands from around the globe come to take in "Haunted Happenings," the town's annual month-long Halloween celebration.

Henry pulled the red Toyota Camry up to the curb in front of their apartment. He ran around to the passenger side, opened the door, took the baby from Joanne, and held out his hand. She looked at it, a crooked grin on her face.

"I have a baby and now you're Captain Chivalry?" She shooed his hand away. "I'm okay, Band-Aid boy, just concentrate on getting her into the apartment in one piece."

He loved it when she called him Band-Aid boy. It was her funny pet name for him, inspired by his profession as an ER nurse, and it always made him laugh.

Henry did as instructed and Jo followed behind, carrying two duffel bags full of stuff from the hospital. They entered the lobby, took the elevator up to the second floor, exited, and ran straight into their neighbor, Mrs. Greenblatt. And, again, both had the same thought at the same time. *Does this woman ever sleep?*

"The prodigal son returns! Faith and begorrah!" she said.

"Hi, Mrs. G. How are you?" Henry asked.

"I'm fine, Henry and Mrs. Henry. And I see all those nights I heard the two of you bumpin' uglies has finally paid off! Let me see that little bundle o' joy!"

Henry and Jo exchanged amused glances, and he brought Delilah over to Mrs. Greenblatt. The look of pure joy as she looked over their baby was completely out of place on her usually stern face. And the cooing noises and baby talk she made as she touched Delilah's nose and ran a finger along her cheek... they just didn't sound right coming from her. To Henry, it was like hearing the sound of a smart car engine coming from a dump truck—just wrong. He smiled anyway.

"Alright, I'll let you two go. It's been so many years since there's been a little one anywhere near a place I call home. Brings back so many wonderful memories."

Henry noticed Mrs. Greenblatt getting misty around the

eyes. He didn't want to embarrass her, so he smiled, took his little girl back, and said goodnight.

Jo was already turning the corner and heading toward their apartment. That's when she screamed. Henry knew whatever caused that scream had to be bad. Jo wasn't the type to scare easily. And yeah, it was bad.

Written on the door, in what Henry was pretty sure was not red ink, were three words: *Delilah Is Ours!* And hanging from a spike buried into the eyehole of the door was an effigy that could only be one person.

The doll was dressed in a purple cloak, bathed in smears of the blood used to write the message on the door. Its kinky, dirty-blonde hair was a crude match for its human counterpart's. The hanging figure of Wanda Heinze, leader of the *Foedere In Luna* (aka League of the Moon), sent chills down Henry's spine.

"Who in the fuck do these people think they are?" Jo asked.

Well, Henry thought, *she didn't exactly stay scared for long.* He knew his wife pretty well, considering they'd been together for roughly a year. And he knew the dumb bastards who decided they were going to pick a fight with Jo, especially threatening her baby—well, he actually felt a tinge of fear. For them. Joanne Andersen Trank was not one to take a threat lying down. God help them.

Mrs. Greenblatt shuffled around the corner, stopping short when she saw the new decoration on the Tranks' front door.

"What in the hell is that all about, Henry?" asked Mrs. G.

"It's a long story, Mrs. G. But I don't have time at the moment to get into it. Have you seen anyone in the building today that didn't belong here?"

"I've been sleeping most of the afternoon, Henry. And you know me, I don't need a ton of sleep."

Truer words were never spoken, Henry thought.

"You know, I couldn't swear to it, but I have a fuzzy memory of hearing whispers outside my door not long before I fell asleep. But I don't recall actually lying down on my blasted couch. And I wouldn't even *think* about *sleeping* on that lumpy piece o' shite. No, something ain't right. I would have seen or heard whoever did that." She pointed at the door.

Henry believed her. He'd been living in the building for almost a year and a half, and he'd rarely been able to slip by Mrs. Greenblatt unnoticed. He seriously doubted someone who didn't belong here would escape her all-seeing eyes.

Shit just wasn't adding up... or maybe it was. Solomon Dobson was dead and gone, but the *Order Immortalis,* his group of "Immortal Asshats," as Wanda called them, were alive and well, and more than likely beyond pissed at the loss of their leader.

Yeah, it didn't take a rocket scientist to figure out who'd done this. But knowing didn't change things. He knew the group responsible for the threat, but that didn't narrow it down to any one person. There was no telling how many members of the group still existed in Salem or around the world.

The apartment building's manager lived off-site. Henry planned to call him as soon as they put Delilah to bed.

Mrs. Greenblatt said her goodnights to Jo and Henry and headed back up the hallway. Henry and Jo slipped inside their door and bolted it from the other side. They put Delilah in her crib and stood over her for a few minutes until she fell asleep. Both parents, though they didn't know it, were thinking the same thing. *I hope they can't get to her in her dreams.* It was how they'd tried to get to Henry when he'd arrived in Salem back in July 2018.

The *Order Immortalis* were skilled in traveling the astral plane and using it for whatever ends they deemed necessary. They wouldn't hesitate to invade the dreams of an infant if it meant they could get what they wanted.

Once the baby was asleep, Jo and Henry went into the living room, unpacked, and put away the items from the hospital. With that done, they settled down on the couch. Each with a mug of coffee.

Henry pulled out his cell phone and called the building manager.

"Gino, it's Henry Trank. How are you?"

"I'm good, Henry! How are you, the wife, and the new bambino?"

"We're all good, Gino. Thanks. Hey, listen..." Henry told him about the mess he'd found on his front door when he came home.

"You gotta be shittin' me!"

"Nope. It's got us all worried. Mrs. G. included."

"Mrs. G. didn't see him? I find that hard to believe!" Gino said.

"So did I. But she said she heard some whispering outside her door before she fell asleep on her couch. There are two things wrong with that statement..."

"Yeah, I know. You don't have to tell me. I've been the building super for a long time, man. There ain't no way she fell asleep in the middle of the day without some fishy stuff happening, and she would never sleep on that crappy old couch. I believe she calls it the *'lumpy ole piece o' shite,'* or something like that."

Henry asked, "Do you have the video feed available over there, Gino? I would *really* like to see who the hell is threatening us."

"I'm at home right now, Henry. But I can log in from here. Gimme a sec."

Henry waited for a couple of minutes until Gino came back on the line.

"Okay. It's seven twenty-six right now. How long you been home, Henry?"

"Half an hour... maybe a bit more."

He could hear Gino clicking and typing away over the phone.

"Son of a bitch!"

"What?" Henry asked.

"About 3:13 in the afternoon, there's a guy in a black hoodie. Only it ain't like a regular lookin' hoodie. It kinda goes down to his ankles. The idiot isn't even wearing shoes. He's standing in front of Mrs. G's door; he's pulling out some kinda pouch and putting it on the floor. Looks like he's chanting or praying over it or something. He's opening the pouch and spreading some shit all over the floor right in front of her threshold... Looks like powder, or salt maybe? He's knocking on the door from his knees, and then he blows on the powder. And now Mrs. G is opening the door."

Henry was getting nervous. This was *not good*.

"She's talking to him, only she ain't acting like Mrs. G.—looks like some kinda zombie or something. Now she's nodding at him and then just shuts the door. Must've been when she went to lie down on the couch that we *both* know she never sleeps on. Hold on, Henry, I gotta switch to the camera aimed at your door."

Henry held. He was getting that nervous feeling in the

belly. Jo watched Henry—a mix of concern and anger on her face.

"Okay, Henry, he's reaching into his pocket, he's pulling out a little hammer and now he's bangin' on your door. Looks like he put a big nail right in the eyehole. He's reaching back into the pouch and writing with his finger on your door. Is that blood?"

"Yeah, it's blood, Gino. Keep going."

"I can see what he wrote. You call the cops yet, Henry?"

"If I thought the cops could help us, I would have already called them, Gino."

"Yeah, but..."

"Trust me, Gino, the cops can't help. But I need to know what's on the rest of the tape. Please, Gino."

"Okay, he looks like he's hangin' something on the spike. It looks like a doll. Now he's reaching into the bag again. He just rubbed blood on the doll. He's closing up the big pouch now. He's turning around to leave and..."

About ten seconds went by and the line stayed silent.

"Gino, you okay? Gino?"

"Um, Henry. I know why you can't call the cops now."

Henry knew the reason he couldn't call the cops. But he wasn't about to tell Gino why. So, he found it really interesting Gino had figured this out all on his own. He waited. Finally, Gino spoke.

"It's kinda hard to give them a description of the perp when the perp doesn't have a face."

"You mean it's blurred out from the camera?"

"No, the camera works fine. It's 1080p, as a matter of fact. I can see the lint on the guy's hoodie. He doesn't have a face, Henry. It's. Not. There."

CHAPTER 2
MERCY

The hooded figure stood outside Wanda's Wicca'd Emporium on Essex Street in Salem. The night was warm, humid, and quiet. Few people walked the streets at this hour on a Sunday. Businesses closed earlier today than the rest of the week. The being in the cloak lurked across the street in the shadows and just out of reach from the streetlights—watching and learning.

The message was delivered to the Tranks. Now it was time to pay their leader a visit. Time to exact a little revenge for the loss of the leader of the *Order Immortalis*, Solomon Dobson. Although the being outside the shop of the white witch knew him by his real name, Inanis.

He chuckled when he thought of the name Inanis. It literally meant *void*. The place Inanis was supposedly sent. The being in the hood had his doubts, though. If pressed, he couldn't honestly tell anyone why he believed Solomon still existed. It was just a feeling in his soul. He chuckled low. His *soul!* If they only knew! Nobody knew, though. And he liked it that way... for now.

The lights of the shop were still on. It was closed, but not empty. He could feel the power of the witch all the way out here on the street. Hatred consumed him when he thought of her. And revenge was so close! But patience was the watchword of the day. To confront her head-on was the errand of a fool. And as much as he revered Inanis, part of him despised his leader for the foolish pride he'd shown when he thought he could defeat Wanda in a head-on assault. She'd proved more than equal to the task. Indeed, she'd lured him into the very trap Inanis had assumed he'd set for her.

He studied the shop. Wanda's Wicca'd Emporium, when viewed through learned eyes, was a fortress protected by powerful white magic. If you knew what you were looking for, you could see the protections she'd set as though they were neon signs. To the ignorant—the gold-flaked letters, the broom, the half-moon with the black cat at its bottom— all appeared as innocent decoration, a clever display of signage. To those who knew, to those who could *see*, they camouflaged protective sigils. The term *sigil* is derived from the Latin *sigillum*, meaning "seal." It's an expression of a desired outcome. And her desire was quite clear to him and those like him: *Keep out.*

He smiled—well, at least on the inside. Soon, old woman. Soon.

∽

WANDA SAT in the middle of the gold-flaked pentacle emblazoned on the gleaming obsidian floor in the back room of her store. She plopped down into the black leather beanbag chair at the pentacle's center. Time to relax after a busy day. She'd done several tarot card readings, and she was spent. The amount of energy it takes to read for so many wonderful and inquisitive souls can leave a practicing witch drained beyond belief by the end of the day. And that was the state she was in now—happy exhaustion.

The smell of herbal tea hit her nose, and she sipped the hot drink with care. Chamomile tea was how Wanda liked to unwind. Barely two sips in, she felt it. Something pulled her toward the front of the store. She'd learned a long time ago not to ignore intuition. Wanda sighed, hauled herself up from the beanbag chair (not as easily as she used to), and made her way to the front of the store.

Mercy Glass, her newest employee, was tidying up the shop. She brandished a feather duster and attacked the shelves holding a myriad of multicolored crystals.

Mercy was one of the most meticulous employees she'd ever hired. In the few months she'd been working at Wanda's Wicca'd Emporium, Mercy had to be guided very little, if at all, in the shop's running. It was not exactly a surprise to Wanda; she knew Mercy practiced witchcraft. For a new employee, however, she was uncannily aware of the ins and outs of the business end of things. Almost as if Wanda's old friend Delilah were still here, running the shop with her. She was *that* good.

"Mercy, honey, it's late. You should get on home now. The place looks fantastic!"

"Oh, no problem, Ms. Heinze. I just wanted to clear the dust from those obsidian pieces. No matter how much I clean them, they never stay that way."

"Mercy, it's Wanda. *Please* call me Wanda. You've been here how long? Three months now? Give or take a week or two?"

"One hundred eleven days, to be exact."

Wanda said, "That's more than enough time to qualify both of us to be on a first-name basis, sweetie."

Mercy looked uncomfortable.

"What's the matter, honey?"

Mercy wrung her hands. "It's just not the way I was brought up. I was taught to respect"—she paused, apology writ large on her face—"my elders."

Wanda broke into a grin.

"Mercy, I'm definitely your elder, no doubt about that. And I get *and* respect the way you were brought up. It's obvious your parents did a wonderful job—"

"Ms. Heinze? Wanda?"

Wanda stopped mid-sentence. She held up a finger, a polite shushing of Mercy. Mercy stayed silent and watched.

Wanda stepped around Mercy and crept toward the front of the store. She flipped the lights to off, her bangle bracelets softly clattering. Darkness enveloped the store, save for the blueish-silver glow of LED streetlights leaching through the multi-paned picture window at the store's front. She couldn't see whoever or whatever was out there, but she could feel it.

Wanda concentrated on a spot directly across from the store. Through her eyes she saw only the dark-green, cotton-ball glow of leaves reflecting the streetlights. She could feel the presence hiding within them, just beyond her vision, and sensed a malevolent intelligence, probing—looking for a weakness, a way in. Wanda faced it for a long, silent moment.

Mercy moved without a sound and took position to Wanda's left, training her eyes in the same direction. Both witches could feel it now, though Wanda was oblivious to all things not related to the spot she was watching. And then, quiet and steady, Mercy spoke.

"It watches the store. It knows it can't get in yet, but it's confident it will find a way. It hates you, Wanda. It wants you dead. It wants revenge."

It startled Wanda when Mercy spoke. She pried her eyes from the spot across the street and toward her employee. What she saw shocked her. Mercy's eyes rolled back to the whites. A trickle of blood, black in the soft light, rolled its way from her left nostril and made acquaintance with her upper lip. Both of Mercy's arms were held slightly away from her sides. Her palms faced out, her fingers splayed, and her feet left the floor. Wanda watched in awe as they ever so slightly rose above it. Not a lot, but enough to see she had risen from the broad planks of wood that comprised the shop's walking space.

Wanda put her hand, gentle as she could, in Mercy's left palm. When they connected, a mild and not unpleasant jolt of energy transferred into Wanda's body. In that moment, she saw through Mercy's eyes, though it was not exactly what normal, everyday vision looked like. If Wanda had needed to describe to someone what she saw, it would be akin to a thermal camera, much like the shots you'd see in the ghost hunting shows on television or YouTube. Only, Wanda knew better than that. She was seeing the aura of the being across the street. It was red and black—murky and disturbing. It was an aura of hatred and anger. And it fled when it sensed the two witches homing in on it.

Wanda released Mercy's hand. Mercy's feet reunited with the floor and, as Wanda went to turn on the lights, Mercy leaned her back against the counter and exhaled. She looked unsteady. Wanda rushed behind the counter, grabbed hold of the office chair from behind the register, and wheeled it over to where Mercy stood. She guided Mercy into the chair, steadied her, then ran into the bathroom and grabbed some tissue for Mercy's bloody nose. She went to take the tissue, but Wanda nudged her hand away and tended to the leaky nostril. She smiled a weak thank you and let her boss take care of her.

"Well, my dear. It appears there is more to you than meets the eye."

Again, Mercy offered a weak smile and began explaining herself, but Wanda would have none of it.

"No talking just yet, honey. Let's take care of this bloody nose, then you can tell me all about what just happened."

Nodding gratefully, she let Wanda finish.

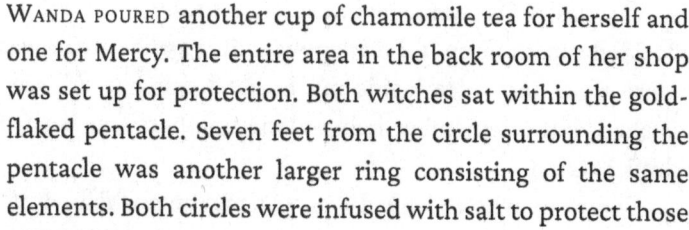

Wanda poured another cup of chamomile tea for herself and one for Mercy. The entire area in the back room of her shop was set up for protection. Both witches sat within the gold-flaked pentacle. Seven feet from the circle surrounding the pentacle was another larger ring consisting of the same elements. Both circles were infused with salt to protect those within from evil.

The belief that salt could protect one from evil spirits or influences dated back centuries and was used in many religions, not just witchcraft. That Wanda was still alive, indeed all the members of the *Foedere In Luna* were alive, was the only proof she needed it worked. It was why she took no chances tonight and had brought Mercy to the room.

"Feeling better, honey?" Wanda asked.

"Much. Thank you, Ms. ... thank you, Wanda."

Wanda smiled at Mercy's use of her first name.

"See? That wasn't so hard. Now, what just happened to you out there?"

Mercy took a deep breath.

"It all started last year. Myself and a bunch of friends went to a quarry to go swimming. It was at the end of July and it had been over ninety-five degrees for, like, a week straight. If I had to guess, the ledge we were all jumping from was maybe fifty-five or sixty feet straight down to the water. Everyone had already jumped in and it was my turn. I was alone up there, and I don't mind telling you, I was not all that thrilled about doing it. And the little voice inside my head, the voice I now listen to regularly, was screaming at me not to do it. And I *remember* deciding not to."

"That sounds absolutely terrifying."

"It was! What happened next is a blur. Even though I'd decided not to jump, I did it anyway. It was like there was more than one voice inside my head. It felt like I'd been pushed, but I remember being alone up there—at least, I think I was.

"Anyway, when I leaped—or was maybe pushed—from the cliff, my body went every which way, and my arms and legs seemed to be under the control of someone else. I flailed all the way down and then hit the water flat." Mercy clapped her hands together. "Just like those belly flops you see on all the YouTube videos. Except I'd done it from about five times higher than most of those. I hit that water so hard it knocked me unconscious."

"Oh, my God!" Wanda said.

Mercy nodded. "Yep, and the worst part of it was, no one realized I wasn't coming back up."

"How is that possible?" Wanda asked.

"Because all my friends were high or drunk. They all laughed and just continued on drinking and partying. They must have assumed I would pop back up. No big deal. I still can't believe it, but it's true. Then, light finally dawned on Marblehead, and the guy I was seeing, who left his lighter in my purse, asked where I was. Everyone assumed I swam over to the beach and was chillin' in the sun. That's when they finally realized I was nowhere to be found.

"I don't know how long I was under the water, but I was told it was close to seven minutes by the time they got me to shore. I died, Wanda. I didn't have a pulse when they started CPR on me."

Wanda reached out and took Mercy's hand in hers. Mercy squeezed back and held on.

"I don't know exactly how to describe what happened next, but... as strange as it sounds, it was wonderful. I'd never felt so at peace, so content. I saw the tunnel everyone talks about. I saw silhouettes of people walking through mist that was lit by a light from the end of the tunnel. No faces, though. I didn't recognize anyone, but I had the feeling there was someone there with me. Someone who knew me. And whoever it was, they cared deeply about me. I cried, but not because I was sad or afraid. I was crying because I felt completely and utterly loved and understood."

The bottoms of Wanda's caring blue eyes were brimming with tears, threatening to spill over at any second. Mercy's eyes were in the same state.

"Then, a voice came to me out of the mist. It was soft and gentle. She said, 'It's okay to let go. Go into the light.' But I didn't want to die. There was so much more I wanted to do! Whoever said those words was *not* happy with my choice—I could *feel* it. The voice went away then, and others took its place. I think it was the voices of the EMTs, maybe? Who knows? That was when I started falling. It was like I was crashing back to earth. And right before I woke up on the beach, something dark flashed before me. It touched me on the forehead, then disappeared. Ever since that day, things like what you saw up front have happened on occasion. Although nothing quite as dramatic."

"What did you want to come back to earth for? Was there a clear reason?" Wanda asked.

"I think I'm here to protect someone. Maybe you? I feel like I've done it before."

"Done what? Protect me?" Wanda asked.

Mercy nodded.

The first feelings of recognition stirred in Wanda. She remembered the saying from the AA meetings she attended every Tuesday night at St. Theresa's church basement. It rang true now, as it had countless times in her life already. *Your Higher Power puts people in your life for a reason*. She sent a silent prayer of thanks to Hecate.

"Well, thanks for listening to me ramble, Wanda. I better get going."

"Going? I don't think that's such a great idea tonight, honey. Not with whatever the hell that thing is out there still on the loose. You can stay here. I've got an air mattress I can set up for you. You can sleep right in here."

"But I have an early class in the morning, at the U."

Wanda knew the answer before she asked the question, but she asked anyway.

"What class are you taking in the morning, honey?"

"It's called"—she searched the ceiling for an answer—"Demons, Demigods..."

"...and Greater Mortals," Wanda said.

"That's right! How did you know?"

Wanda smiled and told her all about her friend, Dr. Archibald Love.

CHAPTER 3
ALWAYS A CRITIC!

Dr. Archibald Love sat in a plush leather chair behind his disaster area of a desk. Strewn across its top were dozens of photographs. Each picture was of a different supernatural entity. He was organizing the photos into a cogent display for his students in the Demons, Demigods, and Greater Mortals class.

Dr. Love's Parapsychology course at Salem University was one of its most popular courses. His lectures were always packed and his students eager to soak up his knowledge on all things paranormal. Of course, this bred jealousy among the other faculty at the school. Where Archie always spoke in front of packed lecture halls and students listening with rapt attention, most of the other disciplines were lucky to be at half capacity. And of the students who showed up for their classes in other subjects, most were more interested in what was on their iPhone or Android screens than what was on the screen at the front.

This jealousy was no more evident than in his relationship with the head of the physics department, Dr. Darren

Biltmore. In Archie's learned opinion, Biltmore was a douche bag of galactic proportions. For fuck's sake, the guy's initials were DB. Talk about appropriate! *And today*, Archie thought, *would send that colossal ass hat into new realms of douchebaggery*.

He had just about put Biltmore out of his mind when his phone rang. It was Annie, his receptionist.

"Archie, got DB on line two. You wanna talk to him or should I blow him off?"

Archie rolled his eyes to the ceiling, leaned back in his chair, blew out a long breath, and said, "God, just what I need right now. Put him on, Annie. Might as well get it over with."

"Okay, Arch. Remember, deep breaths."

"Thanks, Annie."

Click.

"Hello, Dr. Biltmore, what can I do for you today?"

"Good morning, Love. I noticed you filed for more funding for that class of yours. What's it called? Demons, Devil Dogs, and Dildos, something like that?"

"Yes, that's exactly it. It's perfect for you too, DB! Given your proclivity for talking out of your ass, we have the dildo. And for those times you just can't shut up, we can plug your pie hole with a Devil Dog. And finally, we will summon a demon to usher you to hell, where there will be a conspicuous scarcity of milk with which to wash the Devil Dog down. So please, by all means, stop by!"

"You know, that was a remarkable retort for someone in the *esteemed* field of Parapsychology."

Archie pictured the idiot making quote fingers.

"What do you want, DB?"

"I want you to rescind your request for funding. There

are a lot more legitimate disciplines that need the money. A lot more 'real world' applications those funds could be applied to instead of this goddamned mumbo-jumbo you keep filling these kids' heads with."

"Yes, I suppose that's true. I'll tell you what, DB. When you guys can actually prove what quantum gravity is, I'll be more than happy to release that funding to you. Until then, you just send those kids over from your class who are, undoubtedly, bored out of their minds, and they can take in something that's actually interesting. Oh, wait, can't do that. No room in my lecture halls, they're all full."

"Love, you *do* realize that parapsychology is the burger and fries of the science world, right?'

"Beats the hell out of being the tofu burger. Have a nice day, DB."

"I'll get that funding from you, Love. This is *not* over."

"Knock yourself out."

Click.

Just another day in the life. Archie gathered up the photos and stuffed them into his briefcase. It would be another fly-by-the-seat-of-your-pants lecture. No problem. He'd done it a million times. Some of those lectures turned out to be the best ones he'd ever done. *Ordo Ab Chao*—Latin for Order out of Chaos. It was one of his personal mottoes. He reached out and tapped the foot of the triple-goddess statue of Hecate sitting in the only uncluttered area of his desk. She always brought him strength.

Archibald Love was not one to dwell on the negative. The conversation with Biltmore was quickly in his rear-view mirror and fading fast as he made his way down the hallway toward room 111. By the time he opened the door to the lecture hall, the conversation with Biltmore was filed away in his mind. Not forgotten but put in the file marked "nuisance" to be dealt with when the time came.

He opened the door to the lecture hall and stepped through. It was the standard lecture hall you'd see on any of a thousand different campuses around the country. Tiered seating, narrow at the bottom with expanding rows leading to the top and forming a half-bowl, focusing all attention toward the front.

It made Archie think of the studies done on the psychology of seating in lecture halls. Almost without fail, students chose seating that revealed their levels of anxiety, their capacity to focus, their willingness to engage others, and even who to study with based on similar ability. Except for the times when similar abilities were not compatible.

These things mattered when dealing with parapsychology. Most of the students who came to his class (whether they knew it or not) had some type of psychic ability. And he found it fascinating that those of similar ability, say someone with empathic tendencies, would separate themselves from other empaths. He'd always assumed they would attract each other. And for sure they did, from time to time. But relationships between two empaths, unless founded on solid footing and well-defined boundaries, almost always crashed and burned.

Strangely enough, he'd found empaths drawn like magnets to narcissistic people. The adage, opposites attract, was so true with empaths and narcissists. It pained him when he saw these relationships bloom in one of his classes. Nine times out of ten, the empath wound up with the short end of the stick. He should know. He'd gotten out of one of those relationships not too far in the distant past. Archie pushed Mondra Tibbets from his mind. She, too, was a subject he had also put in the "nuisance" file for later.

He recognized one of his new students sitting in the front row. Wanda's new employee, Mercy Glass, did not look good. In fact, she looked like an emotional Mack truck had run her over. He made a mental note to talk to her after class. She was such a great kid, and he wanted to reach out to her and find out what was wrong. Or maybe he would just get in touch with Wanda and find out what was up. Archie mulled it over and chose the latter. Better to get the scoop from Wanda first.

He walked over to the left of the giant display screen and dimmed the lights. The room was silent. He opened his briefcase, removed an image, and placed it on the projector stand. Archie knew about PowerPoint presentations, but he was old school.

On the giant screen, for all to see, was the silhouette of a figure in black. It was a figure Archie was quite familiar with, since it had tried to kill his son and daughter-in-law less than a year ago. It was the image of a demon named Chesrule. This particular demon was a shapeshifter. When busy trying to kill his son Henry and Henry's wife, Joanne, it had morphed back and forth between its demon form and that of a Rottweiler, depending on what the situation called for. And it would have succeeded too, if not for the foresight and cunning of his best friend in the world, Wanda Heinze.

Archie then placed the image of a Rottweiler next to the one of Chesrule. He asked the class, "Can any of you tell me what these two images have in common?"

There was silence for a few moments, and then a voice floated down from one of the upper rows of the lecture hall.

"Um, they're both black silhouettes?"

"Thank you, Captain Obvious," Archie said. "Care to elaborate, young man?"

"I don't really see what they have in common, sir. One's some dark, evil lookin' dude and the other is just a dog."

"Hard to argue with that," Archie said. "But try to use your imagination. Try to think of a way they might relate. Remember, this is a class on parapsychology and the supernatural. Jumping to odd conclusions is *not* frowned upon here."

A voice from another area of the hall, "One is a servant and the other its master?"

"That's better. Wrong, but better. You're starting to get the feel for how I want you to think about things this semester. Anyone else?"

Mercy Glass raised her hand.

"You can speak freely here, Miss Glass. No need to raise your hand."

"I think they may be one and the same, Dr. Love."

"And by that you mean, Miss Glass?"

"I mean, the dog and the demon are both one being—a shapeshifter."

Snickers and soft laughter floated down from the gallery. Archie couldn't see it in the dark, but he was sure Mercy was blushing.

The immaturity of some of his students perturbed him. And he decided he would make them feel a bit of it back.

"For those foolish enough to laugh at that answer, please take out your cell phones, make sure they're off, and look at the reflection in the glass."

Puzzled looks sprang from the faces around the room, but the students did as asked.

"Now you know what an idiot looks like. *Mercy* is right.

And not only that, this particular entity is also real. And it is exactly what miss Glass said it was, a shapeshifter. But, fortunately for all of us, it no longer exists. My son killed it, and ultimately, its master later that same day!"

Murmurs of disbelief rolled from the front of the hall to the back. Archie expected as much. And maybe he was being presumptuous about the open-mindedness of his students. It *was* a lot for them to swallow, especially on the first day of class in a new semester. But he also had another goal in mind for this year.

Archie was not above using his class to draw out his enemies. God knew this town was filled with plenty. One of them was in the room right now. He just couldn't tell who it was yet. But he could feel it. The moment he'd announced his son was the one who'd killed the demons, he felt a searing stab of anger shoot toward him from within the hall. He knew the *Order Immortalis* had infiltrated his workplace. He'd have been more surprised if they hadn't.

Dr. Love looked down from the raised platform at the front of the room to the first row. Mercy Glass looked back at him. Her eyes were wide with surprise and her posture was rigid and alert. She felt it too. It didn't surprise Archie— Mercy, like himself, was an empath. Someone in this room was quite unhappy about the annihilation of Chesrule and his master.

Archie noted her reaction and planned on asking her about it later. He made his way over to the light switch and flipped it back on, casually scanning the faces of the students, looking for anyone who seemed uncomfortable or perhaps angry. No one fit the bill. Whoever had reacted emotionally to the announcement of his son's victory over the demon had quickly tamped down those feelings or had otherwise left the room.

CHAPTER 4
A HAND FOR HENRY

Monday morning came much too fast for Henry's liking. He'd been up and down all night with the baby. As predicted, she didn't stay quiet for long. He did the best he could to calm her down and get her back to sleep. About an hour later, it would start all over again. He handled it like a trooper, but he really had little choice. The hours of labor Joanne had gone through had wiped her out, and there was no way he was going to let her handle Delilah on the first night. Jo needed rest—badly. Besides, he wanted to stay up and keep an eye on both of them after the incident with the faceless creep in the hood.

When 7:00 a.m. rolled around, Henry was sitting on the couch, Delilah in the crook of his left arm, her bottle in his right hand, and a towel on his shoulder in case his new daughter yacked up.

Joanne came out of the bedroom, poured herself a cup of coffee, and sat on the edge of the table across from her husband and daughter. She said nothing, just watched the two of them with a smile on her face. She sipped her coffee and closed her eyes, savoring that first taste.

Jo was about to say something when Henry held up a finger in front of his lips, got up as gently as he could, walked into the baby's room, and returned—sans child.

"Weren't you just about to feed her?" Jo asked.

"I was, then I noticed she was asleep. And I was *not* gonna take another chance on her waking up again. This is the fifth time since last night I've been up with her. I gotta take my shots when I get them." He smiled.

"Thanks for letting me sleep." She bent and kissed him. Then curled up on the couch next to him.

Henry said, "Thank God for paternity leave. If I had to go into work today, there would be a lot of innocent life at risk."

"Speaking of that, where did you leave off with Gino?"

"You heard it all on the phone last night. He hasn't gotten back to me yet. To tell you the truth, I don't think he believes in what he saw. And who could blame him?"

"So, what do *you* think it was?" Jo asked.

"We both know I'm the wrong guy to ask about that. And we both know who I'm going to go talk to once I get a nap. It's seven now. I'm gonna head in to bed for about three or four hours, and then I'm going over to Wanda's shop."

Joanne nodded. "Yeah, I figured as much. When in doubt..."

∾

HENRY HOPPED in the Camry for the five-minute ride down to Wanda's Wicca'd Emporium. He parked at a meter in front of Rockafellas, his favorite restaurant in Salem. He paid for the parking meter through the app on his phone, hit the alarm on the Camry, and made his way on foot the rest of the way down Essex Street.

He loved everything about this area of town—the brick-covered street, the various new age shops like Omen and The Magic Parlor. Then you had the Witch History Museum right across from Angelica of the Angels, Witch City Ink for the tattoo-loving crowd (he wondered if that was where Jo got her tattoo), and diagonally across from that, Wanda's Wicca'd Emporium.

He opened the door to Wanda's shop and was hit by the smell of dragon's blood incense. He loved the smell of it. Ever since he'd met Joanne, and whenever he smelled it, almost all he could think about was her—almost. The scent now represented so much more. It brought back the memories of all that had happened from July, when he'd moved to Salem, and right up to the pre-dawn hours of Halloween 2018, when Henry, Joanne, Wanda, Dr. Love, and Henry's mom had battled for their lives against a foe that was *much* more than he appeared to be.

He stood at the front of the shop and took in the items for sale. To his left were bookshelves filled with new age titles, books about witchcraft, wizardry, tarot cards, how to read tarot cards, spell books, and numerous other tomes related to the craft.

Unlike his first time coming to this shop, he actually understood much more about what he was looking at. And that was thanks to Joanne and Wanda. They had helped him immensely over the last year in reclaiming the power he'd once had in a time and place long ago. He was just starting to understand how to use it.

To his right there were glass cases filled with statuary to the gods and goddess, placards and charms adorned with pentacles, black cast-iron cauldrons, mortar and pestle sets, and hundreds of jars filled with different herbs and concoctions. And dead set in the middle of the room was the crystal display case. It was a polished, wooden, hexagonal-shaped case. Its top was a bed of black velvet with inlays for all kinds of charms, bracelets, rings, earrings, and various pieces of Wicca related jewelry. Suspended above the case, pendulums hung from chains, reflecting the bright display lights set into the beams above them. They sent sparks of brilliant, prismatic light lazily about the room's walls. It was like Wanda's own little slice of Oz. He loved it here.

He was so lost in his thoughts and taking in all the little details of Wanda's shop that he never noticed Mercy Glass standing at the register a mere five feet from him.

"Can I help you, sir?" she said.

He jumped.

"Sorry." Her face reddened. "Didn't mean to startle you."

"No, no. I was just lost in my own little world." He reached out his hand. "I'm Henry Trank."

"Hi, Henry, I'm Mercy Glass."

When she took his hand, Henry was surprised how small it felt in his. And even more surprised at the amount of firmness she packed into her handshake, causing him to examine her a bit more closely.

Mercy Glass was beautiful, he thought. She was about five feet tall, with a compact frame—a dancer or a gymnast's body. She had platinum-blonde hair streaked with black highlights, giving it an odd, three-dimensional effect. Her hazel eyes were intense and ringed with black around the edges of the iris. They almost looked like costume contact lenses. Maybe they were, but he didn't think so. And Mercy's eyes were brimming with intelligence, but cast slightly downward in much the same way as Wanda's eyes—they made her look kind and sympathetic. Black ankle boots covered her feet, zipped at the sides and swallowing the bottom of her strategically torn blue jeans. She wore a plain, black, long sleeve T-shirt with the sleeves rolled up to her elbows, and a silver chain hanging halfway down the front of it, terminating in a silver pentacle.

He let go of her hand after what seemed like a few beats too long. Now it was Henry's turn to blush, and he immediately felt a pang of guilt as he thought about his beautiful wife at home. But why was he feeling guilty? It was just a handshake. At least, that's what he told himself. Later, he would understand why it was so much more than that.

"Um, is Wanda around?"

"Yes. I'll go get her for you. Be right back."

He watched her as she walked down the hall to get Wanda. Henry tried to stare at the top of her head as she went, but gravity seemed to pull his eyes lower. Again, he felt guilty. He grabbed a book from the shelf to his left, making a concerted effort to actually read the words on the page.

Mercy came back to the front of the store with Wanda trailing her.

"Good morning, Henry! How are you, sweetie?" Wanda walked right up to him and hugged him hard. After all they'd been through together, the attachment she felt toward Henry was like a mother to her son.

Henry let go of Wanda, smiled, and said, "I'm doing great. I just left Jo with the baby after pulling an all-nighter. I thought newborns were supposed to be kinda chill for a few weeks. She's full of energy!"

"Let's not forget who she is!" Wanda winked. She liked

Mercy, but the details of Delilah's birth were not, for the time being, something she thought Mercy needed to know, regardless of how much she liked the girl.

"So, what brings you to my shop of horrors on this fine Monday morning, honey?"

Henry flashed a quick look toward Wanda's back room, and they headed in that direction.

"I'll be in the back with Henry for a bit, Mercy."

"No problem, Ms.— Wanda. I can handle the front."

Wanda led Henry down the sigil-covered hallway, through the beaded door, and to the middle of the room. Henry followed behind, dragging two of the black leather beanbag chairs and the Market Basket plastic bag he'd brought with him from home. He plopped the chairs down in the middle of the inner circle.

"So, what's on your mind, sweetie?"

The smile faded from Henry's face.

Wanda said, "Uh oh."

"I brought Jo and Delilah home from the hospital yesterday. When we got to the apartment Mrs. G. was, of course, there to greet us."

"Really? Does that woman ever sleep?" Wanda asked.

"I think she's a vampire. Though I have seen her when the sun comes up too, so who knows for sure?"

Wanda smiled. She'd been to Henry's apartment to visit and help with Joanne as the baby's due date approached. She'd met and talked with Mrs. Greenblatt on many occasions. It amazed Henry how well the two of them had hit it off. Then he reminded himself that it was Wanda—you'd have to have a heart of stone not to love her. And everyone did.

Henry continued, "So, after Mrs. G. got acquainted with Delilah, I took her back and that's when Jo screamed."

"What? What happened?"

Henry told her about the blood-smeared words on the door. Wanda put a hand to her mouth in an "oh dear" gesture.

"That's pretty bad. There's more, though. Whoever this bastard was, he hung something from the door."

Henry reached into the Market Basket bag and pulled out the bloody effigy of Wanda hanging from a rope.

Wanda motioned for him to hand it to her. She studied it for a few moments. Henry watched her reaction. It was not what he expected.

"Ha ha ha. Isn't that funny? They did a pretty good job with the detail. Although the hair could have been better."

Wanda looked at Henry and said, "Don't worry, honey. I'm not gonna lose my shit over something like this. I'm more concerned about their apparent interest in the baby. I can handle myself just fine."

"I know, better than anyone, that you can. But there's more to the story." He described what Gino had revealed to him about the hooded figure on the tape.

Wanda took in that tidbit of information with a little more seriousness than she'd given the bloody doll. She cupped her right elbow in her left hand and stroked her chin, pondering the situation.

"What time of day was it when you discovered the message and the doll, Henry?"

"I'd have to say about seven thirty. Maybe eight, at the latest."

"We close at eight on Sunday night."

Henry looked at her, puzzled. "What's that got to do with it?"

"I think your friend in the hood paid us a visit after he left your place. We were closing up the shop, around eight thirtyish. Mercy was just tidying up the place and I was in the back, settling down after a very busy day of readings. Almost as soon as I felt comfy, I got a nagging feeling something wasn't right. And you know me, I don't ignore things like that."

Henry nodded as Wanda continued.

"Well, I felt something tugging me toward the front of the store. So, I followed my gut and went up front. Mercy and I were talking, and that's when I felt it."

She told him about the events that followed. Including Mercy's apparent abilities. It blew him away.

"She actually rose above the floor?"

"I shit you not, Henry. But that's not all. When I touched her hand, I could see through her eyes! It was the strangest damned thing I've ever felt. And that's saying a lot."

Henry thought back to the feeling he'd gotten when he'd shaken Mercy's hand.

"But I saw the bastard. Talk about a polluted aura! It sensed we could see him, and he took off pretty quickly after that. And, in my opinion, that's a good thing. It knows we *know* about it. *That* is a mistake."

"How so?" Henry asked.

"I think it was counting on the element of surprise. I could feel the rush of anger it felt as soon as we discovered it was there. You know how these creeps are—prideful to a fault. I probably wouldn't have known he was there or at the very least dismissed it as just some random negative energy. But neither it... nor I, for that matter, counted on Mercy. I don't know where she came from, Henry, but she's got some seriously powerful abilities. It's like I always say, your Higher Power works through people."

Henry nodded. It was hard to deny it, given the events of the recent past. When the coincidences keep piling up, sometimes you have to admit maybe there are forces beyond your control setting things in motion. What was the old saying? 'We make plans and God laughs.' Henry couldn't remember who said it, but it was an eternal truth.

"So, what do we do about it?" Henry asked.

Wanda thought about that for a few moments. "You know, I think it's time we bring your father into this. I'll call Archie and we can all meet here tonight. And bring Joanne and the baby. I don't want them staying by themselves at night."

CHAPTER 5
ON THE MOVE

He rested during the day. Night was fast approaching and the slumber he'd gotten was much needed. Events had unfolded almost according to plan—though he'd made a careless mistake. True, it was a mistake that could not have been foreseen, but a mistake nonetheless.

Assumptions in matters spiritual were how things went wrong. Inanis had assumed far too much when dealing with the witch, and that had cost him. A trickle of fear crept through the entity's entire being. Was he following the same path as his former master without knowing? But how could he have foreseen *the coupling*?

The girl's power he had seen firsthand, *and* it was much more than a common ability to read auras. The problem was the girl could transmit what she saw out of her own eyes into the eyes of another with a simple touch. And when that touch transmitted to a witch as powerful as the old woman —that was dangerous.

He rose from the hideaway. The tomb where he hid in

the daytime was at the very back end of the Salem cemetery. The current occupants wouldn't be a problem—souls long since departed seldom complained.

The sun pulled on its purple blanket, and the moon made its first hazy appearance on the horizon. There was much work to do, but before he could begin the night's work, he must feed.

Raising his nose, he sniffed. West. There was food west.

HENRY ARRIVED home just as the sun was going down. He told Joanne about what he'd discussed with Wanda.

"She wants all of us to come down to her shop *tonight*?" asked Jo.

"That's what she said. It's probably a good idea. We don't know what we're up against just yet. Archie is gonna be there, too."

"Have you talked to Archie lately?"

Henry was a little uncomfortable, still, with the idea that Dr. Archibald Love was his biological father. It had nothing to do with Archie himself. He thought he was a great guy—interesting to talk to, fun to be around. But the man who had raised him, Dominick Trank—*he* was, as far as Henry was concerned, his real dad. It still made him feel a little guilty when he would spend time with Archie, while he'd hardly seen Dominick at all over the past year. In an odd sort of balancing act, whether consciously or not, Henry had been avoiding Archie lately.

Joanne picked up on Henry's uneasiness. "Henry, you know it's not a competition, right? Neither one of them is jealous of the other, and they both love you... a lot."

"I know. And you're right... damn your intuitive ass," he said with a smile.

Jo smiled back and said, "It's only gonna get worse from here, Band-Aid boy. Remember, this is at least our second lifetime together."

"And you were the dude last time, Big Red."

She shot him a wicked grin. "Maybe I'll get a strap-on and teach you who's boss!"

Henry had been sipping a Diet Coke, which was now all over the coffee table, his shirt, and burning the inside of his nose. He wiped the soda from under his nose as he giggled and coughed.

Jo was laughing so hard tears formed in the corners of her eyes.

"You always get me when I'm drinking something!" Henry said.

He made a sudden leap, grabbed the back of her neck, and smeared the soda left on his face all over hers. Jo tried pushing him away, but not too hard. And then she gave up and gave in. Henry ran his hands through her hair and kissed her, and she immediately matched his intensity. She grabbed the bottom of his T-shirt and pulled up with her left hand, then started working the button on his jeans with her right. They kissed and tangled and undressed. The lovers frog-walked backward into the bedroom. Jo pushed Henry down on the mattress so hard he bounced. Every time she did this, it always made him laugh—even though he knew it was coming. Jo crawled slowly over him and settled on top. Henry ran his hand over the triple-moon tattoo on her left thigh and... the baby started to cry. Jo collapsed down on Henry, and they both laughed.

"Maybe next time, sailor," Jo said.

"The perks of being new parents." Henry laughed.

He kissed Jo, rolled from the bed, got dressed, and took care of his daughter.

Jo got dressed and ready to go to Wanda's shop as Henry was feeding Delilah. She put together a bag of supplies for the baby and left them by the door. Wanda's Wicca'd Emporium closed at nine o'clock on weeknights. The digital clock on the stove read 8:37.

ARCHIE HOPPED in his 1967 VW Microbus, started it up, and was getting ready to pull out of the University parking lot when his phone started playing "Doctor Love" by Kiss. It had been his personal ring tone ever since cell phones could *play* ring tones.

"Love here, who may I ask is calling?" He knew it was Wanda. Her name was lit up in bright white letters on the screen. He just loved to tweak her a little bit. And, of course, she loved that he thought it was funny. So, she played along.

"Is this *The Archibald Love?*" she asked. Mock admiration dripped from every syllable.

"The one and only!"

"My dear professor, the honor of your presence is requested at the humble establishment known as Wanda's Wicca'd Emporium this evening. Your adoring public *must* make your acquaintance. Any answer other than *yes* is simply unacceptable!"

"Duly noted, madam!"

"And, Archie, do you have your pendulum with you, by any chance?"

"Never leave home without it. What's up?"

"I'll tell you the whole story when you get here. See you at nine o'clock?"

"You bet."

~

AT ABOUT THE time Archie was making his way over to Wanda's shop, Salem Police Officer Raul Martinez was investigating a call that had come in to 911 at 7:59 p.m. A homeowner near the southeast end of the Salem cemetery had called in about someone "screaming their friggin' lungs out" somewhere within the borders of the town burial ground.

Martinez dreaded having to roam the grounds of the cemetery. The last deep-yellow light of the blistering August sun painted the ground with long, black, tombstone-shaped shadows. A patch of white, about thirty yards ahead of him, caught his attention.

Raul followed the path of an elongated, crucifix-shaped shadow. At the very end of it, he saw a pair of sneakers. The white high-tops appeared luminescent in the twilight. He made the sign of the cross, pulled the crucifix from inside his uniform shirt, and kissed it. As he got closer and his eyes adjusted to the darkness, he could see there were jeans attached to the sneakers. Whatever was attached to the jeans was hidden from the knees up by a large, slate-gray tombstone. The polished stone was inset with granite in its middle. The name "Graves" (*how appropriate*, Martinez thought) was inscribed on it back in 2007—the year the owner claimed it for eternity. Martinez feared what he would find behind that stone, steeled himself, and poked his head around its side.

"*Ay, Dios mío!*"

On the dark carpet of grass, on the other side of the grave, a young man and woman—his date, Martinez assumed—lay face up. Both were dead, their eyes wide open. Two youthful faces appeared to be screaming their way into eternity. And both poor souls each had a hole in their foreheads, about an inch above their eyebrows and dead center in the middle, directly north of their noses.

Martinez called for backup, explained the situation to dispatch, and then pulled the LED flashlight from his belt to examine both bodies. What he expected to see—lots of blood pooled behind their heads, or maybe the obvious singe marks of a bullet hole fired at close range—were not there. He recalled there was no mention of shots fired on the 911 call. The hole in each forehead was neat, clean, and bloodless. The skin on their faces was completely drained of color. They looked like terrified photo negatives of the people they used to be. It was the oddest damned thing he'd ever seen in his seventeen years on the force.

CHAPTER 6
SOMETHING'S WRONG

Archie was the first to arrive at Wanda's Wicca'd Emporium. He parked the VW bus in the rear and made his way to the door leading directly to the pentacle room at the back of Wanda's shop.

Wanda sat in the middle of the room—eyes closed, candles lit, dragon's blood incense burning away. She was deep in meditation.

Archie grabbed his own beanbag chair from the side of the room near the back door and dragged it next to Wanda's, sat down, and joined her.

Archie and Wanda had both been meditating for years and realized the value of the practice a long time ago. And it was something Archie liked to encourage the students in his classes to take up. When one of his students would ask him why he thought it so important, Archie would fill them in on all the benefits. He thought about one such conversation now as he quieted his mind.

The kid's name was Hendricks. This student stood out in his mind for two reasons. The first was that his name sounded like Archie's favorite guitarist's last name, Jimi Hendrix. The second reason—the kid asked damned good questions...

"So, why is it so important to meditate, professor?" Hendricks asked.

"Well, Aaron, I'm glad you asked. One of the first and most important effects meditation can have on you is it provides emotional balance. What I've noticed, through the years, is that when I make it a regular practice, I don't react... or let's say over-react, to any situation—positive or negative, dangerous or innocuous."

"But how does it DO that? I'm not sure I can buy it at face value."

Archie replied, "Nor would I expect you to, Aaron. That's why I recommend you investigate it for yourself. But I think I can put a little science and history behind my claim, if you prefer."

"I do."

"One cannot start a conversation about meditation without mentioning the physical location in the body that is of ultimate importance to the practice. The pineal gland is a small, pea-sized gland, shaped like a pine cone—thus the name—in the middle of your brain, between both hemispheres. It handles the production and regulation of various hormones in your body. Chief among those that it produces and regulates is melatonin. Melatonin, Aaron, is the hormone that plays a huge role in your circadian rhythms, or sleep patterns. If your melatonin levels are off, you don't sleep well. And we all know, especially those of you who like to party a bit too much, you don't perform all that well on exams when you haven't slept. Or maybe pulled an all-nighter?" He wiggled his eyebrows and the lecture hall rippled with knowing laughter.

"But one of its other functions is its relation to the development of your third eye, or ajna chakra. The chakras are the energy centers throughout the body. The way spirit 'moves' through the body, if you will. When one or more of those energy centers are not functioning as intended, your body manifests that outwardly in both physical and psychological ways. Physically, it can show up as diseases of varying kinds. Mentally, in my experience, it can present itself as cynicism, a pessimistic attitude, mental confusion, or indecisiveness—i.e., a lack of confidence."

Aaron asked, "So, I get the melatonin thing, that's obvious, and I've actually read a lot about that. My mom has a melatonin deficiency, among other things. She's been sick for a while. But what effect does meditation have on the pineal?"

Archie weighed the question before he spoke.

"I know not all of you are religious, and I'm not promoting any religion. That is NOT the purpose of this class. But, throughout time and in many religions and philosophies, there are references to the pineal gland, or the 'Third Eye.'"

"In the Bible, Matthew 6:22 reads, 'The light of the body is the eye: if therefore thine eye be single, thy whole body shall be full of light.'"

Archie watched the reaction of the class. He noticed a lot of raised eyebrows at that one. He continued.

"Herophilus, an ancient Greek anatomist, described the pineal gland as the 'Sphincter of Thought.'

"The French mathematician, René Descartes, wrote in Treatise of Man: *'My view is that this gland is the principal seat of the soul, and the place in which all thoughts are formed.'*

"Anyone here familiar with ancient Egyptian hieroglyphs?" He scanned the class. "In particular, there is one that looks like an eye with an eyebrow above it, and something resembling a jester's boot sticking out from its bottom?"

Aaron asked, "Isn't that called the 'Eye of Horus'?"

"Exactly, Aaron. And its similar ancient Egyptian symbol, the 'Eye of Ra.' You know more than you're letting on, I think."

"Nah, just read about it on one of those conspiracy websites. You wouldn't believe some of the nutty shit you find on those sites."

"I'll bet," Archie said. "There is, however, one uncanny coincidence about the 'Eye of Horus' and the actual physical structure of the pineal gland. When dissected, the physical structure of the pineal gland, pituitary gland, and the corpus callosum region of the brain LOOKS like the 'Eye of Horus.'"

Archie produced a slide from his briefcase and slapped it down on the projector. There was an audible intake of breath from the lecture hall collective, indicative of their agreement that, yes indeed, they bore a remarkable resemblance.

"Now," Archie said, "the pièce de résistance—the structural composition of the pineal. When you dissect the pineal gland, you'll see structures called pinealocytes covering its interior lining. These structures are very similar to the rods and cones, or photoreceptors, that you find in the retina of your eyes! Not only that, the pineal contains retinal tissue AND the same connections to your visual cortex as your regular eyes!"

Jaws around the lecture hall dropped open. Nothing could be more satisfying for a professor. Archie felt warm inside at the memory of it.

"Now, whether this structure was actually capable of sight along the evolutionary path of our species is a debate for another time. And another class... perhaps biology. I only point it out to you because, in my opinion, there is a significant similarity to the eyes we view the waking world with.

"Another thing I've noticed, during my own meditations is that, although my eyes are completely closed, and the room I'm in

is completely dark, I still see color. Often muted waves of purple or green or blue, but color nonetheless. And, scientifically speaking, color is simply light hitting an object, said object absorbing parts of that light and reflecting back the rest, producing a red or a green or a blue, dependent on the wavelength reflected at us. If that's so, then how are we able to observe color with our eyes closed and no light source available? I submit to you, dear students, that there is much more to the pineal gland than, pardon the pun, meets the eye."

"That's all incredibly interesting, professor. And I mean that sincerely. But my question still stands. How does meditation affect the pineal gland?" Aaron insisted.

"And now your answer, Aaron. When you first meditate, you'll find that your mind is a whirlwind of activity. Quieting the mind is definitely not the easiest thing in the world to do, and it takes practice and patience. I've found the easiest way to begin this discipline is to sit in a dark and quiet room, close your eyes, and focus on your breathing. Your breathing should naturally calm and become steady as you focus on it, but force nothing. Let it happen naturally... it will. The next thing I do is rest my focus slightly above and between my eyes. This is the third-eye region. Remember, above all else, force nothing. Your thoughts will slow with time and practice.

"This passive concentration will ultimately release neuropeptides and nitric oxide. That will trigger a relaxation response in your body. These biochemicals released into your system allow for a deeper meditation and will stimulate the third-eye region. In the brains of those who meditate regularly, melatonin increases. There are actual brain MRIs of individuals showing meditation increases pineal gland activity. And, as I've mentioned earlier, one of the first benefits of meditation is emotional balance. And science and biology prove this."

He put a link up on the screen for his students to copy down. It connected to a website backing up his scientific and historical claims. Aaron gave Dr. Love a thumbs up.

"So, in conclusion, Aaron, the way meditation works, in a scientifically based sense, is a chain reaction initiated by the person willing to indulge in it. You calm the body, the body responds by releasing chemicals that relax you. That relaxation response promotes the production of melatonin by the pineal. The pineal functions at a higher level, mental and physical health increase, and the circle continues the more you practice.

"I would like those of you—who are willing—to try it. It's not mandatory, but if you are open-minded enough, let's see what happens. Keep a journal from the start. Note how you felt when you first tried it and then, at the end of the semester, how you feel now that you've done it for three months. If you are honest in your efforts, I guarantee you will feel differently at the end of this brief experiment."

HENRY AND JOANNE left the apartment at 8:55 p.m. The ride to Wanda's was only five minutes at that time of night. Traffic was light, and they parked in the back of the shop and next to Archie's VW bus at exactly 9:00 p.m.

Henry took Delilah from her car seat and Jo grabbed the diaper bag from the back. As they approached the back door, Jo stopped. Something felt *off*. "Henry, wait."

Henry turned and noticed the odd look on Joanne's face. "What's the matter?"

"Something isn't right. I can't put my finger on it, but the vibe around the shop feels... wrong."

He didn't question it. Henry had witnessed far too many

of Jo's intuitive moments and knew better than to doubt her. He stood with his hand on the doorknob and waited.

"Let's get inside," she said.

ARCHIE HAD SETTLED down into a comfortable rhythm with his breathing, setting his focus, eyes closed, on the area just above and to the middle of his eyebrows. The fruits of years of practice showed themselves almost immediately. Undulating clouds of alternating colors collapsed in on themselves in gentle waves—purple, then indigo, then dark green, and then... something new. An angry red hue inserted itself amidst the peaceful tones. This had never happened to him, and the feeling was nothing close to peaceful.

"Archie, are you seeing what I'm seeing?" Wanda asked.

In a relaxed yet cautious tone, Archie answered, "Mmhmm."

"I think whatever came calling last night is in the area again. If this thing has penetrated the room, and can affect us in meditation, it can only mean one thing—we've sprung a leak."

Archie's eyes popped open. "How is that possible?"

Wanda kept her eyes closed. "It's not. Unless someone did it from in here."

"Who would do such a thing?"

"Good question," Wanda said.

CHAPTER 7
THE CHIEF

A perimeter was set up by the Salem Police Department around the bodies Officer Martinez had found. Bright yellow police tape wrapped around stakes set into the ground in a large, uneven rectangle. The wind had steadily picked up, and the tape rattled in protest. The first drops of rain tapped the hood of Raul's windbreaker. *Funny*, he thought, he'd heard nothing about rain in the forecast today. Looking up, he saw no stars in the sky where there had been a few twinkles here and there only moments ago.

"Martinez, over here." It was his boss, Chief Byron Miller.

He made his way over. "Sir?"

Dispatch called the chief away from his house after he'd just settled down with his wife to watch a little TV. He did not look happy. "You sure they didn't hear any gunshots?"

"That's what dispatch told me. And I asked them again to make sure. Nada."

"Doesn't make any fuckin' sense."

"Nope. But I noticed something weird, sir."

Miller stood a foot taller than Martinez. He reminded Raul of Fred Gwynne, who played Judge Chamberlain Haller in My Cousin Vinny or, as many knew him, Herman Munster from the old TV comedy, The Munsters. The only difference was Miller had a full goatee. Other than that, he could have been the guy's twin brother. Miller rolled his hand, urging Martinez to continue.

Martinez said, "Well, sir, the wounds aren't at all like gunshot wounds. You see here"—he knelt down next to the deceased male—"the ridges around the wound, they're raised around the edges. It almost looks like a crater. Like something you'd see on the moon."

"So?"

"Well, if it was a gunshot wound, there wouldn't be any ridges, or if there were, they would most likely be puffy and folded toward the inside of the circumference of the wound. These... they're raised and all along the outside. This is an exit wound, sir. Like something pulled from the inside out. And there's no blood."

The chief's eyes went wide. He motioned the coroner over and told him to get the bodies to the morgue the second the scene was processed. He wanted autopsies on these two as soon as possible. Miller put his hand over his forehead and massaged his temples. It was gonna be a long night.

HE WATCHED THE WITCH, the warlock, and their child from a distance. The dark-haired witch stopped and stared in his direction. He knew she couldn't see him, but all the same, he backed off. Her stopping and looking in his direction sent another sliver of doubt through him. Again, he cursed his master for his overconfidence. The witches belonging to this coven were far more powerful than they appeared, and they hadn't survived through the centuries without good reason.

The weather was turning. Rain fell as he climbed soundlessly up a tree and settled in a spot for the task ahead. He sniffed the air, taking in the ozone smell that signaled the coming storm. Magical events of this magnitude energized the earth, bringing on foul weather.

He was well fed by the two he'd taken in the cemetery, and his senses were sharpened. It was only a matter of time before he would gain entry into the witch's shop.

MERCY FLIPPED the sign that hung from the nail above the store's front door window from "open" to "closed." She set about her usual routine and spruced the store up from front to back, getting it ready for the next day. With that done, she headed to the back, per Wanda's request. When she got there, she saw Wanda and Archie seated in their black beanbag chairs in the middle of the room. The two appeared to be in meditation, but she noticed they were whispering to each other as they did so. She found that odd, but to each their own.

She grabbed a beanbag chair, placed it next to them in the inner circle, and was just sitting down when the back door opened. Mercy recognized Henry right away. She liked him and knew Henry found her attractive, and was pleasantly surprised at how much he fought the urge to run his eyes up and down her body. But, like most guys (and a fair amount of women) when they met Mercy, the battle was over before the fight had even begun. She knew this, but didn't let it go to her head. The old saying was true: beauty was only skin deep. But she lived her life, especially after the accident, in a quest for deeper spiritual meaning. And the attention, though nice and something she really enjoyed pre-accident, was not something she gave much thought to anymore.

Then her eyes settled on Joanne. She was stunning. Tall; not as tall as Henry, but not much shorter. Mercy guessed her to be five seven or five eight versus where she pegged Henry at about six foot two. Her straight, jet-black hair glowed, even in the soft lighting of the back room. Her face was perfectly symmetrical and her green eyes sparkled with an intelligent curiosity. She reminded Mercy of a beautiful—but dangerous—bird of prey.

Joanne wore, it appeared to Mercy, practically no makeup. And her build was the total opposite of Mercy's. Where Mercy was squat and compact, curvy in all the right places, Joanne was athletic and powerful. The black yoga pants she wore rippled with tone in both her calves and thighs. You'd never know she'd given birth just a couple of days ago. They were a beautiful couple, and Mercy was attracted to both of them. It was good to have options, even if she never intended on acting them out.

Joanne's eyes settled on Mercy's. For both of them, there was an instant connection. A dizzying feeling of déjà vu came over each of them simultaneously. Mercy stood from her beanbag chair, smoothed her shirt, and extended her hand.

"Hi, I'm Mercy. You must be Joanne. Wanda has told me so much about you."

"Really? Wanda, you talkin' about me behind my back again?"

Wanda opened her left eye in Joanne's direction. "Yes. Every single sordid detail, in fact." Then she closed her eye and resumed her meditation.

Joanne shrugged and smirked. "It's all true. But don't hold it against me, I'm not as bad as she tells everyone. Have we met before, Mercy?"

"Not that I know of, but I can't shake the feeling we have."

"Same here," said Jo.

"Maybe in another lifetime?" Mercy shrugged and smiled at Jo.

Henry noticed Joanne held on to Mercy's hand longer than normal—just as he'd done. There was something about Mercy that made you want to hold on for just a bit longer—some undercurrent of attraction that he couldn't quite put his finger on. He'd let his subconscious work that one out for now. It was one of the new things he'd learned to let happen naturally over the last year. Putting a problem or a question on the back burner for a while sometimes allowed the problem to work itself to a boil and pop to the surface... almost like magic.

∽

BY THE TIME the scene was processed and the bodies transported to the morgue, it was 10:02 p.m. Martinez had hitched a ride to the morgue with the chief. Neither man said a word to each other on the way, lost in their own thoughts about the odd wounds on the two victims.

They got out of the cruiser and shut their doors simultaneously with a soft fwump as the rain fell harder. Little clicks and clacks sounded from the cruiser's metal body as small hailstones fell from the darkened sky.

The chief reached the door first and held it for Martinez as he ran through. Miller took a deep breath and watched the hailstones as they bounced on his car. With the piss-yellow light cast from the fixture above the door, they reminded him of teeth.

He was stalling for time. Getting a little rained on was no big deal compared to what awaited him inside. He hated this part of the job. Corpses creeped him the fuck out.

Martinez looked back through the glass at the chief. His expression said "Are you coming?" The chief motioned with his hand for Martinez to keep going. Raul did as instructed and Byron pulled a cigar from his shirt pocket, leaned under the awning, and lit up. Just a couple of puffs. He wanted the cigar smell all over him before he stepped into the room with the sawbones.

Martinez reached his destination, gowned up, and stepped through the wired glass doors and into the room where the coroner was already hard at work.

Both of the deceased had their heads opened up wide in the area of their wounds. The coroner was leaning over the male, his headlamp glowing brightly. In his hands were shiny metal instruments Martinez assumed were used to cut, pry, and probe. His stomach lurched a little at the thought of it and he understood, now, why the chief took his time. With age comes wisdom and experience. Seventeen years on the force and this was the first time Martinez had stepped foot in here. He wouldn't be so quick to rush in next time. Bodies didn't bother him too much; he'd seen them once or twice from afar. But it hadn't ever required him to be *here*.

The coroner looked up. "Who are you?"

"I'm the guy who found the bodies in the cemetery. The chief sent me in here. Martinez."

"He's outside still." Not a question.

Martinez just nodded.

The coroner nodded back with a knowing smile. "He doesn't like this part. He's probably still having a smoke right now, thinks the cigars cover up the smell in here. It works for about ten seconds. But whatever floats his boat." He shrugged.

"So, any idea what happened to these two?" Martinez asked.

"Not yet. These are the strangest wounds I think I've ever seen. And I've seen a lotta wounds."

"Strange in what way?"

"Well, considering what's missing from inside this guy's noggin, you'd think there'd be more damage. Something that far in, it should have ripped up his frontal lobe on the way out. It's almost like it was sucked out with a straw and then the hole closed back up—neat and clean. Well, except for the holes in their skulls. But even those are almost bloodless."

"What's missing from inside their heads, Mickey?" Martinez jumped at the sound of the chief's voice from behind him.

"Hi, Byron. I think you scared the shit out of Martinez here."

Martinez could tell by the way the coroner's face mask moved he was smiling.

"Sorry, Raul," said Chief Miller.

Raul had his hand over his heart, trying to keep it in his chest. He swallowed and nodded, his mask moving in and out with his adrenaline fueled respiration.

"Well, Chief, it's the weirdest damned thing I think I've seen. You see here, once you get past the frontal lobe," Mickey Schmidt said as he parted it with the instrument in his hand, "and then you divide the hemispheres in half." A sickening, squishy sound came from the young man's nonfunctioning head—prompting both the chief and Martinez to put the backs of their hands in front of their masks. "And you peek inside, you can see the missing part right here."

Mickey looked up at both of them. Neither was any closer than five feet from the table. He was gonna smile but decided against it when he saw the "stop fucking around" look on the chief's face.

"Just get to the point, Mick," Miller said.

"Okay, okay. They're both missing their pineal glands. And I'll be fucked in the ear by a spider monkey before I can figure out how it happened."

CHAPTER 8
INFILTRATION AND ACCUSATION

They turned the lights down low. The members of the *Foedere In Luna* sat in a semicircle around the gold-flaked pentacle in the middle of the back room. Dragon's blood incense filled the air while white candles glowed softly at the four compass points on the edges of Wanda's safe space—their flames reflected on the surface of the shiny obsidian floor. The rest of the room was bathed in darkness. All four members and Mercy were deep in meditation, continuing for several minutes until Wanda broke the silence.

"I'm glad you all could make it here tonight. The remnants of the *Order Immortalis* are somewhat upset their fearless leader has departed this plane of existence. Well, he's departed *any* plane of existence."

Soft laughter from all.

Delilah coughed from the carrier near the bar at the back of the room. Joanne got up to check on her, made sure she was okay, and returned to her beanbag chair.

Wanda continued, "I guess now we have to deal with the

fallout." She filled Mercy and Archie in on all the details they weren't already privy to surrounding the events of Sunday night.

"So *that's* what all that was about last night. No wonder you didn't want me going home, Wanda." Mercy said.

"It would have been far too dangerous, honey."

Joanne asked, "Were you able to learn anything else from the thing outside Wanda's shop when you homed in on it, Mercy?"

"Just that it was full of rage and wanted Wanda dead. The only other thing I felt, though it was probably my imagination, is that it knew me... or at least it felt familiar to me. And it scares me a little to think I might have a connection to it."

"I wouldn't worry too much about that, sweetie," Wanda said. "There's no way that I can see, at least right now, that it could possibly be connected to you. But I'm not gonna rule it out either. When Archie and I were in meditation, right before you came into the room, Mercy, we both felt the presence of the being. That means only one thing—it's found a hole in our protection. That doesn't mean it's because of you, sweetie, but it needs further investigation."

"What kind of investigation, Wanda?" Henry asked with a raised eyebrow.

Wanda looked at Henry, mild surprise on her face.

"It seems your intuition is getting sharper by the day, Henry. I was just about to suggest that Archie send you to the astral plane and see if we can glean a bit of information about our red-tinged friend."

Henry nodded. A show of two things: he did indeed sense what Wanda was about to suggest (it still amazed him that this power was within him all along), and second, he agreed with her decision to send him out into the astral realms. When you got right down to it, that was where the game was played when you were dealing with the *Order Immortalis*.

Over the last year, Henry and Archie had, until recently, practiced sending Henry into the astral plane. It was a two-part strategy. The first was getting Henry familiar with leaving his physical body behind. Astral travel was jarring when you weren't used to it. To the novice, the scariest part *was* exiting the body for a new dimension. The shock of it was enough to send someone instantly back to the physical plane.

The second was *being able* to send Henry out of his body and into the astral plane so they could keep an eye on the *Order Immortalis*. No one knew more than Henry the kinds of things the *Order* tried to get away with *over there*. Upon Henry's arrival in Salem last July, they'd stalked him in his dreams. They were trying to discover the secrets his former incarnation, Madeleine, had taken to her grave. And they'd almost succeeded. They *would have,* too, had Henry not had the good sense to seek help from Joanne.

Archie didn't need anyone to tell him what came next. He got up from his beanbag chair, made his way to the south corner of the room, and returned with a black leather massage table Wanda used for Reiki treatments. He unfolded it and set it upright. The rest of the members and Mercy dragged their beanbag chairs out of his way so he could place the table within the pentacle.

Wanda, Joanne, and Mercy moved over to the bar area next to Delilah. The baby slept, but not soundly. She would occasionally kick out one leg or the other or move her head from side to side. It seemed to Joanne she may be having her first nightmare—or whatever passes as a nightmare for a three-day-old. Jo leaned down and gently stroked the baby's head, calming her a little.

Henry turned to Joanne. "Here we go again."

Jo smiled. "Come back safe, Band-Aid boy."

Henry made his way to the middle of the room, sat on the edge of the table, swung his legs up, and lay back—face up to the skylight directly above the pentacle. He heard the rain falling and the hailstones ticking off the glass above. The storm was picking up.

Archie removed a deep-purple amethyst pendulum from his jeans pocket. He started at the top of Henry's head, dangling the pentacle over his crown chakra, and waited for it to hang still. The pendulum then rotated clockwise in an ever-widening circle.

"I see someone has been keeping up with his meditation work lately," Archie said.

Henry smiled and kept his eyes closed, focused on calming his mind, body, and soul.

Archie moved through the seven chakra points in succession—crown, brow, throat, heart, solar plexus, sacral, and root. The pendulum swung in wide, clockwise circles. It showed all of Henry's chakras were unobstructed. Optimal conditions for the next step into the astral plane. With that done, Archie guided Henry down, down, down, into deeper and deeper levels of relaxation. When he finished speaking, Henry was in a total and complete state of wellbeing and ready to ease out of his body.

He felt the first gentle tug of the realm beyond. There was a brief, high-pitched sound, and then a briefer moment of disorientation. Then he was there.

Immediately he felt the weightless peace of the astral

plane. The colors were much brighter here. All his senses worked much the same way as the ones in the physical world, but they were stronger, sharper, and more attuned now.

He ignored the lower beings that moved through the realm with their own agendas—astral plane equivalents of squirrels hoarding nuts and getting ready for winter was the way Henry thought of them. Then there were beings of higher intelligence. Most of them kept to themselves and seemed to like it that way. Others were confused, like they didn't really get where they were or why they were there. These were common, average people in the middle of dreams. Occasionally, he would run into other beings wanting something from him. He wouldn't acknowledge their presence. The only thing they could do for Henry at the moment was serve as a distraction. And he had bigger astral fish to fry.

He gently rose from the area Wanda's shop occupied in the physical world. Ascending, he noticed a dim red light far off in the distance. It was tough to make out the form of the entity from this far away through the milky-blue haze of the astral plane, though he was intuitively certain it was the being who had stalked Wanda's Wicca'd Emporium the night before.

It emanated a negative vibration Henry could feel, even at a distance. With caution, he moved in that direction. If it was the being who tried to attack Wanda's shop, he didn't want to give himself away by approaching too quickly.

He got as close as he dared and settled in a spot giving him a view of the being without revealing himself. The entity crouched high above Henry's position, in the astral plane equivalent of what looked like a tree—a tree in no other sense save it was tall and had protrusions Henry's mind interpreted as branches. He watched and waited.

The being dropped something to the ground. It slithered its way toward and past him, wiggling along the path Henry had just traveled. Henry watched with a dawning dread as he realized what was going on. In Wanda's shop, where he knew the members of the *Foedere In Luna* stood just on the other side, there was *another* red light. The glowing red snake pulsed brighter as it approached the shop, matching the rhythm of the red light within the Emporium's perimeter. Someone in Wanda's shop *was* a target!

Henry's mind raced. A decision needed to be made now: attack the entity, trying to kill it—or hop back into his body and warn the others. It only took a split second for him to decide. The snake was too close to the shop now, leaving him with little choice. The moment the snake penetrated the shop, the figure in the tree vanished. Attacking it was not an option anymore. He'd realized, too late, what was going on to stop it.

He needed only to think about returning to his body, and he was there. There was a moment of disorientation, and then he was back on the physical plane. Henry sucked in a deep breath, like a man coming up for air after a deep underwater dive, then sat up and looked over at the other members of his coven. His eyes settled on Mercy. She stared back, uncomfortable under Henry's gaze.

Wanda spoke, "What's the matter, Henry?"

Henry said nothing at first. He stood from the table and walked over to Mercy, looking in her eyes for what, to Mercy, seem an agonizingly long time. Henry wasn't sure what he was looking for, and if he'd been honest with himself, he should have deferred to Wanda or Joanne. But he considered himself the de facto leader of the *Foedere In Luna* now, since Madeleine had been its leader back in the late 1600s. And he made a decision in that moment he would regret later on.

He drew his eyes from Mercy and looked at Wanda. "It's connected to her. I could see it reaching out and now it's in here with us. It's part of Mercy now."

Mercy's mouth hung open. She looked shocked and hurt, as if Henry had accused her of a heinous crime.

"How can you be sure of that, Henry?" Wanda asked.

"It connected with someone in here. I saw it as it connected, but not to who. It was too late to stop it from happening on the other side, so I had to come back here as quick as possible and warn everybody. I'm sorry, Mercy. But you're the only one in this room that could possibly be compromised. I don't know how, but it has to be you."

"I don't feel any different than I did before you left, Henry. I'm pretty sure I would know if something or someone tried to enter my body," Mercy said, "but if you think I may pose a danger to you all, I'll leave now. I want nothing bad happening to any of you on my account."

For the first time in years, Wanda was at a loss for what to do. And that's when Joanne spoke up.

"She has to leave. There's no way around it. Even if it's only until we know what's going on for sure, she can't be within the walls of this building. It's too dangerous."

Wanda looked at Archie. The two of them communicating by eye contact alone.

Archie said, "Come with me, Mercy. I'll take you home. I'm the only one that's not, as far as I know, in any danger at the moment."

Wanda wanted to cry. She'd grown to love Mercy in the short time she'd been working at the shop. Tears were forming in the bottoms of her eyes. Mercy looked to her for help—her own eyes on the verge of tears.

"Does this mean I can't work here anymore, Wanda? Does this mean I lose my job? I love it here..." Her voice cracked, her words cut off as she was overcome with emotion.

"No, honey. And I'll make sure you keep getting paid until this is all sorted out. But for the safety of all, I have to agree with Henry. I'm so sorry, Mercy."

Red-faced and unjustly ashamed, Mercy made her way toward the back door of the shop. Archie followed. The door hissed on its pneumatic hinge and closed with a soft click. Wanda, Joanne, and Henry stood silently together around Delilah, watching them leave. The baby coughed.

CHAPTER 9
PENNY

Chief Byron Miller swung the cruiser into his driveway, killed the headlights, and blew out a deep breath. By the time he'd arrived home, it was 11:11 p.m. He made his way from the car, through the torrential downpour, and into his garage. He couldn't remember the last time it had rained this hard in Salem. Strike that, he remembered. It was last Halloween Eve and into the pre-dawn hours of Halloween. That was bad... this was much worse.

He thought back to that night. Rumors had spread throughout the town that snow had fallen. No big deal, it snows sometimes in October in the Northeast. But not usually in a one-block area in a single city. Most of the reports centered on the Essex Street area.

Haunted Happenings, the town's annual month-long celebration culminating in a massive, town-wide Halloween party, had been canceled for that night. The chief assumed most of the call-ins reporting snow on Essex Street were sent in by drunks bored and frustrated the festivities had been called off. He'd seen one or two videos posted on YouTube that actually showed it snowing. In the age of digital editing, who knew what was real anymore?

The moment the chief walked into his garage, the power went out. He wasn't surprised. The storm had been raging since he'd arrived at the cemetery, and it showed no signs of slowing. He made his way, by feel, over to his workbench, grabbed the police-issue flashlight from its peg, and entered the house.

Byron tried to be as quiet as possible. He didn't want to wake up Penny. His wife was usually up until eleven o'clock, at the very latest, on most nights. Tonight was TV night, and he felt a twinge of guilt for missing *Ghost Adventures*. Byron wasn't really a big fan of the show, but Penny loved it. And she always got a kick out of watching Aaron freak the fuck out over something. Even Byron got a good laugh when it happened. Some of the Aaron freak-outs were epically funny.

He thought he'd made it safely to the living room until he caught a faint flickering glow at the top of the stairs. It was Penny. She was in a white nightgown and carrying a white candle in a glass holder.

"I'm sorry, honey. I didn't mean to wake you up."

"You didn't, By. I couldn't sleep. I've got a bad feeling about something, and I just can't put my finger on it."

"Did you call the kids?"

"Yep. Tina's fine. It's not even raining in Swampscott. Michael, Angela, and the kids are down the Cape. Not raining there either. They're more worried about us being up here in this monsoon."

"A monsoon is the perfect word to describe this shit. I

think I saw Noah floating down Derby Street in the ark." He laughed, though there was little humor in it.

"Why were you called out, honey?" Penny asked.

He didn't enjoy talking about work at home on a *good* night. Telling her about what he'd seen tonight was not something he was ready to do now. But his wife was sharp, and he'd hesitated too long. She picked up on it.

"Don't try to soft-pedal me, Byron Miller. I'm not some shrinking violet. I don't need electric lights to see it was bad. It's written all over your face, and your aura is a mess."

He was at a loss for words. What he'd seen tonight was like nothing he'd seen in the entirety of his career. He looked up at Penny and said, "It was bad, baby. Real bad."

She made her way down the rest of the stairs, took him by the arm, and guided him to the kitchen. She put the candle in the middle of the table. Penny had prepared for the power outage. They were frequent on this side of town during foul weather. She brought a thermos and two mugs to the table and poured steaming hot coffee for both of them.

"Okay, By. Spill it."

He didn't even bother trying to sugarcoat it. Penny would know instantly if he was bullshitting her. You don't stay married to the love of your life for thirty-two years and one day figure out how to put one over on her. And, truth be told, he knew he was just being protective. His wife had seen a lot over the years they'd been married. And, he suspected, she probably had shielded *him* from some things. She and her brother had both seen things that would have turned his hair white.

So, he told her everything—gory details and all.

"And there was no blood?" she asked.

"Not a drop. Not at the scene and not at the morgue. It's as if their blood stopped pumping the minute they died."

"That makes no sense, By."

"Tell me about it."

"And the coroner, he said they were missing what, again?"

"Both pineal glands. With no damage from extraction. Like some sick fuckin' magic trick."

Byron sipped his coffee and watched his wife as she turned what he'd just told her over in her mind.

When Penny churned something, it was a site to behold. He was amused by the faces she made as her sharp mind wrangled with something that made zero sense. He could predict the faces, in order, she would make.

She'd start by looking up at the ceiling. As if the answer was up there in tiny letters... she even squinted. Next came the nose pinch, as if she were coping with sudden-onset migraine. It would send wrinkles crawling toward her temples like an earthquake's fault line. Finally, she'd drum her fingers faster and faster on the table, her nails clacking all the while. No answer? Rinse and repeat. It could go on for quite some time. He knew better than to talk. He sipped, watched, and waited.

When no answer came, she threw her arms up and tossed her head back, like a preacher beseeching a higher power. It was the only time he allowed himself a smile. When she leveled her gaze, the smile vanished. It was probably the only secretive thing he did, in thirty-two years of marriage, he could truly call his own.

"I'm stumped. Well, almost. I seem to recall reading something about the pineal gland and the third eye."

Byron's eyebrows shot up. "Come again?"

"The third eye... you know, the one that opens up when you meditate?"

He stared at her, his face a billboard of skepticism.

"I know, I know. But there are things in this world that are beyond science and reality, By."

He sat up, rubbed the back of his neck, and grimaced. It was one of *his* telltale signs when a subject was uncomfortable. Byron was a facts and reality kind of guy. When things got beyond those parameters, he had a hard time going to the same places his wife's mind went. He'd rather massage the facts until they released the answer he was looking for. Only problem was, the world *wasn't* always ready to cooperate. Tonight was exhibit A.

"I think I need to ask my brother about this. It's right up his alley."

Byron was uncomfortable with that. Penny knew he would be. Her brother and Byron were friendly enough to each other, but they saw the world in two completely different ways.

She saw the look on his face and ignored it. They'd been down this road before. Penny got up and went into the living room. The soft glow of the iPhone lit the left side of her face. He could hear the ring coming from the other end. It rang five or six times and went to voicemail. Her brother's phone hardly *ever* went to voicemail. Especially when his little sister was calling. He *always* dropped whatever he was doing and took the call. It was one of the things she found endearing about him. That, and his belief in all things spiritual. He had an open mind, but not so open that his brain was about to fall out. She left a message.

Penny's name came up on Archie's phone. If the weather weren't an absolute horror show, he would have picked up immediately. He always loved talking to his little sister. But the wipers were barely keeping up with the rain as it was. He didn't dare take his eyes off the road. He let it go to voicemail.

"This is terrible. Worse than the storm we had last Halloween," Archie said.

Mercy was quiet. Her eyes had almost dried. Her eyeliner had run, and she'd smeared it haphazardly with a Kleenex. She looked like a pretty, sad raccoon. Archie felt horrible for her.

"Wanda meant what she said, Mercy. If there's one thing I know for sure, she'll get to the bottom of what's going on."

"I just can't understand it. I'm pretty sensitive to most anything of a spiritual nature. I'm one hundred percent positive if anything *had* tried to enter me from another realm, I'd have felt *something*. I've been that way since the accident."

"You don't have to convince me, Mercy. I saw your face when I mentioned Henry had killed the demons. Someone in that classroom was *not* happy."

"Yeah. It was like a hot iron spike flew through me. That's always the feeling I get when I'm in the presence of anger. Only that day it was *much* more intense than usual," Mercy said.

Archie was about to say more when he noticed something in the middle of the road. He slowed the VW bus to a crawl until it was close enough for him to make out what it was. A man. He was lying in the middle of the road. His face was turned away from the bus and down the street, a flashlight still in his hand. Its beam pointed at the curb, illuminating raindrops pounding the pavement so hard they sent up little rings of water.

Archie pulled his hood up, told Mercy he'd be right back, and went to check on the man. Mercy tried her best to watch through the wipers, though at this point they were smearing the rain instead of clearing it. She had no problem following Archie's progress, however. He was wearing a florescent orange rain coat. A big peace sign and colored dancing bears adorned the back of it. Underneath the dancing bears was a skull with a lightning bolt across its top. Archie loved to advertise to the world he was a Deadhead. One of millions who loved the Grateful Dead.

Mercy watched as Archie bent over and gently shook the man's shoulder. She knew what was about to happen a split second before it did. She could feel it, but she was helpless to do anything about it. Almost at the same instant Archie had shaken the man's shoulder, the flashlight came to life and connected with Archie's face. The next second, Archie was a bright orange lump in the road and the man sprang up, bolting to the driver's side of the VW. He hopped in behind the wheel, turned to face her, and said, "Hi, Mercy!"

And then he introduced her to Mr. Flashlight.

CHAPTER 10
WHERE'S ARCHIE?

Henry made the rounds of the entire store after the power went out. He pulled the metal shutters down, protecting the shop's enormous picture window, then locked the front door. It wasn't much in the way of security, but it was all Wanda had.

The sigils—the Emporium's true protection—lining the hallway leading to the back room were glowing. Wanda had cast a few spells to shore up the protection for the remaining members of the *Foedere In Luna*. Henry still marveled he could now *see* things like the glowing sigils with his own eyes. The first time he'd entered this hallway, over a year ago, he thought they were merely cute little designs. And he'd also thought Wanda a little eccentric. Lovable, but batshit crazy. Now... not so much.

When he passed through the beaded doorway (another seventies relic of Wanda's to go along with the beanbag chairs) he saw Wanda on her phone. She looked concerned.

"Archie, call me as soon as you get this message. You're scaring me. Love you, honey."

"What's up with Archie?" Henry asked.

"Wanda's been trying to get him on the phone for the last ten minutes. Keeps going straight to voice mail," Jo said.

"That's not like Archie. He's a first-ring kind of guy. Two at the most."

Jo nodded. She looked worried and started nibbling on her left thumbnail.

Wanda didn't hear a word either of them said. She was too busy thinking about the next move in front of her. Whatever this thing was, it was smart. It had infiltrated the store without the use of magic. Or, at the very least, it was using a type of magic or subterfuge she was not familiar with. And *that* was saying something. Now, doubt's sneaky fingers plucked at her from within. It was a feeling she'd not had in quite a long time.

It began with her judgment about Mercy. She was *positive* the girl was not responsible for the breach. But what Henry had seen in the astral realm had put the lie to that. If its strategy was to scare the members into making a mistake, it was getting the job done. Mercy was temporarily banished from the store and now Archie couldn't be reached. Well, not reached by Wanda anyway. She pulled her phone back out from the pocket of her purple cloak.

"Who are you calling now?" Jo asked. Wanda held up a finger.

"Byron, it's Wanda. Archie isn't answering his phone, he... Oh, you tried calling him too. He was driving Mercy home... um, she lives over near Witch Hill Road. I'm not exactly sure of her address, but I know she lives with a couple of roommates." Silence from Wanda, and then, "Okay, let me know when you find him."

She looked up to see Henry and Joanne hovering over her —concern and anticipation all over their faces.

"By is going back out to look for Archie."

Wanda put her right elbow in her left hand and tugged at her lip. It was Wanda's non-verbal way of telling them to leave her alone and let her think. Henry and Joanne let her be.

"I'm going with you, By."

"No way, Penny."

"Why not?"

"Well, I can think of two reasons right off the top. They both have holes in their heads, at the moment. And whoever or whatever did that to them is still out there."

He saw the look on her face and knew he'd fucked up. Byron walked over to his wife and put his arms around her.

"That came out wrong. I'm sorry. Just because Arch isn't answering his phone doesn't mean something bad's happened to him. For all we know, Archie could have dropped his phone on the way to his car. You know how forgetful he is."

She nodded, but she didn't feel any better.

"I'll call you as soon as I find him. And I *will* find him."

"I know you will. I just hate sitting here, waiting around and doing nothing."

He went to the cabinet over the microwave, removed something from it, and handed it to her. It was a Motorola police scanner. He turned it on and set it to the Salem Police frequency.

It made her feel better. At least she would know, as soon as Byron did, her brother was alive and safe. She put her hand on the back of his neck, pulled him forward, and kissed him hard. Penny did this every time he left for work in the morning and every time he went out on a call like this. She would never say it, but being a cop's wife, you never knew if today was going to be the last one together. And she wanted to make sure he knew how much he was loved. He was nobody's fool, though. He knew what it meant. Then he put on his cap, tipped it to her, and said, "Ma'am." It was their private little joke. Byron winked at her, turned toward the door, and walked into the storm.

Once her husband left, Penny walked upstairs, lit some dragon's blood incense, lay down on the bed, and prepared to conduct her own search for Archie—and maybe one other.

CHAPTER II
BOUND AND FOUND

After the kid had driven away, the hoodie dragged Mercy, unconscious and bleeding from the wound on her head, into the cemetery hideaway. The entity, currently in its earthly form, bound Mercy by the hands and looped the rope through a handle on one of the two coffins within the forgotten mausoleum. He tore a rag from his cloak and strapped it around her head, covering her mouth, and tied it tight. Couldn't have the lovely lady crying out and drawing attention to the site. Though he doubted anyone would hear her—even without the gag and screaming at the top of her lungs—it was better to be safe than sorry.

With that done, and a major threat out of the way, he left the mausoleum and slipped back into the raging storm. As he closed the rusted green door—sealing Mercy safely away—he stopped to consider his next move.

It would have been so much easier if he could have just killed Mercy and been done with her. But things were never that simple. He needed to keep her alive now. The one in charge needed Mercy to use the gifts she'd received from the last lifetime—a gift they'd failed to acquire when Mercy, shockingly, survived the attempt they'd made on her at the quarry.

It could backfire on them. He was well aware of that, but it was a risk worth taking. There really was no option. Mercy was the only one with the power they *both* needed. Once the old witch let her guard down, they would be free to set things in motion. They would get what they wanted.

BYRON MILLER SMOKED AND DROVE. The wipers were having little effect on the constant downpour. Radio chatter was at a minimum, per his order. No one with a brain in their head would be out driving on a night like this, anyway. It spared him the usual mundane calls that would come in on a normal night. No DUIs to deal with. No flat-tire calls. No pothole calls. And he prayed for no domestic disturbance calls. Those always pulled resources away. When those calls came in, the only thing predictable about them was their unpredictability.

He rounded the corner on Witch Hill Road, slowing the vehicle to a crawl. The last thing he needed tonight was to turn his brother-in-law into a bright-orange speed bump. He caught motion ahead of him. It was Archie. He was kneeling in the middle of the road, wiping blood from his forehead. Archie tried to stand, wobbled on his feet, and landed ass-first in a puddle. Water splashed up from between his legs and hit him in the face, rinsing some of the blood down the front of his raincoat.

Byron brought the cruiser to a halt ten feet from where

Archie sat, dazed and confused, then turned on the spotlight, exited the vehicle, and helped his brother-in-law up. He guided Archie to the passenger side, opened the door for him, and helped him into his seat. The chief of police reached across Archie, belted him in, and ran around to the driver's side. When they were both safely in the heated compartment of the cruiser, it was Archie who spoke first.

"Mercy Glass was with me. He took her, Byron."

"Who took who?"

"A young lady named Mercy," said Archie between heavy breaths. "She works at Wanda's shop. There was a man lying in the middle of the road, right where you just found me. I went to help him and he attacked me. I was driving Mercy home from Wanda's shop, got out to help him, and that's the last thing I remember. She was in my bus. He took her and the bus. I never saw where they went."

Byron wasted no time. He issued a be-on-the-lookout order for the bus and its two passengers. The BOLO was met with several "copy" responses from four other units patrolling Salem's waterlogged streets.

"We need to get you over to the ER, Archie."

"No time for that now. Could you please take me back to Wanda's shop? Henry is there; he can patch me up."

Byron wasn't about to argue the point. His brother-in-law was a gentle soul, but arguing with him was akin to debating a nun about the existence of God—you could argue why you thought He didn't exist, but in the end all you got was a smile and a blessing. Archie was going to get his way. Byron shook his head and set course for Wanda's Wicca'd Emporium.

∼

Henry, Wanda, Joanne, and Delilah were in the center of the pentacle. It was the safest space in the room, and all agreed there was no point in taking an unnecessary risk being outside of it.

Joanne was getting worried. Little Delilah was coughing a bit here and there, though it had subsided since Mercy and Archie had left. She hadn't liked the sound of it and was considering taking her to the hospital.

Henry, being an ER nurse, was inclined to agree. The baby's cough wasn't normal sounding at all. Not that there is ever a normal-sounding cough when you're talking about an infant, but this sounded hoarse and scratchy. He considered maybe he and Jo were overreacting a bit, as new parents did, but the truth was it had really started to worry him, too.

"I know what you're thinking, Jo." Wanda said.

"And what's that?" Jo asked.

"You're thinking of taking Delilah to the hospital. I don't blame you, but it could be a mistake."

"It's a mistake to want to make sure my baby's not sick?"

"No, honey. It's a mistake to think her being sick is not connected to what's going on here."

"Really? And you know this how?"

"Don't you find it curious that Delilah started coughing almost as soon as Henry came back from the astral plane? And not long after we kicked Mercy from the building, the coughing has mostly subsided. Doesn't that seem a bit odd to you?"

"I don't see the connection, Wanda. It's slowed, but not completely," said Jo.

Henry felt Delilah's forehead. She wasn't feverish in the slightest. It still didn't rule out something being wrong with her, but it did surprise him a bit. If she'd had a fever, he could at least understand why she would suddenly start having coughing fits. It wasn't like the room was dusty or dirty. Quite to the contrary, it was immaculate.

Henry asked, "So what do you think *is* going on here, Wanda?"

"I can't say yet, sweetie. But my gut tells me Mercy has nothing to do with it. I know what you *said* you saw coming from that entity in the astral plane, but you told me you also had to cut the trip short. Maybe Mercy wasn't the target of that rotten bastard. I hope I'm wrong... but what if it was after Delilah? Given what happened at your apartment yesterday, it actually seems to make a lot more sense. Remember what they wrote on the door?"

Henry did. And he already had the uneasy feeling what Wanda was getting at was true. He just didn't want to believe it. And, given how things had gone down last year, he was *afraid* to believe it. He'd lost this beautiful soul once. It sure as fuck would not happen again.

Jo looked angry and defensive. She trusted Wanda with her life, but this was her *daughter*!

"Wanda," Jo began, "I know you see things coming that others don't. And I trust your judgment. But we are talking about the health of an infant here. My *daughter's* health. I can't hang her well-being on a hunch."

Henry was about to say something when the door on the other side of the room opened and in walked a bloody Archie, with the chief of the Salem Police Department following close behind.

"Archie, are you okay?" Wanda asked.

"I'm fine. Just need a little patching up. Can you help me with that, Henry?"

"Of course."

Henry and Archie headed to the bathroom to take care of the nasty head wound.

"I tried to get him to the ER. He wouldn't have it," said Byron.

"Not surprised," said Wanda. "He's a sweetheart, but he *can* be a stubborn bastard when he wants to be."

Byron nodded as he looked around the room. He'd always thought Wanda was a little cracked. Sweet, but a few sandwiches short of a picnic.

"How's Penny holding up during this monsoon?" Wanda asked.

"You know Penny. She insisted I take her with me to look for her brother. Stubborn... just like him." He nodded toward the bathroom.

"What happened to Mercy?" Joanne asked the chief.

Byron Miller looked at Jo. A look Jo interpreted as *"You just had to ask that now."* Joanne was not in the least bit worried about what the chief thought of her question. Her face was a blank slate, waiting for an answer.

"We don't know. The guy who did that to Archie"—he pointed in the bathroom's direction—"took Mercy... and Archie's bus. We have a BOLO out for them now."

Wanda gasped and put a hand to her mouth. Joanne arched her eyebrows.

Byron continued, "Do either of you have any idea what this is all about?"

Jo and Wanda exchanged glances. Byron wasn't a witch, a warlock, or much of a believer in things spiritual. He was a cop, though, and he was trained in observing people. The look that passed between the two witches did not escape his notice.

"Okay, you two. What's *really* going on here?" Byron asked.

"If we told you, Chief, you wouldn't believe us. Penny would, but you definitely wouldn't," Wanda said.

"Try me," challenged Byron.

"I think I can help with that, Chief," Henry said as he returned from the bathroom with Archie, who now sported a large, wraparound bandage on his head.

"You're mixed up in this, too?" the chief asked.

Henry nodded. He filled the chief in on the events that took place at the apartment. Every little detail. Henry took it upon himself to inform Byron about what happened for one simple reason; he was in the same mindset the chief was in now, only a little over a year ago. He felt it qualified him to explain things. Henry knew all about doubt when it came to the kinds of things that seemed to happen in Salem just below everyone's radar.

"Let me get this straight. You're telling me you have this guy on camera, and the sumbitch doesn't have a face? Come on..."

"I know how it sounds, Chief, but it's true. Gino, the building superintendent, has it on camera."

"Any chance you can get him to send you the video? I mean, if it's true, why not?"

Henry hadn't thought of that. He pulled out his cell phone and punched the contact for Gino. The super picked up after two rings.

"Hi, Gino, it's Henry Trank. I have the chief of police here with me at Wanda's shop..."

Henry listened, then said, "I know I told you the cops wouldn't believe me. And, as it stands right now, they don't.

I called to ask you to send me a copy of the video so the chief can have a look at it..."

More talking from the other end, then, "Okay, thanks, Gino."

The chief looked at Henry, eyebrows raised, questioning.

"He's sending it now."

Two minutes later, Henry's phone started playing a sound file of the orgasm scene from the movie *When Harry Met Sally*. He'd put it on his phone as a joke between him and Jo. He'd forgotten about it. The chief was not amused. Henry's face turned ever so slightly red.

"I'll have what she's having," said Wanda.

The video had arrived.

CHAPTER 12
AS ABOVE, SO BELOW

Penny Miller lay still on the bed. Her breathing was steady, slow, and even. The smell of dragon's blood filled the darkened bedroom. Rain and hailstones tapped the windows in rhythm with the wind. Candle flame fluttered as the draft from the storm forced its way under the windowsill and across the dresser. Shadows danced.

Though physically in the room, Penny soared through the Salem night, her consciousness tethered by the thinnest strand of her essence to her corporeal body. She wondered if this was what people saw *way back when*—thinking they'd seen a witch on a broom. It made her smile.

She'd found Archie long before Byron had. And she had sent Byron a warning to be careful as he'd rounded the corner on Witch Hill Road. Byron always felt her warnings as the faintest feather-touch on his ear. He didn't know she did it, of course, but it worked every time. It was her way of protecting those she loved the most in this world. Once she knew her brother and husband were safe, she went in search of the bus, the girl, and the bastard who'd attacked them.

One thing she had working in her favor was time. It was different on this side of the veil. Time and space were the same. Thought could move you when you needed it to, and to *where* you needed to be. But that was only useful if you had a place in mind. Penny didn't have a clue where she needed to go first. Then she remembered something from her conversation with Byron before he'd left the house. He'd told her about the two killed in the cemetery, and she wondered if maybe those two poor souls hadn't realized they were dead yet. She might find out something from them before they passed to the other side. Crossing her astral fingers, she thought about the graveyard.

MERCY REGAINED consciousness in the dark. The only illumination came when flashes of lightning slipped around the frame of the door to the mausoleum. Her head hurt something fierce, and though the light from the door frame was sparse, it still set her head on fire every time it flashed. *Concussion*, she thought.

She realized for the first time her hands were bound above her head and her body rested in muddy earth. She thrashed about and the splashing suddenly registered with her. The water was rising in here! Panic slipped its icy fingers between her ribs. Her heart jackhammered in her chest. Beads of sweat broke out on her forehead—her breath became shallow and rapid. Thinking became muddled. Her mouth ran dry. Terror was slowly consuming her, and she screamed as loud as she could through the cloth that gagged her. And then she stopped mid-scream.

The voice inside she'd relied on so much lately broke

through the wall of confusion. She forced herself to breathe deeply and slowly. Mercy was well versed in the practice of meditation, and being trapped in the dark—in a place that smelled like mildew and rot—was about the hardest place in the world to put her skills to the test. But she knew she had to try. Every instinct told her to she needed to calm down and figure a way out of this place, or she probably wouldn't be leaving it.

Breathe in, breathe out. Breathe in, breathe out. The lyrics from the song "Machinehead" by Bush began playing in her head. It wasn't exactly the meditation music she was used to, but the rhythm of the lyrics got her into a groove. It helped. She could feel her heart rate approaching something close to normal. Her body was feeling the odd yet reassuring calm that always came after an adrenaline rush. Thoughts started slowing down. The pounding in her head that beat in time with her heart faded. She was relaxing now.

First things first. She needed to get her hands loose. Everything would be a lot easier if she could break free of whatever the hell he'd tied her to.

Mercy yanked her hands toward her head as hard as she could. They wouldn't budge. She took a deep breath, tried again, and got the same result. The old quote from Albert Einstein rang through her mind, "Insanity is doing the same thing, over and over again, and expecting different results." She began forming a different plan.

Mercy had been a gymnastics junkie her senior year in high school. And she had stayed in shape since her glory days. It was likely a large part of why she'd survived the fall at the quarry.

Her hands were bound at the wrist to whatever it was behind her, but her fingers were free. She worked her wrists back and forth until her fingers wrapped around something smooth, long, and cold. A handle. To what? She did not know. Nor did she care to guess.

She dug the heels of her boots into the muddy earth and pushed herself from the rising puddle. Mercy crab-walked closer to the object to which she was tethered, took a deep breath, gripped the handle as tightly as she could, and pushed up from the mausoleum floor with all the strength she had. For one dizzying moment, she felt like she was tumbling through the dark—weightless and floating free. Almost as soon as that thought entered her mind, it fled. Reality came in the form of her body crashing down on a smooth, convex surface. Her arms were yanked violently forward and pain rocketed through her shoulders. Her upper body whacked into the top of the surface and her thighs and knees slammed into its side. It knocked the wind out of her.

"Smooth," she moaned. It echoed throughout the waterlogged room. Mercy allowed herself a few moments until the breath returned to her body. Once she felt strong enough, she began thinking about the second leg of her plan.

Her hands were still bound to the other side of the object. She needed some idea of what it was, so she waited until the next flash of lightning leaked through the frame of the door. It didn't take long, and she sucked in a surprised breath when she realized what she was bound to.

She whispered, "A fucking casket!"

Someone whispered back.

BYRON WATCHED the video all the way to the end. He still wasn't sure what he was seeing, but he sure as hell didn't believe he was seeing someone who didn't have a face. He told Henry so.

Henry said, "I don't know what else to tell you, Byron. I don't blame you for thinking it's a bunch of bullshit. A lot of stuff happened last year, to me, that I never would have believed in a million years. I'm just asking you to keep an open mind."

"Having an open mind is one thing. Believing that someone on a video doesn't have a face, that's something I can't do, Henry.

There was nothing more Henry could say to convince Byron what he was seeing was real. And that's when Wanda gave it a try.

"Byron," she said. "You know there are things in this world that can't be explained. I know you don't believe in them, but they happen. And I know you've seen things happen in your own house—with your own wife—you've just conveniently ignored. For you to stand there and continue to deny what you see on that tape is real is nothing more than the same stubbornness you accuse your wife and your brother-in-law of having. What else would it take to convince you what you're seeing is real?"

Byron said, "I don't know. Why don't you think of something that might change my mind? I can sit and watch this video all day long, but there is no way in the world I'm going to buy what I'm seeing. Especially when I know video can be manipulated. I can go on YouTube right now and show you a million videos that'll convince you the earth is flat, the moon landing took place in a movie studio, and Elvis Presley works at a car wash in Memphis. But that doesn't make it real."

Wanda threw her hands in the air, exasperated. *If only*, she thought, *there was something I could do right here, right now, to convince him what he was seeing was real.* Her eyes settled on the Reiki table and something occurred to her.

"Byron," Wanda said, "if you really want me to prove to you something you have no belief in is real, would you allow me to do a brief experiment on you?"

Byron was wary. "What kind of experiment?"

"It's nothing to fear, nothing to be worried about, but it is something that needs your cooperation. All I want to do is use Reiki to demonstrate an ability that I have."

"Reiki? Isn't that the healing mumbo-jumbo you and Penny practice?"

Wanda said, "If you think it's mumbo-jumbo, then put up or shut up."

Byron rolled his eyes. "Fine. Let's get this bullshit over with."

Archie didn't need any prompting from Wanda. Without a word, he went to the back of the room and, for the second time that night, grabbed the black massage table Wanda used for Reiki treatments. He set it in the middle of the pentacle. Both he and Henry retreated outside of the circle and took their seats in the black leather beanbag chairs to watch.

Wanda stood next to the table, waved her hand over it like a magician, and said, "Byron, if you please."

Byron let out a sigh of exasperation, kicked off his shoes, and lay face-up on the massage table.

"Okay, Byron," Wanda said, "I'm going to ask you a question, but I don't want you to answer it. I want you to keep the answer to yourself."

Byron looked at Wanda, his face displaying obvious skepticism.

"Ask your question," he said.

Wanda asked, "Have you had any aches or pains lately? In particular, any part of your body that's been hurting you lately? Now remember, don't answer, just think about it."

Byron nodded and said nothing.

Wanda went through her preparations to treat Byron with Reiki. The first thing she did was flatten her left hand, placed it a few inches above Byron's forehead, and slowly ran it the length of his body. Her hand never came into contact with Byron at any point. When her hand passed over Byron's left knee, she felt a mild jolt of electricity jump toward her palm. And she knew, right away, this was the spot Byron was having pain in.

Usually, people keep their eyes closed during a Reiki treatment, but Byron, being the skeptic he was, kept his eyes open the entire time. Wanda would not fool him. So, it came as quite a surprise when Wanda stopped just above his left knee.

Wanda finished scanning Byron's body down to his toes. She looked back in his direction, smiled, and made her way to his left knee. She placed both hands on the knee, took a deep breath, and began the healing process.

As energy flowed from her hands into Byron's knee, he nearly jumped off the table.

"What the hell was that?" Byron yelled.

"What do you mean?" Wanda asked.

"What did you just do to my knee? It felt like little bee stings."

"Sometimes, Byron, healing energy can feel really strange to someone not used to it."

"Let me see your hands," Byron said.

Wanda held out her hands, palms up. They were, of course, empty. She asked him, "What are you looking for?"

Byron was at a loss for words.

"As you can see, there is nothing in my hands, and nothing up my sleeves. Now, why don't you get your skeptic's ass back on the table, and let me finish what I was doing."

"I don't know," Byron said, "something fishy is going on here."

"What is your problem, exactly? You asked me to prove something to you and I'm doing that. So, if you're not afraid of being proved wrong, I suggest you get back up on the table and let me finish what I was doing."

Byron looked to Archie and Henry for help. None came. Both men stared at him. He reluctantly got back on the massage table.

This time when Byron got on the table, he closed his eyes. It was just easier that way. He was getting the feeling something was going to happen he didn't *want* to happen. It was the curse of the skeptic when presented evidence their dearly held beliefs were about to be proved wrong.

Wanda continued. The first thing Byron felt was the intense warmth radiating from Wanda's hands. That warmth worked its way from the top of his kneecap, through the middle of his leg, and to the other side. The entire process took less than five minutes. When Wanda removed her hands, she repeated the crazy hand gestures again, then ran her hands flat over Byron's body as she did before, closing the healing session.

"That's it," she said.

"What's it?" Byron asked.

"Well, what did you think about when I asked you to focus on something that was hurting you?"

Byron said nothing for a few seconds.

"Byron?"

"I thought about the pain in my knee, but there must be some way you knew about it. I'll bet Penny said something to you."

"I haven't talked to Penny in six months," Wanda said. "Has this been going on for longer than six months?"

Byron croaked out a weak, "No."

"So, how long has this been going on? This pain in your knee I couldn't possibly know about?"

"For about the last three weeks," Byron answered.

"Well, maybe you should be a little more careful when you get out of the shower."

Byron told no one, not even Penny, he'd hurt his knee coming out of the shower.

Wanda saw the look on his face. She winked.

CHAPTER 13
ILLUSION AND CONFUSION

Mercy didn't know where the whispers came from, and she didn't really care. The pain in her shoulders, arms, and legs was all her mind could handle. She needed to figure out how to get loose from the casket—then she could deal with disembodied whispers.

Her arms were still strapped to the handle on the opposite side of the casket. The muscles in her legs throbbed from the pounding they'd taken when she'd vaulted the casket and slammed into its far side, and her knees were red-hot apples of pain from hitting the ground with the weight of her body behind them. So, it was no simple task to stand up, but she managed.

Mercy swung her left leg up and over the convex surface of the casket. It landed on top with a soft *fwump!* A sound not unlike the slamming of a car door. "Let's hear it for flexibility," she said to the empty tomb.

She worked her foot in herky-jerky motions and wedged the heel of her leather boot into the twists of cloth binding her to the casket handle. She braced against the far side with her right foot, pushing back against it with everything she had.

A video clip she'd seen on YouTube flashed in her memory. Batman and Robin, climbing up the side of a building in that old, late-sixties TV show—capes hanging behind them—it made her laugh just as the bindings gave way.

Mercy launched backward and through the air a short distance, slamming into the stone wall behind her. She was dazed and clinging to consciousness when she saw them. A young couple, obviously dead, walked past her and into the wall.

PENNY KNEW this was the spot. *He* had been here. Whatever *he* was. She knew Byron and Archie were both safe. Now she needed to know who'd hurt her brother.

A green, rust-flaked mausoleum door stood in front of her. Rain pounded down. Hailstones bounced against the door and landed in the stairwell, piling up in clumps. She couldn't remember the last time she'd seen a storm this bad. On this plane, thankfully, it had little effect.

She put a hand to the door and let it rest. Whatever the entity was, she should, she thought, be able to pick up some trace energy it had left behind.

Penny quieted her mind. After a time, images formed, hazy and unfocused at first. They became clearer the longer she left her hand against the door. He was dragging an unconscious woman across the threshold and into the mausoleum, shutting the door when both were inside.

Penny removed her hand. She needed to get inside to

learn more and walked forward, expecting her astral body to pass through the mausoleum door easily. Instead, she was blasted backward into the stairwell. It felt like a thousand volts of electricity whizzing through her mind, and it surprised her she hadn't been zapped straight back into her body. She sat up and stared at the door, trying to get her mind around what had just happened.

He floated just outside the window to Penny's bedroom. There was no way to get inside. It was well protected—much like the witch's store. But he didn't need to get inside. All he wanted to know was who had been following him. And now he knew. Another member of the League of the Moon. He thought he'd accounted for all of them. He'd thought wrong. But, unlike his former master, he'd been more cautious. The trap he'd set at the door connected his consciousness to that of Penny's, and it immediately sent him to the area from which her consciousness emanated. She would figure out what had happened, eventually. All it accomplished was buying him some time, but time—on the earth plane—was what he needed. Mercy had to be protected at all costs. Until they finished with her.

"Okay, Wanda," Byron said, "you need to come clean with me. Right now. How did you know I hurt my knee coming from the shower?"

"The same way I knew it was your knee that was hurting you. I just *know*."

"That makes zero sense."

"To you, I'm sure it does. But consider this, Byron. Have you ever had a feeling you knew something was about to happen, and then it *did?* Or, maybe, you travel to a place you've never been, but suddenly the feeling you've been there before crawls all over you. Déjà vu, you know?"

Byron nodded, but his face said he wasn't buying it. "That's a far cry from knowing something like how I hurt my knee."

"Put that aside for now. Just think. When was the last time something like that happened to you? It happens to all of us. Please, just be honest about it."

Byron tried to recall something, *anything*, like what Wanda was getting at. His eyes popped wide when the memory hit him and he tried to hide it, but Wanda saw.

"What was it, Byron? You remember something, I can see it in your eyes."

"It's probably nothing. But... okay." He shook his head, not believing what he was about to tell her. "There was this one night, oh... about this time, last year. No, it was later... October. Night before Halloween, I think. Call comes in, 'bout eleven-ish in the evening. Someone tells the 911 operator they see a flashlight in the library... looks like there might be a break-in. Well, it was my night to cover that area. I take the call and head over. Lights off, don't wanna let 'em know I'm coming. Turns out it didn't matter; the alarm was blastin' and the place was lit up like the Fourth of July. I called Raul for backup."

"Oh, I love that kid. He's one of the good ones," Wanda said.

"Yep, he is. So, we get there, too late, as it turns out. But we gotta check the place anyway. So, me and Raul, we head inside to see what's what. I tell him to take the second floor and I'll take the first. Well"—Byron shook his head, a look of disbelief slid across his face—"I tell Raul to wait. Don't know why, but I just had a feeling, you know?"

Wanda nodded.

"Raul says, 'What's the matter, Chief?' and I tell him I don't know, but something ain't right."

Byron paused for a long time. He looked scared. To Wanda, it seemed the memory had been so overwhelming that Byron might have suppressed it. Whatever it was, he looked shaken. She felt bad for him.

"It's okay, Byron. You can tell us. There is no judgment within these walls."

Byron looked at all of them in turn. He felt embarrassed and vulnerable, but the looks on their faces told him it was okay. They looked like they *believed* him. It gave him the courage to continue.

"I smelled something. It was faint but *there* all the same. It was coming from the second floor. I nodded for Raul to follow me, and we made our way up the stairs as quiet as we could. When you look back on it, it's kinda silly —trying to be quiet. The alarm was blaring but... you know, procedure and all. Well, the smell only got worse the further we went. When we got to the second floor, it was a stench."

Archie chimed in, "What did it smell like, Byron?"

Byron pinched the bridge of his nose, closed his eyes, and gave it some thought.

"If I had to compare it to anything, I'd probably say it smelled like sulfur, or rotten eggs."

Everyone in the room knew exactly what he was talking about. And exactly *who* he was talking about. No one said a word. No one had to. They let him go where they all knew he was going.

"We turned the corner on an aisle of books. And... I saw something. But if I told you, you'd never believe me. Raul saw it, too. Neither of us has talked about it since it happened. I still don't know if I believe what I saw with my own eyes or not."

Joanne said, "You saw a man in black. You saw him leap in the air and turn into a dog."

Byron's jaw hit the floor. And his world shifted ever so slightly in a new direction—slightly, not totally. He focused on Joanne. "How do you know that?"

"I'm the one who broke into the library."

"Come again?"

"It's true. There's a long story behind it, but it was me," said Joanne.

"And what, exactly, were you hoping to accomplish by breaking into the Salem Library?"

"There was a book in there we needed."

"You *do* know there's a much easier way to take books from the library, right? You get one of those little cards with your name on it, they stamp it when you take it out. Then, when you're done reading it, you take it back to the library and they stamp it returned. It's really a lot easier."

"Yes, I'm aware of that. Thanks for looking out for me, Chief." Joanne smirked. "But this particular book couldn't wait for business hours."

"Oh? And why's that?"

Jo continued, "It was a matter of life and death. We'd just returned from Henry's parents' house in Maine. At the house, we came into possession of a note that explained it all. The book contained some information that couldn't wait to be obtained. I suggested to Henry it may not be the wisest course to wait for the morning. It turned out to be true."

"What was *so* important?" Byron asked.

Henry took over. "The note was from my mother. My birth mother, Delilah Davis."

"The real estate lady?" Byron asked.

Henry nodded.

Byron was not aware of the connection between Henry and Delilah. Penny had warned off the entire League of the Moon from telling him. She told them she would let him know when the time was right. Byron, bloodhound that he was, would want to investigate every little detail of what had happened last October. And *that* was not a good idea, given how things had gone down that night.

"Whatever happened to her?" Byron asked. "I never see her or that asshole she was gonna marry around town anymore."

"She was murdered. In this room. Do you remember a man named Solomon Dobson?" Henry asked Byron.

Byron nodded. "Sure do. Nasty guy. Owned half the town, if I had to guess. Mean eyes."

"Well, as it turns out, he owned—scratch that, still owns —half of the souls in this town," Henry said.

Byron's eyebrows shot up. "What do you mean, he owns half the *souls* in this town? I don't even know how to process that, Henry."

Henry thought for a few moments about how to proceed. He knew what it was like to be a skeptic and have others tossing what appear to be crackpot theories and stories at your feet. But he also, through the events of the previous year, understood how you could be persuaded to open up—just a little—in order to accept a different way of thinking. He chose his next words with great care. "Chief, how much do you *really* know about Solomon Dobson?"

"Just what I told you. He was a prick with power."

"But what do you know of his history in Salem?" asked Henry.

"Nothing, really," said Byron.

"What would you say if I told you he'd been here for a real long time? Like, before you were *born*, long?" Henry asked.

"It wouldn't surprise me. He looked older than dirt the last time I saw him."

"And when was the last time you saw him? Do you remember?"

Byron squinted his left eye and looked at the ceiling with his right. "I'd say, oh... 'bout a year ago, maybe less. He was down by the town common, shootin' the shit with the real estate guy. Why?"

"You remember what he looked like that day, correct?"

Byron rolled his eyes. "Yes. Is this going somewhere, Henry?"

"Please, just bear with me. I'm going to show you a video I got from the hospital last year. It was captured late, the night before Halloween. Just watch the video and then we can talk about it afterward. Okay?"

Byron nodded. He looked doubtful and curious at the same time.

Henry handed the chief his phone. Byron tapped the middle of the screen and the video began. It was crystal clear. In it, a large, black Cadillac Escalade pulled up to the rear entrance of the hospital. He could clearly see Solomon Dobson with his elderly, bent posture exit the vehicle, say something to his driver, pull a keyring from his suit coat, open the door, and step inside.

"You recognize Dobson?" Henry asked.

Byron nodded without looking up from the phone.

"Watch real close now, Chief," Henry said.

Time on the video jumped from 10:51 p.m. to 11:17 p.m. The date remained the same. The Caddy hadn't moved, and the driver still sat, now smoking a cigarette, where he'd been when Dobson left the limo earlier. A much younger man returned to the vehicle.

The camera had captured a clear image of his face. Byron paused the video, studying the face and the clothes the man was wearing. And the cane he twirled in his hand that, twenty-five minutes earlier, had been used to support his rickety frame. There was no mistaking the face of Solomon Dobson. His eyes were a shade of blue Byron had never seen shining out from the face of another human being—almost a light purple. They'd always made him feel cold. The eyes hadn't changed, though the body had.

"What am I supposed to get out of this video, Henry?"

Now it was Henry's turn to be impatient. "You don't see what's happened here, Chief?"

"I see a younger guy exiting the hospital dressed like Dobson," Byron said. He was exhibiting the best poker face he could muster, but it wasn't easy. Inside, he was putting things together, but the skeptic in him was holding on to the last threads of its coveted blanket of reality. When Henry took a picture from his pocket and thrust it at Byron, there was a tearing sound from that blanket.

"What's this?" Byron asked.

"Look," Henry said with growing impatience.

The picture was yellowed and frayed at its edges. In the

background, just above the head of the primary subject of the photo, was a banner that read "Salem celebrates Fourth of July 1935." Two men were in the photo. The man on the left was in profile, and Byron couldn't be sure, but it looked an awful lot like Leonard Shrumm, the real estate guy. There was, however, no mistaking the man facing forward. His enormous smile put the lie to the cold, hard, ice-blue eyes. Mean eyes. Solomon Dobson's eyes. And the man in the photo looked exactly the same as the man framed in Henry's video—right down to the clothes and the cane. Inside, Byron heard something rip.

CHAPTER 14
TRADING PLACES

It didn't take long for Penny to figure out what was going on. After she'd been jolted from the mausoleum door, and after her head cleared a bit, she realized she'd been played. It should have been obvious to her, but in her haste to find her brother, and with the rage that came from knowing what was done to him, she had rushed after his attacker with nothing but icy-hot vengeance on her mind.

In the astral realm, anger and the vibrations it sent out were the same thing as slapping a homing beacon on your ass for all to see. And she knew he *saw*. He probably felt her coming a mile away, so to speak. She was not happy with herself; she knew better. Penny had let emotion run the show, and it had caused her to be exposed.

In the past, her greatest ally had been her anonymity. Both in the real world and the realm just beyond it. He knew where she lived and what she could do now. Whatever this being was and whatever its mission might be, it now had the upper hand. Penny thought herself back into her body, got up from the bed, and considered her next moves.

~

BYRON STARED at the picture in his hand. The man at the Fourth of July parade and the man he'd seen exiting the hospital on the video were the same. There was no denying it. He wondered how this could be possible—nothing came to mind. Something inside him shifted again, and the comfy blanket of skepticism tore a bit more.

He stared at the picture for a few more moments, buying time as his mind tried to wrap itself around all that Henry, Wanda, Joanne, and Archie had presented for his scrutiny. The scales were tipping in their favor. It was getting harder for him to deny what was right in front of him. But he wasn't all the way there yet.

"So, you mean to tell me," Byron said, "that Solomon Dobson had been, what? Alive for almost a hundred and twenty years? And that the guy in this picture and the one in the video are the same person? I'll admit, they *look* like the same person. And if you told me they were, and I didn't know the dates of the video and the photo, I would say they're either the same person, or the guy in the photo is the guy in the video's granddad. But that's not what you're saying..."

"Nope, they're the same person." Henry said.

Byron shook his head, and the only thing he could think to ask was, "How?"

"The question you need to ask, Byron, is why?" said Wanda.

"Come again?"

She thought about it for a second, then said, "What is the one thing in the world most people would want if you could grant them one wish?"

"Money," Byron said.

Wanda smiled and nodded in concession. "Granted. I should have been more specific. What is the one thing in the world you would wish for if you had all the money and material possessions you would ever need?"

Byron stared at the ceiling, thought about it, then said, "Time."

"Exactly!" Wanda said, excited. "Now think about it, Byron. It's your last day on earth. What would you do for a chance to live longer? Even just one more day? You'd probably give up just about anything, wouldn't you?"

"I suppose. I guess it would matter how you felt—health-wise, I mean—but yeah, I'll go along with that."

"Now think of it in terms of a greedy bastard like Solomon Dobson." Wanda held up a hand and ticked off a list. "He craves money, power, attention, adoration, and just about anything selfish you can think of. Imagine what someone like that would do to keep everything he's acquired. And imagine if someone like that had found a way to keep himself alive for hundreds of years."

"Okay, Wanda, I'll play along. And I agree, a guy like Dobson, if he could find a way, would try to keep himself alive to keep all the goodies he's collected. There's just one minor problem with your scenario. It's not possible."

"But it is, honey," Penny said.

No one had heard Penny enter the room. It was like she'd appeared out of thin air.

"What the hell are you doing here, Penny?" Byron asked.

"Listening to my stubborn husband defending the wall

of the skeptics." She walked over to Byron and planted a kiss on his forehead.

"I'm sorry, baby, but the stuff they're all talking about isn't possible. I can't deny the guy in the photo and the guy in the video look a lot alike, but there's no way they're the same person."

She nodded, expecting Byron to say *exactly* that. They'd had numerous discussions in the past about all things spiritual. Of course, he would never budge an inch on his stance. He wouldn't belittle her or her beliefs. He loved her way too much for that, but there was no way he would ever buy into the things she believed. Byron would nod and ask questions in all the right places, but that was as far as he would go. To him, the world was black and white, with an occasional allowance for a shade of gray, here and there. When it came to life, he was a lot like Joe Friday in the old *Dragnet* TV show. "All we want are the facts, ma'am." Joe Friday was about to get the rudest awakening of his life tonight.

"By, how did you find my brother tonight?" Penny asked.

"I knew the girl who was with him lived up by Witch Hill Road. So that's the area I headed to first. Why?"

"When you got to Witch Hill Road, did you feel anything funny? Out of the ordinary?"

Byron thought about it and said, "No. Nothing I can think of other than that crazy itch I always seem to get right before something on the job happens. You know, my "cop's intuition" thing we always talk about. Why?"

Penny shrugged. "Oh, I don't know. I was just curious. By the way"—she nodded toward Archie—"when that guy hit Archie in the head with the flashlight, what side was it on?"

Byron looked at Penny, a little worried. Anyone could see the left side of Archie's head was where the blood seeped through his bandage. "Baby, are you alright? Can't you tell where Archie got hit just by looking at him?"

Penny stared at her husband, laughed, and said, "Yes, honey. I can see exactly where he was hit."

Byron was trying his best to remain patient. It was getting a lot harder as the night wore on. "Baby... then why did you ask me—" He stopped mid-sentence when it hit him. His eyes jumped from one face to the next. He'd been in the room with Wanda, Henry, Jo, Delilah, and Archie since he and Archie walked through the door earlier in the night. No one had asked how Archie had gotten the bump on his head. They all knew he'd been attacked. Their only concern was for his safety. Nobody knew about the flashlight.

Penny winked at Byron.

FEW PEOPLE KNOW about the tunnels that run underneath the town of Salem. Well, not many people *other* than those who live in the town. It's fairly common knowledge to the residents who know the city's past that the tunnels are there. It's just not the kind of thing that's talked about a lot. Everyone above ground is more interested in everyday life, the businesses they own, and the tourists that flock by the thousands, year-round, to pay good money for all the wonderful things the Witch City offers.

Mercy knew about the tunnels, but she never imagined she would navigate them during a storm, in the middle of the night, having been led to them by a recently murdered couple. When Mercy saw the two ghosts walking by her, she'd at first assumed they'd walked through the wall and disappeared. When her mind cleared, she noticed it wasn't a wall at all. It was the pitch-black entrance to a tunnel that only *appeared* as a solid black wall in the mausoleum's darkness. When the lightning next flashed, she saw the opening of the tunnel as clear as day. It was the sole way out. She took it.

The only way Mercy could navigate the light-deprived tunnel was by sticking to its left side and keeping one hand in contact with the wall at all times. Her only other "tool" to navigate with was the sound of her footfalls in the shallow but rising water on the tunnel's floor. Any time the frequency of the echoes bouncing from the walls shrank, or dulled down, she knew she was coming upon a turn. She would extend her right hand carefully in front of her to gauge the direction she needed to take next.

"This is going to take forever," she told the tunnel. Echoes mocked her words.

Something splashed in the water, right in front of her. Mercy froze in place and listened. Another splash, followed by the sound of scurrying feet. Several splashes followed, and high-pitched squeaking noises filled the fetid, inky-black air all around her. Rats! Mercy was no longer frozen in place. She broke into a full-out run, her hands extended in front of her to brace against running headfirst into a stone wall. Somewhere, in the dim recesses of the high-function part of her brain she knew to run—to panic—was the worst thing she could do. But there is another part of the brain that takes over in times like these.

Everyone is born into this world through the portal of spirit, but the vessel we're deposited into is made for survival in *this* world. The lower-functioning lizard brain takes over in times like these. It's an unfortunate fact of evolution. Except, were it not for that lower-functioning, fight-or-flight response, we as a species would have ceased to exist a long time ago. In the battle for survival, the lizard beat the shit out of the philosopher every time. Mercy was no exception.

The part of the tunnel her powerful legs propelled her down was a straight run. Panic still consumed her, but luck was on her side. Her lungs burned, her legs ached, and the pounding of her heart was the only sound she could hear. And when she realized the only sound she could hear was the jackhammer beat of her own heart, she slowed. She'd outrun the rats, and the earth beneath her wasn't a splash-fest anymore. Dry ground lay beneath her feet.

Mercy allowed herself a brief rest to catch her breath and slow her mind down. She was bent over at the waist with her hands on her hips, sucking in the mildew-laced air. She straightened up. There was a faint light at the end of the tunnel that moved to the left and disappeared. It was too far away to tell what it was for sure, but she didn't need to guess. She was sure it was the couple she'd seen earlier. Mercy prayed they were helping her and not leading her to a fate similar to their own.

HE ARRIVED at the mausoleum once he'd re-inhabited his partially formed body, satisfied with himself for neutralizing Penny as a threat. The satisfaction was short-lived. When he unlocked the mausoleum door and stepped inside, he saw the tattered and torn rags he'd used to bind Mercy. They lay floating on the surface of the murky water, rising and falling in time with the small waves his movements had stirred up. He kicked at them and sent filthy water across the surface of the dulled silver casket and cursed himself for not anticipating the possibility of her escape. He'd underestimated Mercy's resourcefulness, much as Inanis had underestimated Wanda's. Doubt's itchy fingers picked at his innards. He pushed them away and stormed into the tunnels to find Mercy.

CHAPTER 15
ASTRAL CONFESSION

"Okay, Penny. How did you know Archie got clocked in the head with a flashlight? No one, other than Archie and myself, knows that."

Penny exchanged a look with Wanda. Byron watched as Wanda closed her eyes and nodded. He had a bad feeling about it.

"By, there's something you need to know. It's something I've thought about telling you in the past. Well, it's actually something we've tossed back and forth at the dinner table so many times I've lost count. I always tried to steer the conversation to where I could just come out and tell you the whole truth, but it never got there. We have a lot of things in common, By. We both see the world the same way on almost everything, but those nights when we get into the weeds on the stuff you call "woo-woo"—well, it just always felt that if I came right out and told you exactly what I am—" She paused and tears were brimming in her eyes.

Alarm and concern lit Byron's face. "What is it, baby? You're starting to scare me... what's the matter?"

"I'm afraid if I'm honest with you, you won't look at me the same anymore."

"Baby, nothing in the world could change the way I feel about you. I love you. Now please, tell me what's wrong."

Penny wiped her eyes with the backs of her hands, took a deep breath, and let the chips fall where they may. "When you found Archie tonight, I was with you."

Byron tilted his head like a dog that doesn't quite understand what you're asking it. Then he nodded, closed his eyes, and gave her a smile like he understood. He didn't. "Oh, you mean you heard it on the radio I left behind for you. That's okay baby, that's why I left the radio for you in the first place, I—"

"That's not what I mean, By. I was there. I saw Archie plop down in the puddle. I saw the blood wash from his face when it splashed up. I saw you help him up from the ground and belt him into the car." She laughed, "I even heard the conversation about taking him to the hospital."

Byron's jaw was working, but no sound was coming out. Like a hungry fish in an aquarium tank at feeding time.

"But the funniest thing of all," Penny said, "was I could hear what you were *thinking* about. And yes, trying to get Archie to change his mind *is* exactly like trying to tell a nun there is no God."

Silence descended upon the room. Rain and hailstones peppered the skylight above. No one said a word. Everyone watched Byron as he tried to get a grip on something that didn't have a handle. When he finally spoke, all that came out was, "How?"

Penny walked over and sat next to him on the Reiki table. She gave Wanda a look. They were so in tune with each other, despite the months they hadn't had the chance to talk, no words needed to pass between them. Wanda pulled up a chair and sat in front of them. Henry, Joanne, and Archie did the same. Joanne placed Delilah in front of her in the little carrier, careful not to wake her.

Wanda said, "Byron, I know this is a lot to digest in one night. But every single thing we've been telling you tonight is the truth."

Byron nodded, but said nothing.

Wanda continued.

"All of us in this room are members of a coven. The name of the coven is *Foedere In Luna*. In English, the League of the Moon."

"Coven? As in a bunch of witches?"

Henry and Jo exchanged amused glances. Jo had planted an imaginary gold star on Henry's head when he'd asked the exact same thing in this room almost a year ago.

"Exactly," Wanda said. "I know you've thought of it as a cute little hobby we all engage in together, but I assure you it is *much* more than that."

Byron asked, "Meaning what, exactly?"

Penny said, "We protect Salem from the bad guys, honey. Kinda like you do, but on a different level."

Byron turned to his wife. "What kinda bad guys are you talking about? And what do you mean by a different *level*?"

Henry chimed in, "You remember when I told you my mother was murdered in this very room, Chief?"

Byron nodded.

"Well, Solomon Dobson was the one who did it. Only, by that time, he was no longer Solomon Dobson. He was a demon and his name was Inanis. Now, I know how completely insane this all sounds—it sounded fucking nuts to me, too—but it's true. And I had even *more* time to wrap my head around it than you've had here tonight. But the thing is, whether or not you believe it, and whether or not you accept it... it doesn't matter. What's going down tonight is *real*! And it's gonna happen whether or not you buy in. But I've gotten to know you a little since I became part of your family. We need you on our side, Chief. Whatever that thing out there is, it's not gonna stop coming for us. It won't stop until it gets what it wants."

"Henry, I knew your mom was killed, though I didn't know Delilah Davis was your mother. But I have to ask, what happened to her? And what happened to Dobson? And Shrumm? I'm giving all of you the benefit of the doubt. And for me, that ain't easy. I'm a cop, Henry. I need evidence."

"You remember the fire at the funeral home last year?"

"Yeah," Byron said, "the fire department said it started in the morgue. They left the furnace on. We all thought Dobson did it to collect the insurance money. Then he disappeared. You mean—"

"It was the only way we could end it all without arousing suspicion. My mother and Shrumm were cremated there that night. The fire was cover."

"Wait, who killed Shrumm?" Byron asked.

"Dobson. Blew his brains out in the limo. That was also toasted in the fire at the morgue."

Byron shook his head in disbelief. Then, he remembered something from that night. He said, "That stuff about the snow falling on Essex Street—was that all part of what happened here back in October?"

Everyone in the room nodded.

"Don't suppose you could fill me in on what that was all about?" Byron asked.

Wanda filled in the blanks for him about how they'd

opened a portal to 1692. How they'd sent Henry back to retrieve the items needed to put an end to Inanis. How the raging storm that took place on All Hallows' Eve, back in that far-off time, had leaked into the present and covered the grounds in snow, both inside and out. It didn't seem to convince him totally, but he couldn't come up with a better explanation for how it could snow in one part of Salem while the rest of the town received only rain.

As Wanda was finishing up her summation of the events of early Halloween morning 2018, Archie made his way behind the bar in the back of the room. He came back to the circle in front of Penny and Byron with a cardboard file box, handed the box to Wanda, and took his seat.

"What's in the box?" Byron asked.

Wanda pulled the lid from the box and removed its contents. She showed Byron a flask with the demon's name on it, a small box with a combination lock on its face, and a note protected by a Ziploc bag. Wanda explained how each item related to the events of that night. She saved the note for last and handed it to the chief.

When Byron finished reading it, he said, "Well, that jibes with you two breaking into the library."

Joanne and Henry both nodded.

"Okay, it makes a twisted sort of sense to me, I guess." He turned to his wife. "Now, how in the hell did you see what was happening on Witch Hill Road?"

Penny took her time before answering. How could she explain astral travel to a hardened skeptic like her husband? She dove straight in. "By, when you dream at night, do you know where you go?"

Byron was actually mulling it over a bit. *That* alone was an encouraging sign to Penny. She waited him out.

"Well, I don't know. I never thought of it in terms of actually *going* anywhere. I always figured it was something my brain did automatically, you know, to relieve the stress of the day. Granted, some of the stuff is bizarre as hell, but I think it's that way for everyone. Where do *you* think we go?"

"That answer is partially right, honey. But there's much more to it. When we fall asleep at night, we get into a place between this world and another dimension called the astral plane. And yes, your brain does it automatically. Everyone's does. But you can control it! You can slip into that plane of existence while you're awake. It takes practice, and it's not something you can do right away, unless you're a natural like Henry. I've been doing it my entire life, well, since I was about eleven or twelve years old."

Byron's eyebrows shot up at that revelation.

"Yep. And I've done it our entire marriage, too." She winked. "I keep tabs on you when you're working. And I help you in subtle ways when I can. Tonight, when you turned on to Witch Hill Road, I bet you felt a little tickle right here." She reached around her husband's head and lightly brushed the top of his left ear. It was always that spot for her when she needed to give Byron a heads up.

He was speechless. His mind ran through all the times he'd felt the peculiar sensation right before something was about to happen. And how many times it probably had saved his ass. He'd become a little superstitious about it. Almost dependent upon it. It was a lot like a baseball player going through a ritual at the plate—tap his bat three times, kick up dirt in a certain way in the batter's box, tap the top of his helmet, and so on. He actually felt a twinge of guilt about harboring the superstition and not actually coming clean about it to Penny. Especially since, though he would never say it out loud to her, he thought most of the stuff she was into was a bit "out there." His opinion was changing, big time.

"When you left the house tonight, I went right upstairs to the bedroom, dropped into a meditative state, and started searching for Archie on my own." She looked at her brother when she said this. He looked genuinely touched. And, to Byron, there was not a hint of surprise anywhere on Archie's face about his sister's abilities.

There was no surprise on the faces of *anyone* in the room. It was like they'd heard all of this before, like it was a commonplace thing with all of them. He wished he could just *believe* the way they all seemed to. And in that simple wish, though Byron didn't realize it, the seed of belief was born.

Penny knew her husband well. She could tell from the look on his face, something had shifted ever so slightly. And for now, that was good enough. He would draw his own conclusions. The mountain of "evidence" he claimed to need was piling up in front of him. He'd get there. She suspected the events of the night ahead would take him the rest of the way.

Penny turned to Wanda. "Now, for the bad news."

She filled in everyone about the trap set at the mausoleum, about the vision she'd had of Mercy being dragged in there, and how she, herself, had been compromised. Which, they now understood, was the reason she decided it would be better for her to come to Wanda's safe room.

"You don't know what's become of Mercy, do you?" Wanda asked.

Penny shook her head. "The two who were murdered

there tonight, if we're lucky, might still be around and may help her out. How? I couldn't tell you. But when Byron told me what had happened, especially about their bizarre wounds, I figured it might have something to do with Mercy. That's what led me to the mausoleum."

Archie spoke up, "What was bizarre about the wounds?"

Byron said, "They both had exit wounds in the middle of their foreheads. Not entry wounds, like from a bullet. Something was pulled, neatly and cleanly, from right here." Byron motioned with his hand. "Their pineal glands were removed. No blood at all."

Archie felt an icy wave of fear wash over him. He didn't believe in coincidence. Two seemingly different lectures he'd given—the one on the pineal gland, which came to mind as he'd meditated earlier in the night with Wanda, and the lecture he'd given earlier today, where both he and Mercy had felt the rage of someone in the room at the mention of Henry killing the demon Chesrule—were linked by the events of the past few days. As of now, he couldn't understand how they related, but a hazy picture of their connection was forming in his mind. The possibilities terrified him, and he couldn't stop his mind from trying to piece the connection together.

CHAPTER 16
FOR WHOM THE BELL TOLLS?

Mercy took the left, where the lights had disappeared. It led to another long, dark, but mercifully dry tunnel. *'Get your tickets to Salem's weirdest guided tour. Complete with recently murdered ghosts and a psychotic entity hot on your trail!'*

At least without all the splashing, she could hear. There wasn't much *to* hear at the moment, save for her own breathing and the muted echo of her footsteps. She trudged on, arms outstretched, both hands palms up, praying if she bumped into anything, it was nothing more than a stone wall or a door.

After what seemed a silent eternity, she heard something —the faint but unmistakable ringing of a bell. In the dark, it was hard for her to determine how far away it was, or exactly which direction she might need to go to reach it, but she had the intuitive feeling she *needed* to reach it.

Mercy kept a steady pace and a vigilant ear. The bell rang again, closer, but still far enough away that drawing a bead on it was just out of reach. She fought the urge to break into a run. She kept walking at the same steady, patient pace she'd set for herself and was rewarded when the bell dinged once more. It was now to her left. Keeping her arms up, she turned in the sound's direction. Both flattened hands met with the cool, slimy, moss-covered stones of the tunnel. Mercy adjusted and slid her hands to the right, feeling her way toward an opening. Relief washed over her when she felt the empty space, and turned to outright terror in an instant. She felt several hands clutch her arms and yank her forward. One of the hands released her left arm and clamped around her mouth, stifling a scream a millisecond short of bursting from her lips.

HE HEARD THE BELL. It was barely audible, but *there* all the same. That he could hear anything in the tunnels at all was not a good thing. Others were in the tunnels. Visible to him, but mostly hidden. Souls from long past that were on a different vibration than he was. Spirits closer to the light.

He was an entity straddling two planes of existence, so the reliability of his senses was transitory. A problem magnified by the need to feed. The lack of any live human beings in the tunnels; that was a problem. The two he'd killed earlier were a temporary solution. And trying to accomplish his goal of becoming a material being on this plane, in a world with cameras on every corner, well... you couldn't exactly just pluck someone from the street and get what you needed. You had to bide your time, pick your spots.

He could survive on the pineals of animals, but it wasn't the same. It was barely enough to get by on at all. So, he hunted in out-of-the-way places. Most were far out in the woods, where a stray hiker would disappear, or a hunter would have an "accident." He could ingest their essence and be sustained. Occasionally, he absorbed the essence of an older, advanced soul, and it carried him for weeks before the effect wore off and he started to slip back into the in-between.

Mercy was the key. She might be enough for him, too. Old souls were what he needed, and no doubt about it, Mercy was that. But his current master had plans for Mercy different than his own, and his dependency on his master now outweighed the need to take what he needed from Mercy.

A memory came to him then, something about Mercy from "before," but he couldn't quite grasp it. She had almost been a member of the *Foedere In Luna* once, though she was completely unaware of it at this point in her life.

Wanda would have been able to shield her from detection by Inanis, much as she'd surrounded Henry with protection spells when he'd begun to dream about his past life. But she never got the chance to do so in either of Mercy's incarnations. So, when Mercy had arrived in Salem, the same spiritual tripwire alerting Wanda to the arrival of Henry was simply not there. She'd no idea Mercy was back, and no way to know she needed protection. *Yet Mercy had ended up in her shop all the same*. The strings of past lives wound through time and always ended up knotted together again.

Inanis's protégé knew all about Mercy. And he was almost ready to take what he needed from her when the "accident" at the quarry happened. Instead, he used the opportunity of her near-death experience to mark her, because he had seen the power she possessed. On the other side, it shone like a neon billboard.

It was the power of augmentation—the ability to magnify the powers of others. Usually, this power only worked in one direction. It was a power that a greater witch could use to heighten the powers of a lesser witch, or a neophyte. And Mercy *was* a very inexperienced witch, but only in *this* life.

Back then, she was extremely powerful. Chosen by the guardian of the crossroads to protect the League of the Moon. In the present, she was not yet what she would become. And he intended to keep it that way. But he must risk letting her live now to get the reward. Wanda was the barrier to the prize. He hoped he could use Mercy somehow to take down the barrier.

So lost in thought was he that he never noticed the bell had stopped ringing. He continued down the tunnel in search of Mercy, unaware he'd passed her as she was held quiet a mere two feet to his left.

"Archie, what's the matter? You look like someone just walked across your grave," Wanda said.

"I'm okay. Just something about the way those poor kids died got me thinking about something. There's an obvious connection to what happened to them and the bastard stalking the store and Henry's place, but there's something else I'm missing."

Wanda knew better than to press the issue. Archie was the kind of guy you needed to leave alone and let figure things out. He always did.

The immediate problem was the baby. She'd started coughing again. Wanda knew Joanne could only be asked to be patient for so long. It looked like that patience was running out. Jo started packing things up and getting ready to take Delilah to the hospital. Henry looked worried, but he wasn't about to stop her. Not if he liked his package where it was. But Jo's determination to take their daughter to the hospital presented a problem. There was still a faceless enemy outside, just waiting for the right time to make its move.

"Jo, I know what you intend to do, and I have no plans to ask you again to reconsider. I can see by the look on your face it would be pointless," Wanda said. "But we need to take some precautions. At least let me put a protection spell around the both of you."

"I don't think we have time for that right now, Wanda," Jo said. Then she seemed to think about it. Henry knew she was thinking about the feeling she'd had in the parking lot earlier tonight. Jo had sensed the entity stalking the store long before Henry had sniffed him out on the astral plane. It always blew him away how perceptive she was. But she was also highly intuitive. He knew this was why she would let Wanda protect them. When Jo put the baby carrier on the floor in the middle of the pentacle, Henry breathed a sigh of relief.

Jo nodded and Wanda raced behind the bar's counter and returned with three items. The first was a crude, stuffed doll made of white cloth; next was a long piece of black rope; and the last was a black Sharpie. Since she didn't know the name of their lovely stalker, she had to make one up. It made the spell weaker, but she had no choice. She wrote "fuckface" across the doll's chest.

Next, she began chanting as she wrapped the black rope, from feet to head, around fuckface. "Bound to the left, bound to the right, we bind you now, stay away tonight."

Everyone inside the protective circle, save for Byron, said in unison, "So mote it be." It took every muscle in Byron's face to keep his eyes from rolling. He was starting to believe a little, but this was still beyond where he was willing to go.

Henry grabbed for the baby carrier when Jo said, "What do you think you're doing?"

"Getting her ready for the ride to the ER. Why?"

"You know you can't leave here. They need you in case he, her, it, whatever the hell it is, comes back."

"I'll take Jo to the ER in the cruiser Henry," Byron said. "It's a big old Ford Explorer. Made for this shit tonight."

Henry wasn't happy about it. "Chief, thank you. But I think I should be the one to take my wife and my baby to the ER, don't you?"

Byron nodded. And he agreed with Henry. If he were in Henry's shoes, he'd be wanting to do the exact same thing. But he felt he had to go with his gut on this one. He shuddered to think what Penny would say later when he told her he was acting on *gasp* *intuition!* The chief looked over his shoulder at his wife. For the second time in the last hour, she winked at him. Inside, he cringed.

"Henry," Byron said, "for the last few hours, you all have been trying to convince me what's going on tonight is real. That whoever or whatever is out there is some kinda supernatural bad guy and I should take it seriously. Well, I am. Now, are you gonna argue with me about this? Are the things you and Wanda and Penny have been telling me true? Or are you gonna throw that all to the side because you're afraid? Wanda just said she would protect us. And, if I'm not mistaken, you said 'so mote it be.' I don't have the foggiest flippin' idea what makes it *mote* or why it's *be,* but it sounds an awful lot like what I used to say in church at the end of a prayer. 'Amen.' Which, I believe, is quite similar since it means 'so be it.' Now, I ain't the sharpest tool in the shed, but if you believe in all this stuff, and you believe that Wanda really can protect us from Mr. Fuckface, then I suggest you put your money where your mouth is and let me do my job. I'll get Jo and Delilah there. I can't say I totally believe everything that's been said here tonight, but *I* believe that *you* believe. Or am I wrong?"

All eyes were on Henry and Byron. Both men stared at each other for a few moments until Henry broke the ice. "No, you're not wrong. I don't just believe it, I *know* it. I've *seen* it. And as much as I want to argue with you about it, I can't." He let out a long breath and hung his head.

Byron put a hand on his shoulder. "I know what you're feeling. I wouldn't have much respect for you if you didn't argue with me about it. I promise you, it will be alright. I'm going with my gut on this one, Henry. You should know all about that. Am I right?"

Henry nodded.

Jo came over to Henry, hugged him, and said, "I love you. I'll call you as soon as we get there. It beats what I was gonna do earlier, anyway."

"What's that?" Henry asked.

"Oh, sneak out the back door with her when you were on the table and out there." She pointed up at the skylight, but he knew what she meant.

He shook his head with disapproval, but there was a smirk on his face. "Why am I not surprised?"

Jo returned the smirk. "Gotta keep you on your toes, Band-Aid boy."

He kissed her, picked up the baby carrier, and walked to the door with the chief following close behind. He planted another kiss on her. "Be safe."

"Always," she said.

Byron held the door open with one hand and held an umbrella for Jo and the baby. Jo kept the carrier in front of her and hunched over it to block raindrops from landing on Delilah. They walked in unison into the night. The door clunked softly closed. Henry stood in front of it for a while, saying nothing.

Wanda came up behind him, leaned her head against his arm, and rubbed his back.

CHAPTER 17
A SHIFT IN POWER

Mercy waited for what seemed an eternity. The being in the hood moved silently down the tunnel, away from her. The only way she could know for sure he was safely out of sight was the disappearance of the murky aura he cast. She waited as he rounded a corner.

The hand covering her mouth lifted. Mercy was terrified to turn around and face its owner. When she did, it surprised her to see the smiling and friendly face of an older woman. The apparition stood at eye-level with Mercy. A soft glow surrounded her body from head to toe. When Mercy took in her clothes, she knew immediately the time the woman appeared to have lived in.

A white coif covered her head and reached under her chin. Long strands of wavy, black hair poked from its front, parted in the middle; the rest was lumped up in curls atop the back of her head. A broad, white shift sat across her shoulders and rested on a black waistcoat. An apron was secured around her waist, covering a matching black petticoat. The outfit was rounded out with clunky, brown, anything-but-sensible shoes.

This was the daily outfit demanded of women in Puritanical Massachusetts in the sixteen hundreds. Mercy suspected she was standing in front of a victim of the Salem Witch Trials, but the clothing didn't look right on her. The woman had the face and bearing of a queen, or someone with higher authority.

When the woman's head moved slightly, she appeared to have a face on either side of her head, each with a subtle difference. *Maybe I'm losing my shit down here*, Mercy thought.

Mercy felt she knew the woman. A feeling akin to déjà vu, but not exactly. She was *certain* they'd met. The apparition nodded, appearing to read Mercy's mind.

"Did you ring the bell for me?" Mercy asked.

"Yes. But later, you will be asked about it. Pretend otherwise."

"Who are you?"

"You will know, when the time is right."

"But I—" Mercy started.

"Go! That way." The specter pointed, then disappeared.

HE'D LOST MERCY. The tunnel he'd taken, hoping to find her, was a dead end. He knew it would be, and was hoping to find her trapped and making her way back toward him. Somewhere along the way she'd found another way out.

The bell! It had stopped ringing some time ago, and he'd been so wrapped up in his own thoughts he'd forgotten about it. He cursed his carelessness. Others roaming the tunnels, the ones he couldn't see, must've helped her. When he'd finished the business of *becoming*, he would have his vengeance for their interference.

His thoughts were cut short. A presence was approaching. It was one he knew well. They must have decided to move the child. He could feel it drawing closer, and he knew he'd have to abandon the search for Mercy, for the time being. This development had come sooner than expected. As fast as the tunnels would allow, he raced back in the mausoleum's direction, splashed through the murky water, and shot out into the night.

BYRON CRAWLED the Explorer through the downpour. The wipers could barely keep up. If he ever got the speedometer over ten miles per hour it would be a minor miracle.

"I don't think I've ever seen it rain *this* hard for *this* long in my life," Jo said.

"That makes two of us. At this rate, it's gonna take about a half hour to get to the ER. How's the baby?"

On cue, Delilah started coughing up a storm. Jo gave Byron a worried look. "Is there any chance we can go faster? She sounds horrible."

Byron looked doubtful, but he was worried enough at the sounds Delilah was making to goose the Explorer up to fifteen before he stomped on the brakes. Jo wasn't ready for it. She had to twist her body at the last second as she slid forward on the seat and into the dashboard, turning just in time to spare her baby from the impact. Her shoulder slammed painfully into the glove box. She looked up at Byron, ready to give him both barrels, but stopped short when she saw the look on his face. Wavy, gray shadows from the windshield slid across the horrified expression on the chief's face. Jo pushed herself back from the dashboard and followed his gaze, then understood.

Byron unsnapped his holster, keeping his eyes on the hooded figure blocking their way. He watched as plumes of steam rose from the being's face, drifting upward and dissolving in the LED-lit raindrops. His lips hardly moved when he said to Joanne, "I believe that's Mr. Fuckface."

"It is indeed." Jo did not sound afraid. Byron noted the anger in her voice and couldn't stop himself from taking his eyes away from the being and turning them in Jo's direction. If he was still holding on to a sliver of doubt about the strange things that were going on tonight, Joanne's eyes put an end to it. They were always a deep shade of green, the kind of eyes that were hard to miss because they were so unusual. What he saw now made her everyday eyes seem bland. The irises glowed an iridescent green, lighting up the interior of the Ford. Byron forgot about the gun, the rain, the being, and just about everything else. He could only focus on her eyes. When Joanne offered him the baby and told him to stay put, he obeyed. Slack-jawed, he nodded absently and reached out his arms to receive Delilah.

"I'll be right back, Chief."

"Okay," Byron said, from what felt like the middle of a dream. He had the vague feeling he should be the one heading out into the storm and confronting the man in the hood, but his arms and legs—his entire body—would not obey.

Joanne calmly opened the passenger door and stepped into the storm.

"The child is ours. We only want what is ours."

Jo didn't answer. She strode steadily toward him. Her bright green eyes glowed with fury and magic, turning the raindrops between them into a curtain of bright, falling emeralds that exploded on the ground.

He took a step backward, his confidence waning. She looked a lot like a panther sizing up its prey. He retreated another step. Jo kept pace, a smile playing at the corners of her mouth.

"We *will* have what is ours!" he screamed. Spittle flew from where his mouth should have been. Jo silently advanced. Her smile grew wider. When she bared her teeth, they looked like fangs. The being moved backward; Joanne strode forward.

Byron held the baby in his arms and watched as Joanne challenged the hooded figure. The dreamy feeling had left him, and his senses had returned. Whatever Joanne had done to him, it only seemed intended to last long enough for her to exit the car and avoid his protests. It had worked, and now Byron had a front-row seat for something he would never forget. And later, when he thought back on this night, he would realize how he'd changed, forever, from skeptic to believer.

Joanne stopped, and the figure responded in kind. She pointed at him. "You can't have her. You'll never have her. I could end you right now. Maybe I will. But I want to know something first. What do you want with Delilah? Why are you after my daughter?"

"Something within her lives, witch. Something other than the soul that returned. We want it. We must have it. And you and your coven will die, if need be. But make no mistake, it will be ours."

"Yeah, not gonna happen. But thanks for that little tidbit of information. Time for you to die."

Byron watched as Joanne moved with lightning speed. She raised both arms and brought them down in a sweeping-vee motion. Her hands came together with a thunderous clap he could hear through the storm, the rain, and the closed windows of the Explorer's cab. A brilliant green bolt of light shot from her joined hands and rocketed toward the hooded figure. He leapt to the right and tumbled out of its way, but not before the tail of his cloak caught fire. When he regained control, he bolted for the nearest telephone pole, launched himself upward, and scrambled to the top. He jumped from the pole to the nearest roof, leaving a trail of smoke and ash in his wake.

Joanne followed, climbing the pole quicker than the hooded figure had—a mother's protective instinct driving her. When she reached the top, the roof was bare. The trail of smoke had dissipated. Pounding rain was the only sound as she listened for the slightest noise to reveal her enemy's location. Nothing.

"Fucker!" she said, beyond angry with herself for not taking him out. Jo made her way back to the telephone poll, climbed down it faster than she'd gone up it, and made her way back toward the Explorer. When she got close enough to see the truck through the rain, she froze. The driver's side door was open. A body lay just underneath it. The baby carrier sat next to Byron's head, on its side. Delilah's blanket was pinned under the carrier's edge, flailing in the current. The constant flow of gutter water pulled the blanket free, whisking it down the street where it bunched at Jo's feet. She stared at it, numb. Her baby was gone.

CHAPTER 18
EYES, EYES! GREEN AND OTHERWISE

The tunnel seemed to go on forever. Time was measured in muted footsteps, and Mercy had lost count a long time ago. Her eyes played tricks on her in the dark. Every once in a while, light appeared out of the corner of her eye, but when she would turn in its direction, she was greeted with inky blackness.

Concern nibbled at her insides, and she wondered, again, if maybe she was losing it. *Hopeful hallucinations from a weary mind*, she thought. It took a lot of self-talk to keep the panic at bay, but even that was wearing thin. Just when she felt she couldn't take another moment in this sensory deprivation tank from hell, the bell rang again. A light jingle, but it carried waves of sonic hope.

Mercy had been creeping her way through the dark, her left hand always remaining in contact with the stony wall. Not once had her hand dropped into an empty space, indicating a possible change in direction. Now, her left hand fell from the wall and slapped at her thigh. The bell chimed again, louder this time. She turned to her left, immediately feeling for the wall again, and moved toward the sound. A dim light shone in the distance.

ARCHIE AND WANDA sat behind the bar in Wanda's safe room. Not much had been said since Joanne and Byron had left to take the baby to the ER. Worry filled the room like a silent thief, robbing them of conversation. Henry checked his phone every other minute, hoping for a call or at least a text from Jo. Penny sat in the middle of the room on one of the black beanbag chairs, in the lotus position, breathing in and out in slow, even rhythm.

Archie was the first to break the silence. He snapped his fingers, making Wanda jump.

"I think I may have a little insight into why this entity is killing people, and why he needs their pineals," Archie said.

Wanda waited patiently. She said nothing. When Archie got on a roll, it was best to let him keep rolling. She nodded for him to continue.

"I got to thinking about how it's possible the hooded figure on the video from Henry's place could be faceless. Better yet, how it could be invisible but seem to have a physical form *and* affect events in the physical world. *And* how it seems to be quite proficient at traveling the astral plane, to where it could outmaneuver someone like Penny, a master traveler in that realm.

"When we were in meditation earlier tonight, Wanda, a lecture I gave last semester popped into my head, seemingly unbidden. But we both know there are no coincidences." He gave her a quick wink. "One of my students asked me some insightful questions about the pineal gland and its functions. One thing I told him, and the rest of the class, was that you could be in a dark room, eyes closed, and yet still see light."

Henry and Penny came out of their separate worlds and made their way over to the bar. They took seats opposite Wanda and Archie.

Archie kept rolling. "The thing most remarkable about the pineal gland is its structure is very much like the eyes we view the physical world with. It has rods and cones, but they're dormant. At least, theoretically, they are. But I don't believe that in the slightest. I think they're active and always waiting for someone to activate them through meditation. Waking them up again, so to speak. Many believe they are the physical gateway to the spiritual world."

Wanda's eyes widened. She knew where he was going with this. And she felt foolish for not seeing it earlier.

Archie saw her reaction and nodded. Henry and Penny caught the look between the two and knew something was up. They didn't dare interrupt.

"Whoever or whatever this thing is, it's using the physical structure of the pineals it's removing from the heads of others and somehow ingesting or absorbing them. What its actual method for doing that is? Who knows? But I would bet my life that's the connection! It's caught between worlds. Some of it is within this world, some of it is on another plane. That's how he's able to do what he does! What his motivation is—that's the million-dollar question."

Wanda thought on this for a few moments. "What you say makes a certain sense, Arch. But we still don't know the *why* of it all."

Henry chimed in, "I think we do know the why, Archie."

Archie was Henry's biological father, but he still couldn't

bring himself to call him "Dad." That was reserved for Dominick Trank, the man who had raised Henry since he was a small boy. Archie understood completely, and did not mind in the least.

Henry continued, "Revenge. It's one of the oldest motivations in the world. The message on the door, the hanging effigy of Wanda. I don't want to minimize what you're saying, but I'm having a hard time trying to read more into it than that. What better way to get back at all of us than threatening to steal our child, who is named after, and *was,* my mother—the one who infiltrated their group and was a huge part in the killing of their leader?"

Wanda had started shaking her head halfway through Henry's opinion on the matter.

"I see what you're saying, Henry, but I'm with Archie on this. I agree with you one hundred percent there is a revenge angle, especially when you consider who their leader was and where he came from, but there's something much deeper here, too. And, call it intuition, I think sending Mercy from here was exactly what this being wanted. I also think he's responsible for getting Joanne and Delilah separated from us. It's a divide-and-conquer thing going on. What his end game is? I don't know yet. But there's no doubt we're being maneuvered into something."

Henry nodded, though the look on his face showed he wasn't convinced. He looked down at his phone. It had been over thirty minutes since he'd heard from Jo. Concern was turning to anxiety. He called her.

At the same time he heard the transmission tone in the phone's earpiece, he heard Joanne's ringtone. "You Shook Me All Night Long" by AC/DC sounded like it was playing right outside the back door of Wanda's shop. It was, and less than a second later, Joanne and Byron walked into the room. What struck everyone immediately was Byron leaning on Jo for support.

Blood oozed from a bright-red, zigzagging gash above the chief's left eye. It looked like a drunk tattoo artist had tried to put a Harry Potter lightning bolt on Byron's forehead and missed badly. Joanne guided him over to the bar and eased him onto a stool. Penny ran around from her side of the bar, grabbed a napkin, and gently placed it on the wound.

"What happened?!" Henry, Wanda, and Archie said in unison.

"We ran into the hoodie. He has the baby," Joanne said. Her face wrinkled on the verge of tears, but she fought them off.

No one said a word. The shock of her statement hit them like a thunderbolt. Silence followed, pregnant with unanswered questions. But asked and answered, they must be.

Henry was the first to speak. His tone was gentle. "Tell me what happened."

Jo nodded and wiped at the corners of her eyes where tears still threatened to spill. She took a deep breath and filled everyone in on the incident with the hooded being. She left out the part about the powerful green burst of magic she'd shot from her hands. It was something she'd never been able to do before tonight, and it had scared her almost as much as losing her baby. She shot a quick glance over at Byron. If he *had* seen what she'd unleashed on the hoodie, his face wasn't showing it. He was probably a good poker player, she decided. There was no way he'd missed it.

He brought the baby in from the rain and into the room he'd set aside for her. He carefully placed her down in the crib, covered her with a blanket, turned out the lights, and closed the door behind him with a soft click.

"Is she safe?" the woman asked.

"Yes."

"And she's stopped coughing?"

"Yes."

"Good."

Zachary Villitz loved this room. He loved it now, and he'd loved it back then. He loved the polished, blonde hardwood of its floors, the comforting smell of pine from its walls, the candelabras at both ends of the room that gave off a mellow glow of candlelight, the oak coffee table on which sat steaming cups of tea, and the broad beams that comprised the ceiling. He loved everything about it. What he loved most of all was it hadn't changed one bit in over four hundred years.

Of course, this room was now part of a much bigger structure. Time and progress had dictated that additions be made. It was inevitable. But it was also fortunate. Construction around this room, over the centuries, had provided almost perfect camouflage. The room was nestled within the bowels of a much larger structure. The building was big enough, and the room situated in such a way that its existence was known to only a few. It was protected and hidden by dark magic. And the woman who owned it added another layer to that camouflage. No one would suspect a nun—well, someone who walked around in a nun's habit anyway, to be involved in dark magic. Disguise had served her well more than once over the last year.

"Do you think they've figured out what's going on yet?" she asked.

"No. Not yet. They will."

She nodded.

Zachary sipped his tea. Finally! His reward for procuring the child. It hadn't gone exactly as planned, but it was done. The brew was disgusting, but the taste was worth the price. The essence of many souls had been brewed into it. When he finished every drop, he put the cup down, walked over to the large, oval mirror hanging above the fireplace, and waited.

At first, nothing happened. Lighter and darker shades of orange from the fire danced inside the empty hood. Then, faint and barely perceptible, eyes appeared in the mirror. His eyes. He'd not seen them in four hundred years. Seconds passed like hours. Slowly, the eyes became more solid and real, briefly suspended in midair, floating in the reflection of flaming tongues. A hooded face from hell.

When the transformation was complete, he turned toward her.

Mondra Tibbets laughed, and she thought about Archibald Love.

CHAPTER 19
BACK AND FORTH

Time was not on their side. The members of the League of the Moon sat in the middle of the room, surrounding the pentacle on its floor, and tried to decide what to do next. Top priority, of course, was getting Delilah back from the hooded being. But where to start? He could have taken her anywhere, to do anything. The possibilities were endless. And some were too frightening to think about, or say aloud.

Henry, worried out of his mind but trying to hold it together for everyone, started things off. "First thing to establish is the obvious. Jo, did you see anything that would tip you off what direction the hoodie might have gone?"

Jo was still distracted and upset, but stayed in the conversation with a shake of her head.

"Wanda, is there any place in town that might be a safe space for a creature like that?" Henry asked.

"Several. Too many to count, to be honest. And the toughest part about it is there are many who practice dark magic and appear to everyone to be as sweet as pie. They're like a Tootsie Pop with a rotten center. It can take some time to expose them, but once you do, they're easy to spot."

Archie looked up sharply as Wanda's words penetrated the fog he'd been in. His mind was working overtime on making the connection between the hooded being and its need to collect pineal glands. The creep was no doubt sustaining himself by stealing the gland many considered the "seat of the soul" from his victims. But Archie suspected there was a larger endgame at play.

When Wanda had made the Tootsie Pop analogy, the first person he thought of was his old girlfriend, Mondra Tibbets, and her rotten core. He'd not seen or thought of her for years until the other day in class, when he'd been considering the doomed attraction of the Empath to the narcissist.

They'd met the first year he'd taught at the University. One bright and chilly October morning, during his customary walk to the cafeteria for coffee and a muffin, he'd had his head down, reading a book on near-death experiences. He was enthralled with the subject, and he was considering a lecture series on it for the coming semester. So engrossed was he, he never noticed the tall redhead walking straight at him. She had her head down, same as Archie, reading a book. Fortunately for both of them, when they collided, it was shoulder to shoulder. Each knocked the book from the other's hand. And both offered profuse apologies as they turned around and retrieved the other's morning reading material.

Archie smiled as he read its title. "*The Complete Works of Edgar Allan Poe.* Now that is what I call some good reading! I think I've read every story and poem at least fifty times." He handed it back to her.

She nodded, impressed. "Nice to meet a kindred soul. And one with taste!" She winked.

"My name's Archie, and my game is clumsiness—you might have noticed."

"Indeed. But I think we can both share the blame on this one." She looked at the book in her hand. "NDE's! Now there's a cheery subject for a Monday morning."

"It can be. Depends on which elevator you end up taking."

"I guess it does, doesn't it?" Mondra smiled.

"I'm heading to the cafeteria to grab a coffee. Let me buy you one. It's the least I can do. Consider it my penance for interrupting you in the throes of Poe. Granted, the punishment doesn't fit the crime, but it's all I've got to offer. I'm throwing myself on the mercy of the court." Archie bowed his head.

"The court finds you guilty, sir. Your sentence is to be carried out at once."

Archie held out both hands, waiting to be cuffed. Mondra went through the motions, mock cuffed him, and threw away the key. They laughed and headed to the cafeteria.

Hours went by in what seemed like the snap of a finger. They talked Poe. They talked life and death. They sparred on spirituality, Christianity, Hinduism, and atheism. They both agreed on not talking politics. And they discovered that each had a love for, and deep interest in, all things witchcraft. It was unofficially their first date. At the end, Archie asked her if she'd like to meet him later that evening for dinner.

She looked surprised. "Dinner? You certainly don't waste a lot of time beating around the bush, do you?"

"I'm sorry. If that's too forward or presumptuous, I apologize. I've just enjoyed our conversation tremendously, and I'd like to continue it. We've talked about so much, but I don't even think we've scratched the surface on the things we both find fascinating."

She cocked a dark red eyebrow at him as she considered his proposal. Her hazel eyes danced back and forth as she pursed her lips. "I have a better idea," she said.

She swiveled in her chair, retrieved the black satchel she'd hung over its back, and plopped it on the table. Mondra rummaged around inside until she found a pen and a small ringed notebook. She tore a sheet from it, scribbled something on the page, folded it in half, and handed it to Archie.

She said, "Don't open it yet. Wait until I leave and I'm out of sight. Then open it. If you decide you want to meet me there, then I'll see you tonight. If not, I'll see you around."

Archie was taken back a bit by the issuing of an ultimatum from this mysterious, statuesque redhead. He was also humming with excitement on the inside, dying to know what was on the paper. He'd just met this woman, and the intrigue was almost more than he could bear. And he loved every minute of it.

Mondra stood, slung the satchel over her shoulder, grabbed her Poe book from the table, and tucked it under her arm. "Nice to meet you, Archibald. I hope you come by tonight." She shot him a crooked grin, turned, and left.

Archie watched without a word as she wove, catlike, between the cafeteria tables and out into the sunny courtyard. She turned the corner, looked back at him, and then she was gone.

He looked down at the folded note in front of him. The ink on its front appeared blue and opaque through its back.

THE RED WITCH

The excitement and anticipation he'd felt moments earlier when he was bursting at the seams to see what was on the note was suddenly supplanted by a phantom dread. Intuition was telling him that to open the note and read what was on it was opening up a chapter in his life he might not want to explore. He *always* listened to the sage whisper of intuition. But he had to know! He placed a hand on it, then removed it. He repeated the same motion several times in a row before he finally gave in to curiosity. "Screw that damned cat—the bastard had nine lives, anyway!"

When he opened the note, he wasn't sure what to expect. He was hopeful it was her phone number. It wasn't. It was an address. He knew the address, as well he should. The house at 72 Emerald Lane was a beautiful white house with green shutters, an enormous picture window facing a tree-lined street, and a flagstone walkway winding through an immaculate green lawn. He loved that house as a boy, and when his mother died, he couldn't bear the thought of strangers moving in. So, he bought it. And he'd been living in it ever since. Mondra had invited him to his own home. He shuddered at the memory.

THE LIGHT at the end of the tunnel. Mercy had been moving steadily toward it for what seemed forever. In truth, it had probably been only ten minutes—fifteen tops. Time and space are funny that way. It "flies" when you're having fun. It "drags" when you're waiting for the dental hygienist to call your name for a root canal. *And,* Mercy thought, *it's like fucking wading through molasses in lead boots when you're stuck under the town of Salem, looking for a way out.* So, when she found herself looking up at that light, like she'd been transported to it without her knowledge, she had to fight back tears.

There was a ladder. She hadn't noticed it at first. The light from above was so foreign to her vision it had left saucers of afterimage. They faded, and the ladder appeared from the gloom like a silvery fish rising from murky water. She placed a hand on the rounded, rusty rungs just to convince herself they were real. Flakes of rust coated her hands. Mercy let out a relieved breath and climbed.

She stole brief glimpses as rainwater leaked around the edges of the dim circle above. Most of it ran down the walls in a steady stream, but there was a pinhole of light in its center where drops would fall directly on her head or in her face when she chanced a look upward.

It was a manhole cover. The center, where the water falling on her head was coming from, was for the hook that street crews used to lift the heavy covers. Moving it out of the way was going to be a bitch. She'd heard somewhere the covers could weigh anywhere from ninety to one hundred and fifty pounds. It would put her strength to the test. At this point, she could not give a shit less, and would happily wage war with the cover.

She reached the top, held the ladder with one hand, and gave it everything she had trying to lift the cast-iron lid. It wouldn't budge.

Mercy looked down in the direction she'd just climbed. Though she couldn't see the bottom, she estimated it to be roughly twenty to twenty-five feet from the tunnel floor. A survivable fall, but not a fall she was willing to risk. But how to get enough leverage to push the heavy cover up and to the side?

She climbed up another two rungs, squatting as she neared the top. Mercy gripped the highest rung on the ladder with both hands, let her legs dangle briefly in midair, then swung her right leg over, through, and around another rung three spaces lower. She repeated the process with her left leg and then anchored herself, wrapping her feet around the vertical poles of the ladder's frame, giving her just enough room to reach both arms up and push the manhole cover. It moved the slightest bit. The heavy scraping sound of cast iron on gravel echoed through the tunnel.

She fought with it for nearly ten minutes. All she accomplished was an increase in the amount of water now running down the left side of the walls surrounding her and the ladder. Not nearly enough room to squeeze through and into stormy freedom. Frustration and despair threatened to sap her energy. Mercy fought them off, rested, and wracked her brain for a solution.

She felt better for resting. Calming her mind down in a desperate situation had served her well earlier tonight in the mausoleum. It would prove her saving grace at the manhole cover as well.

She carefully worked her legs free of the ladder and let them stretch for a few minutes. When they felt strong enough again, she was ready to take her last shot at the cover.

Mercy took first her left hand, then her right, and placed them one above the other into the corners of two separate rungs where they met the vertical poles of the ladder. Both hands were on her left side. Her knuckles turned white with the force of her grip, and she swung both legs to her right and pegged them against the wall. With that done, she swung her left hand down and to the opposite corner from her right, now grasping the same rung. Then, with all the strength she could muster, she swung both legs upward and wrapped them around the ladder, anchoring her legs against the poles with her feet.

She was upside down on the ladder, legs pointing toward the manhole cover. She needed to get closer to have enough leverage to lift it. Tightening her legs around the vertical poles, she removed her left hand from the rung and flashed it up to the next level. The ladder groaned and shook. Rust flakes fell into her nose and mouth, and she gagged. Her right hand slipped as her left hand closed around the rung. An electric burst of panic shot through her in the moment it took her right hand to make contact and join her left on the rung above. Her heart thundered. Again, she had to calm herself before she continued. One mistake and she would be part of this tunnel as a ghost, forever traveling its winding passageways with a broken neck.

Deep breaths. Breathe in, breathe out, breathe in, breathe out. Bush played in the soundtrack of her mind once again. She was ready. With great care, she unwrapped her left leg from around the ladder's pole, then the right. Both feet now rested on the underside of the manhole cover. Everything now hinged on the strength in her arms, which were shaking from the strain.

The ladder vibrated, and she had to close her eyes and mouth to keep the rust flakes out. Once the cascading flake-storm subsided, she shook them from her head, took a deep breath, and kicked the bottom of the manhole cover with every ounce of strength she had left. It flew up onto its side and balanced perfectly on the edge of the open hole. It hung on the edge and spun slowly, like the world's heaviest quarter after a quirky coin flip.

Mercy didn't wait to see if it would fall back down and cover the hole once again. She pushed up with both arms and stuck her legs up and through the empty space, hooking either side with her calves. She pushed herself up the rest of the way, one pain-filled rung at a time, until she was free. A gust of wind blew the cover down, eclipsing three quarters of the hole and barely missing Mercy's head.

She rested on her back, sucking in great gulps of air, and staring up into the storm. Rain pelted her face, and she thought nothing ever felt so wonderful. She closed her eyes and took in the sounds of the storm. The steady patter of rain on pavement soothed her soul. It always had. She felt as if she could fall asleep right here, in the middle of the street. And then, as she began to doze, a bell sounded, snapping her out of it. She turned her head in the sound's direction. The woman from the tunnel stood in the doorway to Wanda's Wicca'd Emporium. She smiled at Mercy. The Puritanical garb was gone, replaced by a long, black dress. In each hand, the woman held a torch.

CHAPTER 20
SUSPICION AND SEDUCTION

"I *might* know where they are," said Byron.

Everyone turned toward the bar. Chief Byron Miller held the cloth against his forehead, looking like a pirate addressing his crew. One good eye taking in his shipmates while a pink and white "eye patch" covered the other. It turned pink with the blood still seeping from the wound. Henry did an admirable job of sewing him up with the scant supplies scrounged from Wanda's woefully inadequate first aid kit. It was the best they could have hoped for under the circumstances.

"I'm all ears, Chief," Henry said. He hadn't forgotten the chief's promise to protect his wife and baby. His temper simmered beneath a placid façade.

"Now, I can't be sure of this, but I got a hunch. In this storm, I don't think he's going too far with a baby in tow. Too much of a risk the baby would get sick, or hurt, or injured. I just got a feeling he's operating out of this general area—"

"Is it anything like the hunch you had when you told me

to stay behind? When you promised me you'd take care of my wife and daughter?" The pulse in Henry's neck beat in time with his rising anger.

Byron stared at Henry, his mouth frozen in mid-sentence. There was nothing he could say to defend himself. He was a man of his word, and he'd failed.

Removing the stained cloth covering from his forehead, he tossed it on the bar, took a deep breath, blew it out, and said, simply, "I'm sorry, Henry. I let you down. I have no excuse."

"No, he didn't let you down, Henry. I did," Joanne said.

"What do you mean?" Henry asked.

"I lost my temper. When I saw that bastard blocking the road, I put a spell on Byron. It was a mild one, enough to stop him from getting out of the truck and confronting the guy. I put Delilah in Byron's hands, got out of the truck, and went after him." She neglected to mention the blast of energy she'd shot at her daughter's kidnapper. Not for any reason other than she still wasn't sure how or why it had happened.

"You did what?" Henry couldn't believe what he was hearing.

"I thought I was protecting her, Henry. I thought if I killed him, it would solve at least one problem for tonight."

"Did it ever occur to you that might be exactly what he wanted?"

Now it was Jo's turn to get angry. "No fucking shit, Henry! I just told you I did it because I lost my temper. I know he was baiting me—now—but in the heat of the moment, I wasn't thinking straight. He lured me to the rooftop and doubled back. Byron never saw what was coming. And that's *my* fault, not his."

"Jo, if you had listened to Wanda in the first place, none of this would be happening. She told you it was too dangerous to go outside—"

"What the hell are you talking about? Delilah was coughing her brains out! I'm not gonna sit here while she hacks up a lung and—"

"Stop this!" Wanda yelled. Everyone jumped. "Can't you all see what's going on here? None of this is anyone's fault. I know what he's doing. It's divide and conquer, just like I mentioned before. Only now, there's no doubt."

Henry and Joanne both turned their attention toward Wanda. Henry asked, "How, exactly?"

Wanda walked over to where they stood. She looked first at Henry, then Joanne. "I've known you both for a short time, at least in this lifetime. We've been together through many. In all of those incarnations, and all the moments we've had together, not once did I ever see the two of you come close to an argument, let alone a cross word. Now, tonight, you're practically at each other's throats. That's the first *divide*. And you, Henry Trank." She pointed an accusatory finger at him. "I'm no fool. I know everyone gets mad and loses their cool. But I've never once seen you jump ugly on someone without having all your ducks in a row. Well, except for last Halloween. You kind of lost your shit with Solomon. But the Henry I know always gets the facts before flying off the handle. And even then, you don't lose it like what I'm seeing tonight."

Henry bowed his head. She was right, and he knew it. "You're right. Sorry, Chief. My temper got the better of me."

Byron nodded. "I get it, Henry. I'd have said the same if things were reversed."

Wanda turned to Joanne. "Jo, I know you've got a

temper, and with the things you've endured in your past, it's served you well. This thing knew what would push your buttons. He used your instincts against you. Now he's got you and Henry going at it. And I *know* how you two feel about each other, so I guess we have to tip our hats to the bastard on that one. He's getting the job done. We are going to change that, starting now."

Henry turned to Joanne. She smiled, shook her head, and kissed him. "Now shut up and listen to Wanda."

"I'm not saying any of this to chastise anyone," Wanda said. "There's a lot more going on here than meets the eye. If I'd been smarter about this from the start, we wouldn't be where we are now. And that's *my* fault."

Both Henry and Jo went to say something when she held up a hand. Two mouths clamped shut at the same time.

"Apologies and forgiveness can wait for another time. We need to get our shit together, find Delilah, and figure out what this bastard is after. Agreed?"

The other five souls in the room nodded.

HE WAS ALMOST ALL the way back. The reappearance of his face in the mirror was a good start, but if it was to be permanent, there was much more to be done.

Mondra watched him return from the mirror. She remembered the face well, but it was the eyes she recognized most of all. The eyes of a lover from long ago. She wasn't about to let him get away again.

A knock on the door brought her back from thoughts of the past.

"Come in," she said.

The large wooden door to her hidden inner sanctum creaked as it swung open. Two men stood in the doorway. Rain dripped from their silhouettes, briefly lit from behind by a flash of lightning from the storm. The drops looked like falling diamonds.

"Glad you made it through the storm, professor. I see you've brought your protégé with you."

He strode across the room and stood before her. The professor stared down at her, his face impassive. She rose to meet his gaze. Without a word, he put his hand to her right cheek and caressed it, and she turned and kissed his palm, flicking at it softly with her tongue. Mondra reached up and pulled his hand away from her face, closing her lips around his thumb, sucking its length, then dropping his hand. She smiled and walked away from him, to the bedroom.

Darren Biltmore dropped his raincoat to the floor and followed.

MERCY STOOD under the awning and out of the rain. The store's metallic shutters were drawn. She suspected all the members of the League of the Moon were in the back room, but she wasn't sure they would welcome her. And she felt her heart couldn't handle a second round of rejection.

The apparition of the woman who'd rung the bell, drawing her in from the storm, was nowhere to be seen. Mercy wondered who the woman was and how she connected to everything happening tonight. The feeling she got from the bell ringer was not negative in the slightest. The apparition gave her the same feeling she'd gotten from every member of the League of the Moon—a familiarity that *shouldn't be*, but was.

Regardless of their suspicions, she forgave them. And she felt an unexpected but not unwelcome urge to protect every one of them. But she wasn't ready to face them just yet. There was something left to prove, though she knew she'd done nothing wrong. *They* didn't know that for sure, however. If Mercy could reclaim their trust, she'd feel better about looking them in the eye.

Her arms and legs throbbed, her head was sore, and her whole body ached. It was warm and dry underneath the awning. The air outside was cooler and far less humid than before the rain began. Compared to the rank air of the tunnels beneath the city, however, it was like sniffing a dryer sheet.

She lowered herself against the side of the door well, let her legs stretch out before her, took a deep breath, and let it out. Just a couple of minutes' rest—nothing more—then get to work on how to go about building their trust back. Mercy closed her eyes and within a minute, she was snoring.

ARCHIE SAT in a corner of the room. The arguments and the apologies were background noise at the moment. Lost in thought, he was making connections from loosely related events, trying his best to weave them together. He had a feeling Mondra tied into all of this somehow. When Wanda had mentioned she thought they were being played by the hooded entity, it sparked thoughts of how his old flame had manipulated him in the past.

He thought back to the first night they'd spent together.

The night she had invited him to his own home. How he had been so easily maneuvered. How he had been so blinded by the devastating combination of her beauty and intellect that he'd never put two and two together.

She pulled up to his house just as twilight pulled its silvery curtain over the world. Mondra drove a black BMW. The car gleamed in the soft light. It was sleek and sexy, like its owner. She stepped out and made her way up his winding flagstone walk, pushed her sunglasses to the top of her head, and flashed a crooked grin. He thought it was sexy as hell, but her knowledge of where he lived still freaked him out, and he intended on getting to the bottom of it.

"Good evening, Mondra."

"Archibald, nice to see you again. Glad you could make it."

"It was really no trouble at all, being that I live here. But what I'm infinitely curious about is, how did *you* know I lived here?"

She threw her head back and laughed, then leveled her eyes at him, smiled, and asked, "You haven't figured it out yet?"

"No. Should I have?" Archie asked. Mild irritation had crept into his voice.

"Can I come in?"

Archie thought about it for a moment. It was a moment too long for Mondra.

"If you let me in, I'll slay your suspicion. But I warn you —you're going to feel a tad embarrassed."

Without a word, Archie stood aside, held the door open, bowed slightly, and held out his hand, ushering her inside.

Once inside, he led her to the living room.

Mondra strolled casually around the massive yet cozy

area, surprised at the decor. The way Archie dressed and the way he carried himself were at odds with the room. She took a seat on a large chocolate-leather sofa, its arms studded with nailheads. In front of her was a glass coffee table festooned with reading material. Magazines, books, newspapers, and notes from his classes littered its surface. The soft glow of fire from the enormous brick fireplace cast a muted orange glow about the room. The reflection of flames danced on the polished, knotty pine floors and terminated at the border of a plush, deep-brown area rug sitting between the fireplace and the glass table. On the rug was the book she'd retrieved for him when they'd collided earlier in the day.

Archie returned from behind the bar, a glass of cognac in each hand. He sipped from his favorite monogrammed university glass as he stepped around the coffee table and handed one to Mondra, then offered his up to her. They clinked glasses together and sipped. Both closed their eyes and savored the brandy.

"This is a beautiful room, Archibald."

"Glad you like it."

"It doesn't really go with the blue jeans, black adidas, and Grateful Dead T-shirt though, I have to point out."

"It's not the clothes that make the man. You can never judge a book by its cover... you know, all the old clichés apply." He smiled and wiggled his eyebrows.

"Now, would you like to know how I knew where you lived?"

He nodded.

She got up and strolled over to the rug, picked up the book on near-death experiences, and held it up for him to observe.

"You had a near-death experience and astral traveled to my house?" he joked.

"Not quite. Although, if we had bumped heads this morning instead of arms, it quite conceivably could have ended up that way. That noggin of yours looks quite solid!"

"I'll choose to take that as a compliment." He smiled.

"Oh, and I mean it that way... completely." She winked.

"So, end the mystery for me. How do you know the secrets of the universe, wise mistress?"

"You really wanna know?" she asked. The look on her face was hard to read, but Archie thought he detected mischief and a touch of sympathy.

Mondra held the book up for him with her left hand, then motioned with her right for him to observe like she was a game show host modeling a prize. She held her right hand still, index finger pointing toward the ceiling, and read from the back cover of the book.

"Love, Archibald... 72 Emerald Lane, Salem, Massachusetts, 01970. Property of the Salem Public Library."

Archie sat in stunned silence for several moments. He felt like a complete imbecile—and a complete asshole for being so suspicious. Then, he couldn't help himself. He burst out laughing and gave her a standing ovation. "Well done! Well done!"

Mondra bowed and said, "Thank you, kind sir."

"Kind sir," he laughed, "is not exactly what I would call me, if I were you, at the moment. I think something like what you mentioned earlier about my having a "solid noggin" would be more appropriate."

Mondra smiled her crooked smile, then raised her left foot slightly above the carpet, flexed it, and let her black high heel fall softly from her foot. She did the same with the right. Archie sat motionless on the couch, the only sound in the room the soft crackle of fire, as she reached for the top button of her white blouse and worked it loose. Then five more. It slipped soundlessly to the floor. She turned sideways, her lean silhouette a masterpiece in dark relief against the fire. Her arms reached slowly behind her back and the soft, slow whir of the skirt's zipper tickled his ears. Mondra reached up and removed the clip taming her hair. It fell around her shoulders and down her back. Long, wavy, red hair was the only thing covering any part of her. She cocked an eyebrow at him and crooked a finger in a "come hither" gesture.

She mesmerized Archie. This was the most beautiful woman he'd ever seen. He resisted the urge to look behind him and make sure she wasn't motioning to someone else.

As he rose from the couch, he made a half-hearted attempt to put the glass he'd been holding on the table. It missed by a mile, clattered on the floor, and rolled under the couch. He didn't notice. He joined her on the rug, and she slowly undressed him. And that was how the seduction of Archibald Love began.

CHAPTER 21
COMING AND GOING

"It looks like we're going to have to take this show on the road," Henry said.

Everyone agreed. But where to start?

"I think the most prudent thing to do is to split up. Since there are six of us left, I suggest we group up in pairs and take separate vehicles. We'll be able to cover much more territory and, with the other three units I've got out on the road tonight, if we need any help, I can get them on it as quick as the storm allows," Byron said.

All agreed it was the best way to handle it, and at the moment there wasn't much choice. Henry and Penny had tried their luck taking separate trips into the astral realm, trying to catch any trace energy the entity left behind. They hoped to home in on him, somehow, and match it to an earthly destination. Neither was successful. It felt like he'd removed himself from that plane completely.

"I'll take Wanda with me," Jo said.

Henry nodded. "I'll go with Byron in the cruiser."

"Well, Penny, looks like you're stuck with your brother," Archie said.

"It could be worse." She elbowed him.

"I'll be right back," Wanda said.

She made a quick dash to the front of the store and returned with a black suede bag. It was tied at the top with gleaming gold rope. She opened the bag, placed its contents in the middle of the pentacle on the floor, and set up a purple candle with the words "bad luck recede" carved into its side. Next to it, she placed a white candle on the floor. "Good luck retrieve" was carved into the white candle.

"Gather around quickly, everyone," said Wanda.

Everyone, including Byron, did this without question.

"I'm going to light these candles one at a time. The purple one will be first. Repeat what I say after I light each of the candles. Everyone okay with that?"

All nodded.

Wanda lit the purple one and quietly chanted, "Take away tears with the dying of the moon."

Everyone repeated the chant.

Next, she lit the white candle. "Fortune, bright, come again soon." Again, all repeated.

She lifted the purple candle in the air, moved it above and to the left of the white candle, sprinkling salt over the tops of both candles as she did this, then chanted, "Burn bright and lead the way to Delilah." Everyone followed her lead once more.

She snuffed out the purple "bad luck" candle and said, "Bad luck be gone with the waning of the moon." It was the final chant the group recited together.

"Now, I need all of you to briefly meditate on finding the

baby and channel that energy into the white candle," Wanda said.

They all did this for a few brief moments, infusing the white candle with their intention. Then Wanda licked her thumb and forefinger and snuffed out the white candle. The luck spell was complete.

Everyone headed for the back door. Byron and Henry led the way, followed by Penny and Archie. Jo and Wanda brought up the rear. Just as Jo was about to lock the door to the safe room, Wanda put a hand on her arm. "Don't lock it, Jo."

Jo said, "Why... what are you thinking?"

Wanda looked around the parking lot, up at the roof, and out toward the street. Nothing really jumped out at her, at least visually, but the intuitive feeling the door *must* be left open was so strong there was no way she was going to question it.

"Something we need is coming."

Jo left it open. When Wanda got like that, she knew better than to doubt it. It had saved their lives more than once.

Wanda didn't tell Jo she also heard the slightest tinkling of a bell.

BILTMORE WATCHED as Mondra got up from the bed and made her way over to the walk-in closet. She returned from it wearing a black silk robe cinched around the waist. The disappointment showed on his face.

"Don't look so sad, Darren. There's more where that

came from. But tonight, there are much more important things to be thinking about."

He smiled, but it didn't reach his eyes. Sex with Mondra was incredible. Biltmore was aware, however, it was a temporary arrangement. And he was okay with that... to a point. Mondra was the kind of woman who made you want more. However—and she'd made it abundantly clear—when the freak in the hood had fully "become," whatever the hell that meant, their time together, sexually, was done. In the end, he would get what he wanted from their arrangement. Part of him, however, hoped he and Mondra might keep this facet of their relationship going. *Anything is possible.* Denial can be a man's best friend.

The door to the outer room opened and closed again. Mondra heard it, and left Darren in the bedroom. Biltmore's protégé had returned from his errand.

"Are they gone?" Mondra asked.

He nodded. "I saw all six of them leave through the back. They took off in separate cars, two to a vehicle.

Mondra clapped her hands together. "Yes!"

Darren came out of the room, tucking in his shirt as he went. "What's going on?"

Mondra said, "They've left Wanda's shop. We need to get things ready—wait, did you say there were six of them?"

Biltmore's protégé nodded. "There was the short little witch, the hot brunette, her husband, and Dr. Love. The other two I've never seen before. The man was a cop. I think he might be the chief, but I've only seen him once or twice around town. There was another lady there, too. Not sure who she was."

Zachary Villitz spoke. "The other is the cop's wife. Her given name is Penelope Love. I tagged her when I was on the astral plane. She followed me to the tomb, but I kept her out. I know where they both live, should the need arise to take them down."

Mondra considered the new information. She couldn't see how it would be a problem, but that was how things usually *became* a problem in the first place. There was nothing to be done about it at the moment, but better to know than not.

No more words needed to be said. Everyone in the room knew what came next. Zachary went to the crib room and bundled up Delilah. Biltmore and his companion left to retrieve the group's transportation. Mondra took what she knew they needed for what came next. Four would travel in the car. Zachary would meet them there. He wanted to walk the streets and feel rain on flesh. It had been a long time coming.

THE SOUND of cars leaving the parking lot of Wanda's Wicca'd Emporium awakened Mercy. It was the only sound louder than the unending beat of rain on pavement. They were going away from her quickly. If she hadn't been half asleep when they'd first turned out of the lot, she might have been able to flag them down. Any chance they might see her in the dark, in their rear-view mirrors, and through a torrential downpour, was slim. Better to save her strength and find a way into the shop; if *only* to get out of the goddamned rain.

Just for shits and giggles, she tried the front door in case they'd left it unlocked. For some strange reason, it had never occurred to her to try it when the bell ringing ghost had drawn her to this spot. She pulled on the handle and got what she expected—locked.

Mercy pulled the back of her shirt up over her head and ran around to the parking lot, confident of the same result. When she pulled the handle, she had been bracing her body for resistance. There was none, and when the door flew open, her hand slipped from the handle and she shuffled off balance and backward, landing butt-first in a puddle. The door began to close, and she scrambled up from the puddle to snag it just as it was about to seal her out. When she got inside, she checked the lock and found it set to open. *Weird.* Wanda never left this open.

Mercy scanned the room. All was quiet, the lights were out, and the only sources of illumination were the softly glowing candles at the four compass points of the room. It smelled like something had burnt recently.

She looked at the bar and noticed a bandage lying on its top. It was stained, and she hoped against hope the stain wasn't what she assumed it was. She took it close to one of the candles and confirmed her suspicions. Blood. But whose?

For reasons she wouldn't understand until later, Mercy held onto the bandage, closed her eyes, and waited. Her breathing slowed, her pulse dropped to half its usual pace, and images formed on the dark side of her eyelids. They were like dream images, blurred at the edges. In them, Joanne handed over Delilah. Her eyes glowed bright green! Whoever's eyes she was looking through looked down at the baby but didn't fully understand how she got there. But the hands holding onto Delilah were, unmistakably, male.

Joanne was in the middle of the street, calmly but aggressively walking toward a man in a hood. The man who had taken her to the tomb! Through the eyes of the bandage's owner, she watched as Joanne made a quick motion and green fire shot from her hands! The man in the hood was struck, but barely. He climbed a telephone pole and Joanne chased after him. Mercy was awestruck!

The images for the next few moments were jerky, back-and-forth movements of views from the side window, to the windshield, and back to the side window. Then, before the viewer of these events could react, the hooded figure appeared at the door. He had no face. He had hands, though. One of them touched the viewer's forehead. A bright light blinded him and all went blank for a time. When the images resumed, all she could see was Delilah's blanket carried in the gutter's current and bunching up at Joanne's feet. Then all went black.

Mercy dropped the bandage on the floor and scrambled backwards like she'd just realized it was a cobra. She didn't know what to make of the vision. Was it real? And if so, how was she able to see it? Ever since her near-death experience at the quarry, she knew things were different from before. This was something new. It scared the hell out of her.

As Mercy sat on the floor, thinking about the images, her eyes took in the rest of the room. They settled on the pentacle area. There were several small objects in its center, but the room was too dark to make out what they were.

Soreness swept through her legs as she got up to investigate. When she got close enough, she saw the candles and the salt, and knew instantly it was a luck spell that had taken place here. That explained the burning smell she noticed once she'd entered the room, though it had taken a quick back seat to the bloody bandage.

She considered the visions from the bandage, the used candles from the luck spell, and the open door. To her, they meant one thing. They had gone after the baby and those stupid enough to take her. After that, she couldn't be sure what was going to happen. The best she could do was be ready to help when the time came. She pulled a beanbag chair into a darkened corner, assumed the lotus position, and tried to be the calm before the storm.

CHAPTER 22
THE TWO SIDES OF MAGIC

"—But I just can't believe I was that dumb," Jo said.

"Honey, dumb is the last thing in the world you are," Wanda assured her. "Like I said before, he's been working to divide us from the beginning. If I were in his slimy shoes, I'd be doing exactly the same things."

Jo piloted the Camry slowly through the downpour. Since they'd entered the car, Joanne had taken to self-flagellation like a duck to water. The responsibility for Delilah's kidnapping was hers and hers alone.

Wanda was trying her damnedest to get her in the right frame of mind, with little success. It wasn't easy to put yourself in the place of a mother whose child was taken from her by being outmaneuvered. And it was *doubly* hard to convince her it wasn't her fault when you didn't have children of your own to lend credibility to your arguments.

"Something else happened out there tonight, Wanda."

The pint-sized witch in the passenger's seat turned to look at her young friend. Her face was hard to read with the wavy, rain-smeared shadows sliding across it through the windshield. She didn't bother trying to read her for too long, either. It was more important to keep her eyes peeled for any sign of Archie's van, hoping to home in on the whereabouts of Delilah's kidnapper. Wanda asked her question as she scanned the darkened, rain-soaked streets. "What was it, honey?"

"That's just it. I don't really know. All I can do is describe to you what happened. Maybe then *you* can tell *me*."

Jo described the encounter with the hooded entity, including every detail. When she finished, Wanda was quiet for a long time. Jo knew better than to interrupt by asking what she thought.

After a nerve-wracking eternity, Wanda finally spoke. "Well, on the bright side, for discovering and using a new power, you've got damned good aim."

Jo was not amused.

"I'm sorry, honey. Sometimes trying to stay positive about things can be a piss-off—I didn't mean to downplay what happened. But I have a theory on *why* it happened."

"I'm all ears."

"When you and Henry came into the room earlier tonight, if I remember correctly, Archie and I were still in meditation. So, let me ask you—did you shake hands with Mercy tonight when you introduced yourself?"

"I did. And it's funny you mention it. When I touched her hand, there were a couple of things that went through my mind almost immediately. I don't know if you were listening closely, since you were still in meditation, but I asked her if we knew each other. And she said something like, 'I don't know, maybe in another lifetime.' And, before I even shook hands with her, I had the déjà vu crawlies all over me."

Wanda nodded as she looked out the window. "I think she's one of us, Jo. For the life of me, though, I can't figure out who she is. It's the reason I, against my better judgment, agreed to send her home tonight. I'm still kicking myself in the ass for that one."

"Hey, weren't you the one who told me, just about ten minutes ago, none of this shit is anyone's fault? That he's been working to divide us from the start?"

Wanda saw herself smile in the faint reflection of the passenger side window. She loved Joanne with all her heart. Jo was a smart-ass, but she was a brilliant one. "Touché, my dear. And you're right, enough of the 'blame ourselves' game tonight. So, what else did you notice about Mercy?"

"When I shook her hand, I didn't want to let go. It was like there was... how to describe it... a magnetism. But it was more than that. It was like an electric current. Not like sticking a knife in the toaster and trying to get your burnt toast out of it—"

"Are you speaking from experience on the toaster thingy?" Wanda needled her.

Jo looked quickly over at Wanda, then back at the road. The bitch was smiling at her. She cracked a smile of her own and said, "I'll plead the fifth on that. Anyway, the feeling was nice. It also left me feeling—" She stopped, fishing for the exact words.

"Loved?" Wanda asked.

"Yes! It was real brief, but strange as it sounds to say, that's almost exactly it. But more than that... there was another layer to it. The only word that comes to mind is forgiveness."

"Did you know Mercy had a near-death experience?"

Jo whipped her head in Wanda's direction. "You're shitting me!"

Wanda shook her head. "I'm not." She filled Jo in on what had happened at the quarry.

"I heard about that on the news. They said something about her dying on the beach and being resuscitated. I didn't realize it was her, though."

"That was her. And I think she came back—different. I mean, she told me as much the night after we'd encountered the entity. When I touched her hand that night, I had the exact same feeling you did."

"Hmm, I wonder—" Jo said.

"I have a good idea what you're thinking about, Jo. But I'm not gonna say what it is. I want to hear it from your lips. I want you to confirm what I've been thinking since the night I connected with her."

Jo took her time. She wanted to frame it in the right words. After a few moments, she said, "I think whatever she brought back from the other side... I think touching her, if you're someone who has innate magical power to begin with, I think she amplifies it somehow. I think that's her gift. I'm pretty sure I was able to almost kill that hooded asshole because I connected with Mercy."

Wanda nodded. "Yes. I've heard of it. It's called the power of augmentation. It's usually the power of a much more experienced witch. That had me confused until I thought about it some more. I think Mercy, in another incarnation, was a massively powerful witch. And I also think she was a member of the *Foedere In Luna,* or was going to be. Combine that with what happened to her on the other side, when she died—the possibilities are breathtaking."

Jo dwelt on that for a few moments. Other possibilities

swirled in her mind. They scared her. It showed on her face, and Wanda picked up on it right away.

"What's the matter, honey?"

Jo's eyes met Wanda's. "Magic works both ways."

Wanda's eyes widened. Mercy had come in contact with more than just light magic tonight.

CHAPTER 23
HENRY ENLIGHTENED

Byron drove and Henry searched with the spotlight, aiming it down alleys and into backyards. Neither man had said a word since they'd left the Emporium. Byron was the first to break the ice.

"What in the hell would these psychos want with a baby, anyway?"

Henry kept his eyes glued to the streets. "I think it's simple—revenge—but Wanda seems to think differently."

"Oh? And what's her theory?"

"She thinks what happened at our apartment earlier tonight, the murders at the graveyard, and what caused Mercy to be asked to leave the store, are all connected somehow. Wanda sees it as some grand scheme intricately woven together."

Byron was quiet for a bit while he considered all the angles. He was inclined to agree with Henry's conclusion about revenge, except there were too many things happening at the same time that seemed, to him, to be much more than just coincidence. Topmost among them being everything happening on the same night. But he needed more information first. "Why was Mercy asked to leave the store? I never heard more about that. I only know Archie got the job of driving her home—but not why."

Henry wasn't sure how Byron would handle his explanation of what led up to Mercy's being asked to leave. But what Henry *knew* for sure—Penny *had* gotten to him. He could see it in the chief's eyes, and he knew in his gut what had happened out on the road with Jo had gotten to him, too. If he asked him about the incident with Jo first, maybe it would break down his defenses and make him more apt to believe what he had to say about Mercy.

"Let me ask you a question, Chief?"

"Shoot."

"What happened out there tonight with Joanne? I saw her steal a quick glance over at you when she told us about Delilah being taken. You didn't bat an eye. To me, that means one of two things: either she thinks you saw something and you were playing dumb, or you *know* you saw something, but you're still too much in denial to admit it."

Byron squirmed a bit in his seat, but he kept silent.

Henry continued, "Come on, Chief. Even after everything you've seen tonight, and even after Penny admitted to you she's been traveling the astral plane since she was a child, you're still gonna hold out?"

Byron tapped on the steering wheel and kept his eyes straight ahead. He took a deep breath, then blew it out. "Okay, Henry. I've seen some weird shit in my time. Number one being the goddamned dog in the library last October. Still not sure what that was, but it freaked me the hell out. Enough so that I told Raul to clam up about it. That's my usual reaction to things I can't explain. If it doesn't fit neatly into my view of the world, I just push it off to the side or try to forget about it. What I saw your wife do tonight... I can't just push that off to the side. And I know I'll *never* be able to just forget about it."

"Chief, I'm not gonna judge you or think you're nuts. If anything, you probably still think I'm a few sandwiches short of a picnic. If this were a year ago, I'd think the same thing. I've seen and done too much now to go back. I know the things I've seen are real. And I've learned to do exactly the same things your *own wife* told you *she* can do. So, if you tell me about something you think is unbelievable, trust me when I tell you, I'll believe it. And I won't think you've dropped a screw here or there."

Byron let the chips fall where they may. "Joanne was telling the truth when she said she put a spell on me. It was the weirdest goddamned thing I've ever felt. It was like having your body put in a jar of molasses, but I could see and hear everything... just couldn't react fast enough to change her mind. Which, come to find out, is exactly what she intended. I ain't never seen a woman *that* angry be as calm as she was when she got out of that cruiser. I almost felt sorry for that hooded dickhead... almost."

Henry nodded. He loved Jo with everything he had. But man, don't get on the wrong side of that woman.

"It was like she was playing with him. Letting him think there was gonna be a way out, or a deal or something. At least, that's the feeling I got watching from inside the truck. And then it happened so fast."

"Yeah, she can lose her shit pretty quick."

Byron shook his head. "No, Henry, I don't think you're picking up what I'm putting down. She did a whole hell of a lot more than just lose her shit. Joanne did things I don't think even you—or *Wanda,* for that matter—have ever seen."

Henry *thought* he knew what to expect when the chief was reluctant to tell him about the incident. Now he was nervous. What in the world could she have done that even Wanda wouldn't have seen?

"You see, that's the part I left out at the beginning. When she put that spell on me, her eyes glowed green. And when I say glowed green, I mean brighter than a friggin' traffic light. They stayed that way, too. She and the hooded thing talked in the street... he was backing away from her, and then it happened."

"What?"

"Joanne shot something at him. It matched the color of her eyes, Henry. I saw a huge, green bolt of... I don't know, energy, fire... something. It almost got the bastard, too. Caught his robe on fire, though. Then she chased him. He climbed up the telephone pole like it was nothing. She did it even *faster*. The whole thing looked like a scene from a goddamned movie."

Henry was reeling. He wasn't completely sure what to expect from the chief, but it sure as fuck wasn't *that*. And he believed every word. The *how* of it? That was another question.

"Then," Byron continued, "the next thing I know, he's right next to my side window. I was still looking up at the roof when he ripped the door open. All I saw was a bright flash of light, then the next thing I see is Delilah's blanket floating in the gutter, headed for Jo."

Both men were quiet after that. Henry resumed his sweeps with the light and Byron pulled double-duty, watching the road and whatever else he could safely take in without killing them both.

In the silence, Byron thought about Delilah. The question still gnawed at him, the information he sought about Mercy now an afterthought. *Why the baby? What's so special about her?*

"Henry, I'm curious about something. I asked you earlier why you thought they wanted Delilah. And I know you said you think it's about revenge. I'm trying to approach this from a cop's point of view, so please forgive me if the questions seem too personal."

Henry answered without turning around, "Ask away, Chief."

"Is there anything unusual about Delilah? I mean, something out of the ordinary that would make them want to take her?"

Where to begin? "Remember when I told you Dobson was the one who killed my mother?" Henry asked.

"Yep."

"Well, when she died that night, one of the last things Dobson said to me, when he was in the form he ended up taking—as the demon, Inanis—was that she was headed where he was, because she'd done terrible things, just like him. And I believed him. I was distraught, thinking she would suffer the same fate as him—that when she died, she would cease to exist at all. Not in heaven, not in hell, not anywhere.

"When Delilah was born, all that doubt vanished. My mother had left clues for me all along the way, right up until the night we faced off with Inanis. And that helped me, in the last moments, realize she had been on our side all along. Up until that point, I didn't know she was my mother. The clues had to do with the word swan. She left an image of a swan in that book from the library, then on the street the day I met her and Shrumm, she made a point of saying, 'I sleep well at night,' an acronym with the word swan in it. The swan thing kept showing up. She was telling me who she was in code—which I figured out as shit was going down at Wanda's. You follow?"

Byron nodded, then realized Henry was still sweeping the street with the spotlight, not looking at him, and said, "Yep, with you so far."

"Well, Jo had a rough time in labor. It was hours before the baby finally came. I took a break from the room and called Wanda. She set me straight on a lot of things."

"She's good at that, ain't she?"

"You have no idea. And it was a good thing I called her. It put me in the right frame of mind when I got called back to the delivery room. I had hope. That hope was rewarded."

"How so?"

"One thing Wanda said was she believed, if there was a Higher Power, that It couldn't possibly condemn a mother protecting her child to—as Inanis called it—'the void.' And she was right. After the redhead nurse brought her back from being cleaned up, we named her after my mother and Wanda, right on the spot. Well, Jo named her—credit where credit is due. Jo was nuts about her, and so was I. That's when Jo, being a great mom right from the start, checked the baby out from top to bottom. She slid the blanket from Delilah's shoulders. On my baby's back is a little, brown birthmark. It's a swan, Chief."

It took a minute for Byron to process it. "Wait a minute. So, you're telling me your baby is, what, the reincarnation of your mother?"

"That is *exactly* what I'm telling you, Chief."

"Now ain't that a fuckin' head scratcher."

Henry smiled at the window. He sympathized with Byron—the poor bastard was being bombarded by one unbelievable revelation after the next. And in far less time than Henry had gotten to process things last year. This was all in one night!

"You know, Henry," Byron said, "I'm really getting past the point of questioning any of this right now. So, let's say, for saying's sake, I accept everything you've told me tonight as gospel. Can we agree on that?"

Curiosity and hope got the better of Henry. He turned to Byron to make sure he wasn't shining him on. Byron's face was all business. Henry turned back to the passenger window and resumed searching. "Okay, Chief."

"Now, I'm gonna do my best to apply some 'cop logic' to some of what you've told me tonight. First, you said this demon guy—what's his name again?"

"Inanis."

"Okay, this Inanis. He died when? Before or after your mother on that night?"

"Before. Why?"

"Hold on, let me just get things straight first. I'll get to the why."

"Okay."

"Now, when he died—"

"I killed him."

"Fine. When you killed him, what happened to him after that?"

"His body disintegrated. It was like ash floating up to the ceiling and then disappearing. There wasn't a trace of him left. And it *felt* different in the room. The heaviness, or the evil, or whatever kind of vibe the bastard gave off seemed to vanish."

"What happened next?" Byron asked.

Henry thought for a second. "I went over to check on Jo. She was unconscious and bleeding on the floor. I woke her up, sat her on a barstool, and tended to the wound on her stomach. Jo pointed out my mother lying on the floor. I didn't even know, at that point, my mother had been hurt. Jo was fine, so I rushed over to Mom."

Byron licked his lips as he thought about the sequence of events. He was forming a theory, but he needed a bit more. "Was your mom still alive?"

"Yes. She didn't have long, though. I could tell right away the wound was fatal. But she held on long enough to say goodbye."

Byron nodded to himself. He stayed silent as he ran through it all, analyzing it the same way he would a crime scene. But something had to be added to *this* particular crime scene. If he were considering the events of the night of Delilah's death, and painting it with the brush of the supernatural events of *this* night, then he could make a leap of logic he would never consider under any other circumstances.

"You ever seen a mouse caught in a glue trap, Henry?"

"Um, I'm gonna go with no. Why?"

"It's sad to watch. I had to set some traps a few months back. Ever since our cat Binx died, we've had mice up the yin-yang. Most of them traps worked like they were supposed to. The mouse gets stuck in the trap, usually ends up face down. Suffocates 'em. I stopped using those 'cause they seemed too cruel. I don't want them suffering, just want them gone. Anyway, I was cleaning them up from the cellar when I came to the last one. The only thing I could see in the trap was a tiny red speck. Mouse chewed his foot off to get out of that trap. I couldn't believe my eyes, but there it was. Just goes to show you what a trapped animal will do for survival."

The story puzzled Henry at first. Then, butterflies began buzzing in his stomach, and the moral of the story hit him like a freight train. The chief pulled the car over, put it in park, and turned to face Henry.

"I think Inanis might have found a way out, Henry."

CHAPTER 24
ARCHIE'S GIRL

The pain in Archie's head from his encounter with, as he had dubbed him now, "flashlight boy," had receded to a dull throb. The fog from the blow was clearing and he could concentrate much better than even twenty minutes earlier. Certain facts about the events of the night so far were becoming clearer, and they organized themselves in his mind. He was not happy with the picture they painted.

Penny piloted the brand-new, black Toyota 4Runner through the storm. Archie swept the streets with the Maglite the chief had given him. The never-ending rain beat a steady rhythm on the roof, reminding him of bacon frying in a pan —only without the heavenly aroma. He was grateful he'd not smoked any weed tonight. The thought of bacon set his stomach rumbling. The munchies would have only made it worse.

"Was that you?" Penny asked.

"Hmm?"

"Was that your stomach I just heard? Or was that thunder?"

He laughed. "It was me."

"I second that emotion, then." She shot him a quick smile.

"Penny... what are your thoughts on everything going on tonight?"

She took her time, then said, "I can only speak to what I know so far."

"Of course," Archie said.

"From what I've been able to learn, the hooded guy has got it in for Wanda—that's a given though, who doesn't lately? And, for some reason, his focus is on Mercy. Big time. I know she's in a mausoleum in the graveyard, or was. It kept me out by setting some kind of energy trap on the door. But I could feel her presence through it, anyway. That girl has got it going on. And if I had to guess, that trap had more than one purpose."

"What do you mean?"

Penny shook her head, disgusted with herself. "I should have known what he was up to. I know better than to go after things like *him,* half-cocked. I let my anger about what happened to you get the better of me. I wasn't thinking straight. When I touched that door and it blew me back on my butt, he probably homed in on me right away. He knows I'm part of the *Foedere In Luna.* I'm sure of it."

"So? Is it supposed to be a big secret?"

"Wanda wanted me to always keep as much anonymity as possible. She always felt if there were a member that stayed, for lack of a better term, 'off the radar,' then we could use it to our advantage someday. And *now* would have been a perfect time for me to be used in just such a way. I blew that. I let her down."

"Is that what all that back and forth between you and Wanda was about back at her shop?"

Penny nodded. "Yes. That, and she pretty much okayed me letting Byron in on what I've always been."

Archie's eyebrows shot up. "You understood all that from just a look between the two of you?"

"Yes."

Though parapsychology was his specialty, the power of intuition—indeed, all things spiritual—never ceased to amaze him. He envied, in a good way, the things of which Penny was capable. He'd always admired what his little sister could do. Ever since they were kids, Archie had watched, time and again, Penny telling their parents about the things she could see. About the people who would visit her at night, and the things they wanted her to do for them.

Of course, her parents would lovingly brush her off and chalk it up to imagination. And Archie, still at the age where his parents were the sole and complete authority on everything, was inclined to agree with them. He thought Penelope might just be a wee-bit tetched. That changed in an instant on Archie's thirteenth birthday.

It was hot that August thirteenth. The party was in the backyard of his parents' house—a pool party. Archie was extremely popular at school. He was one of those kids who had an innate interest in just about everything, so he was never at a loss for words. When he talked to someone, he always made them feel like whatever they had to say was the most important thing in the world. It was that way with boys *and* girls. So, the day of the party, the driveway was packed with the bicycles of at least thirty of his classmates.

Everyone was having a great time. The smells of barbecued meat, fresh-cut grass, and chlorinated water filled the humid air. The Rolling Stones blared from a radio in the background. Boys and girls took turns on the diving board. Water flew around the yard, carrying screams of joy and wetting the light-grey cement surrounding the pool, turning it a few spotted shades darker. It was the kind of day you took for granted as a kid, but remember with longing fondness as time passes: carefree and without the demands of adulthood. Magic from childhood fades if we let it.

Archie and a friend were standing waist-deep in the pool, debating each other about the superiority of Batman versus Spiderman, when he noticed Penny sitting in a lawn chair and staring toward a shaded corner of the yard. Penny, no doubt, had done some weird stuff up to this point, but this was something new—enough so that Archie excused himself from the debate to check on her.

"What's so interesting over there, Pen?"

"You don't see it?"

Archie shaded his eyes with a flattened hand on his forehead and squinted. "I don't see a thing but fence and grass."

"There is an old man standing right there. You can't miss him. He's wearing light brown pants, a red flannel shirt, and black shoes. And he's bald."

"Didn't Mom and Dad tell you to stop with this stuff?"

His words stung Penny. "You still don't believe me?"

Archie saw the hurt in his baby sister's eyes. "I want to

believe you, Pen. But this is like the thousandth time you've told me you see something, and every time... there's nothing there. If you could somehow prove it to me, you know I would believe you."

"Who's Roger Murphy?" Penny asked.

"A friend of mine. Why?"

She pointed in the direction she claimed the bald man stood. "He says for you to watch out for the redhead. He says she's dangerous. He told me to tell you to ask your friend about his sister. And he said to tell Roger that Grumps says hi and he loves him."

Archie stared at Penny, speechless. His mouth hung open, his jaw working like a fish out of water, but words were nowhere to be found inside.

Penny said, "Well, don't stand there like a goof. Go ask him. I'll wait right here."

Archie turned around and walked, zombie-like, to the pool. Penny watched her brother as he sat on the pool's edge, lowered himself into the water, and slowly made his way over to Roger Murphy.

Archie turned back and looked in Penny's direction, as if unsure he should ask what he was about to ask. Penny held out a hand and shooed him forward. Dreamlike, Archie obeyed.

Though she couldn't hear them over the din, she didn't need to. Roger tilted his head, appearing not to understand what Archie was saying to him. Maybe Roger thought it was some kind of cruel joke. Then, when understanding dawned, Roger snapped his head in Penny's direction. She wasn't sure what to expect. Roger made his way to the pool's steps, then over to the lawn chair where he'd dropped his belongings. He gathered up his things and left, never looking back.

Archie stood in the middle of the pool for a long time. He stared down into the water, looking like someone who'd maybe forgotten to take his wallet out of his bathing suit and was carefully searching for it. But the answers he sought were not at the bottom of the pool. They were contained in the newly uncovered mystery of his sister.

When he finally snapped out of his funk, he returned to Penny. He pulled another lawn chair over, placed it in front of her, and sat down without saying a word. Penny broke the silence.

"What did he say?"

Archie was staring off into the distance, lost in thought.

"Archibald Love," Penny said, "you tell me right now what Roger said, or so help me—"

"Grumps is his grandfather's name." Archie nodded, seeming to confirm it for himself, not Penny. "I told him what you said."

"Did you mention the redhead?"

"I did."

"What did he say to that?"

"He said he didn't know about any redhead."

"What about his sister?"

"He told me his sister was a few years younger than him. And that she has a crush on me. I've never met her, though."

"Is she a redhead?"

"No," Archie said. "She's blonde. He says he doesn't really get along with her all that well. Says she's mean to him and always wants things her way. Her name is Rhymendara."

"That's a weird name," Penny said.

Archie nodded absently. "I said that, too. He said it's from his mother's side of the family."

"So, do you believe me now?"

He looked up sharply, focus returning to his gaze. Archie took in Penny with fresh eyes. He rose from the lawn chair, took two steps forward, and bent down to hug his little sister. "I do believe you."

Penny's eyes filled with tears, weighed down by relief and joy. Archie stroked the back of her head and said, simply, "I'm so sorry, Pen. All these years you tried to tell me and I didn't listen."

ARCHIE WAS LOST in the memory of that day as he scanned the streets for any sign of his microbus. As he searched, he asked Penny, "Do you remember my thirteenth birthday party, Penny?"

"Of course, I do. It was the day I finally got through that thick skull of yours. Why?"

"I just got to thinking about it. The thing with you and Wanda back at the shop reminded me of that day. Do you remember the look on Roger's face?" Archie asked.

She smiled. "He looked like he'd seen a ghost. I felt bad about having to do that, but I was desperate for anyone to believe me. It was a pretty lonely existence up to that point."

He nodded. "I wasn't any help until that day, that's for sure."

Silence hung in the air for a few moments, then Archie asked, "Do you remember the things you wanted me to ask him?"

"I do," Penny said.

"I remember the grandfather thing. And I remember the

sister with the weird name. What was it again?" Archie asked.

Penny thought about it. It was on the tip of her tongue. "Rhymendara. Sounded like the words Rhyme-End-Dara smashed together."

Archie nodded in agreement. "You know, I never met her. Roger didn't have friends over to the house. He said she saw me in a picture. Years later, at my high school reunion, he told me he was too embarrassed to have friends visit. His dad was a mean alcoholic." He waited a beat, then asked, "Do you remember the other message the old man gave you?"

"Yep. He wanted me to warn Roger about a redhead. I thought he meant his sister, but it turned out she was blonde, right?"

Archie said, "Yes. The blonde part isn't what made me think of the warning about his sister, though."

Penny shot him a quick glance. "Not sure I follow, Arch."

"I think that warning was meant for me, Penny."

"How could that possibly have been meant for you?"

"You remember the conversation we had a while back about how time is different on the 'other side' of the veil?"

"Of course," Penny said.

"Think about it, Pen. What if he knew about someone in my future and that warning was meant for me? The way things work over there, he might have been giving me a heads-up."

"Still not following. Help me here, Archie."

"I'm thinking about Mondra."

"Your psycho ex-girlfriend?"

Archie nodded.

Penny asked, "What about her?"

"It's not much of a stretch to turn Rhymendara into Mondra, don't you think?"

Penny's eyes widened. Though the names didn't sound alike at all, there was a certain logic to it. Roger *had* mentioned the sister's crush on Archie. The warning about the redhead, now that she thought about it, was not directed at Roger specifically, either. She just assumed where the old man had mentioned the sister, the warning was intended for Roger. The old man meant it for *Archie*. It was the only way it to interpret it, looking back. And if there was a redhead in the world that needed to come with a warning label attached, it was Mondra. She said, "Oh, shit!"

"Indeed," Archie said.

"You really think she has something to do with what's happening tonight?"

"I do. Do you know what the last thing Mondra said to me was, right before I broke it off with her?"

"No, what was it?"

"I'll never let you go."

Penny knew well the history of Archie's relationship with Mondra. And she was quite aware Wanda was the one who'd finally figured out Archie was not willingly in love with Mondra Tibbets, and that Mondra had performed dark magic on him. Wanda had laid it all out for Penny one day at her shop.

THE DAY THEY "MET," Mondra had planned, in advance, to bump into him that morning. And, according to Archie, she had a reasonable excuse as to how she knew where he lived. The library book he'd been carrying bore his address, but they all found out later Mondra had known where he lived all along. She knew everything about Archie, right down to the smallest detail. That included his nightly glass of cognac.

Mondra had sneaked into his house when she knew he'd be giving a lecture at the University. She'd tainted his drinking glasses with a concoction containing a powerful black magic love spell. After the night in Archie's living room, the two had been inseparable.

Wanda was skeptical of their relationship from the start. She knew full well Archie was a charmer, so it wasn't like he was desperate for love. Women were naturally attracted to him. Not because of his physical appearance—he wasn't exactly the American version of Sean Connery, but he was handsome enough. His personality always won them over. Slowly but surely, most of the women Archie met grew to love him through his wit, his knowledge, and his self-deprecating humor. But the key word here was slowly. And that was why Wanda was suspicious. She knew Mondra was, as the kids in town put it, hot as fuck. It made her suspicious enough to think there was more going on here than met the eye. And she was, of course, right.

Wanda invited them both over for dinner one night. She'd given Archie a made-up story about how she would have to have them meet her at the shop to eat because her two cats, Samantha and Darren, were both covered in fleas and the apartment was being flea-bombed. It was convincing enough, as it had happened twice before and Archie knew about it.

Before her guests had arrived, Wanda set up a table in the middle of the room and right over the pentacle at its center. A golden outer ring, already infused with salt to keep evil out while protecting those within it, surrounded the pentacle. She was extremely curious to see how Mondra reacted to that protection.

Next, she had prepared a protection amulet for Archie. Wanda would present it as a gift for his recently receiving the Professor of the Year award from the University. Archie's class was hugely popular, and the award was a sore spot for many other more "serious" disciplines. And it was a damned fine excuse for getting the blasted thing around his neck.

The amulet was a pendulum. Archie used one any time he needed to hypnotize a subject and work on past-life regression therapy. This pendulum had been infused to protect against black magic with the help of the four elements.

Wanda had placed it on an altar and surrounded it with salt, representing earth. A cone of dragon's blood incense was lit, signifying the air element. And a burning white candle resting in a saucer of water completed the fire and water elements.

Once the elements were in place, Wanda went into a deep meditation. When she came out of it, she set her intentions for the pendulum amulet and passed it through each of the four elements. She recited a different incantation for each. For earth she said aloud, "Absorb the earth, for it is solid and supports against any dark practice." Next came air. "May you carry away negativity from whichever way it passes." For fire, she held it as close to the flame as she dared, without burning herself, and said, "May you purify and burn away all that may harm." She took the warmed pendulum and immersed it in the water. "May the water hide you from those that mean you harm." Finished with the elements, Wanda raised the newly infused pendulum amulet to the sky and said, "We are all energy, from the divine and sacred."

She then let loose a breath across the object and finished. "With this breath, I infuse you with life." The protection was complete.

The new couple arrived at Wanda's Wicca'd Emporium two hours after Wanda had finished her work with the pendulum amulet. Archie burst through the door with a bottle of wine in his right hand and Mondra nervously clutching his left. Wanda thought she looked as skittish as a long-tailed black cat in a room full of rocking chairs. And, she knew, with good reason! Inside, she laughed.

"Thank you both so much for coming!" Wanda said. "I'm sorry about the accommodations, but my two little beauties were fraternizing with some unsavory neighbors. And it's not the first time, either!"

"That's okay," Mondra said. "Archie's told me so much about your little shop."

Strike one, Wanda thought, and forced a smile.

Archie empathetically picked up on the tension right away. Mondra, ever the narcissist, missed it completely.

Wanda guided them toward the middle of the room, following close behind—her attention fully on Mondra's body language. And, as expected, each step closer to the center made Mondra stiffen up ever so slightly. By the time they reached the table, Archie's date had to be almost folded into her seat.

"Are you okay, Mon?" Archie asked.

Mon? A pet name already? Inside, Wanda was gagging.

"I'm okay, Arch. Just a little stiff and tired from working out."

Wanda coughed, erasing the *bullshit* comment that came perilously close to escaping her lips.

All three took their seats.

"This looks great, Wanda! Thank you so much," Archie said.

"No trouble at all, honey. I know how much you love stir-fry. And you deserve it after winning that award."

"What award is that?" Mondra asked.

"Archie won the Professor of the Year award at the U."

Mondra raised an eyebrow. "Really? That's news to me."

Archie shrugged. "It's no big deal. It's mostly a popularity contest held by the students. They love my class, I guess. But I take some satisfaction knowing how it goes right up the ass of some of those stuffed suits in the physics department."

"When were you going to tell me about it? Or was it just something between you and Wanda?"

Wanda kept silent and watched.

"Why are you getting upset, Mon? It's no big deal."

"I'm not upset. Just a little hurt that I had to find out something like that second-hand. Wouldn't you be?" Mondra said as she crossed her arms.

Wanda decided this was a good point to strategically break the tension. "I've got a little gift for you, Archie. Just something to celebrate your achievement."

She pointed to the gift-wrapped box in front of his plate. The wine bottle blocked it from view. Wanda reached across the table and shifted the bottle so he could see it.

"What's this now?" Archie asked.

"Open it, find out," Wanda replied.

Archie was in his late fifties on the night of that dinner, but he looked like a kid on Christmas. He always looked that way whenever anyone gave him anything. It was, Wanda thought, one of his most endearing qualities. And it was one of the reasons she loved him and protected him.

"A pendulum? But you gave me one of these not too long ago," he said, confused.

"This one is special," Wanda said.

"How so?"

"Try it on. I made the chain extra-long to fit it around your fat head."

They both laughed. Archie removed it from the box and offered it to Mondra. "Would you slip this over my head for me, Mon?"

As Archie had been removing his gift from the box, Mondra stared daggers at Wanda. It was all the confirmation Wanda needed. She could tell right away Mondra knew exactly what the pendulum was really for, and that Mondra was exactly what she thought she was—a dark witch. Only someone highly skilled in the practice of dark magic could tell what the amulet represented just by looking at it.

"No, Arch, I wouldn't want to take that honor away from Wanda. It's *her* gift to *you*, after all."

Archie looked stung. He offered the pendulum to Wanda. "Care to do the honors?"

"I would love nothing more."

Wanda got up from her seat, took the pendulum from Archie's hand, walked behind him, and slipped it over his head. Her eyes never left Mondra's the entire time. The barely contained rage showed on Mondra's face, and with the residual effects of meditation, her aura appeared blackish-red to Wanda. Archie was blissfully unaware of the spiritual warfare taking place at the dinner table.

Wanda sat back down. Archie looked dazed. Mondra looked defeated.

"I'm not feeling well, Archibald. Could you take me home?"

Archie looked over at Mondra, almost as if he were truly seeing her for the first time. He didn't look like a love-struck puppy anymore. He also didn't look like he knew exactly where he was at the moment. Wanda could not have hoped for better results. It was just a matter of time now before Archie would come to his senses and see Mondra for what she really was.

Wanda knew the course of events that would unfold over the next few days. Love built on such a false foundation, once exposed, always crumbled. Love was a two-way street. Narcissists preferred one-ways. They always did.

"I want to go home, Archibald. Now!"

"Okay, okay." Archie got up, apologized, hugged Wanda, and followed Mondra to the door. Right before Mondra reached for the handle, Wanda said, "It was lovely meeting you, Mondra. We must do this again sometime."

Mondra turned slightly back toward Wanda, her hand still on the doorknob. "You can count on it, sweetie."

∽

"What was that?" Archie asked.

Penny was confused, and it showed on her face. "What was what?"

"You just said—out of the blue—'You can count on it, sweetie.'"

"I was just recalling the story Wanda told me about the night she exposed Mondra for what she is. I didn't realize I said that last part out loud."

Archie shook his head. "You don't know the half of it. When I brought her back to her place that night, all hell broke loose. By the time we'd gotten there, the amulet had taken full effect. I saw her true colors and couldn't believe I'd been so easily conned into loving her. If there's only one compliment I can give her, it would be she really knows her stuff. Thank God Wanda was wise to her."

"You never told me how things went down when you finally left her," Penny said.

"When we'd finally gotten home, the amulet had done its job. The spell broke, and Mondra knew full well it had. I told her I was done with her. Of course, being the self-centered egomaniac she is, she couldn't accept it. Spell or no spell, she never believed I would actually leave her. I told her very firmly and plainly what she had done was unforgivable, and that she was basically nothing more than a spiritual kidnapper holding me against my will. I told her never to call me, or speak to me again. It was really all I could do. It's not like I can go to the cops and press charges."

Penny laughed. "No, I suppose you couldn't. Not many laws on the books for dark magic love spells. Then again, I could work on Byron for you."

He smiled and continued, "Her last words to me were—"

"I'll never let you go... you just told me that."

"Yes, but there was something else before that. Talking about this tonight has brought more of it back. She said, and I quote, 'You think this is the first time I've done this, Archibald? We're meant to be together. You've just forgotten. I'll never let you go.'"

"What do you think she meant by 'you've just forgotten'?"

"If I had to guess, it goes back to the time surrounding the witch trials. It was the time of my last incarnation."

"Do you remember who you were back then?"

"That's what scares me. I've never been able to figure out

who I was back then. Any time Wanda helps me with past-life regression to that time, there's a strange blank spot. It's like I never existed there. When I travel backward past my birth in this life, I can see scenes and memories from that time, but something stops me when I get close to the truth. Almost like there's a guardian at the gate."

CHAPTER 25
HOLY PLACES

Cars were pulling into the lot. Doors slammed shut. By their sound, Mercy determined three car doors in total had been opened and closed. Out of an abundance of caution, she remained seated and out of sight. If it was Wanda and the other members of the League of the Moon who were returning, she wanted to gauge their mood. But Mercy was anything if not observant. The door to the safe room had been left open for a reason, but she wasn't entirely sure *she* was that reason. If it was someone else meant to walk through those doors, she wanted the advantage of being unseen.

Her caution paid off. Through the entrance to Wanda's safe room came three figures. Two of them shook off the rain, removed their coats, and stashed them behind the bar. The first was a tall, redheaded woman she'd never seen before. The second was her physics professor, Doctor Biltmore. *What the hell is he doing here?* The third was the man who'd hit her in the head with the flashlight, his face still obscured by his raincoat's hood.

Mercy got up from the beanbag chair without a sound, crawled under the opening where the 1970s beaded door from Wanda's past divided the safe room and the store, careful not to rattle a single bead, and slipped into the hallway leading to the store's front.

When she got to the door at the end of the hall, she turned the knob slowly. Locked! She was trapped in the sigil-covered hallway. Mercy knew the sigils provided a certain amount of protection. She hoped they would be enough to keep the new visitors from entering this space.

Quiet as a mouse, she crept toward the beaded doorway, put her back against the wall next to it, and slid down until she sat on the floor, hoping to pick up any tidbits of conversation she could.

MONDRA MADE her way to the center of the room with great caution. The last time she'd been here, it had taken all her strength just to sit at the dinner table with Wanda and Archie. She was pleasantly surprised. There was hardly any resistance at all. *Maybe Wanda has lost a little of her mojo?*

There were items at the pentacle's center. Mondra knelt down and observed the remnants of a luck spell. Smiling, she stood and kicked them to the corner of the room. *So much for that spell.*

She motioned to Biltmore's protégé. "Bring the baby over here. Darren—grab that black Reiki table and drag it to the center. I want the first thing they see to be the child when they walk through that door."

Both men did as they were told. Delilah was placed on the table.

"What next?" Biltmore asked.

"We wait," said Mondra.

Delilah coughed. Right on cue, Zachary Villitz walked through the back entrance to the safe room.

"Why does the baby cough every time he gets near her?" Biltmore's protégé asked.

Mondra considered how much she wanted him to know. At this point, she couldn't see the harm in letting him in on at least part of what was going on. "Zachary is connected to the child. I made sure of that the day she was born."

"And how did you manage that?"

"Running around in a nun's habit isn't the only thing I'm capable of. In matters like this, being... flexible... has its advantages. I was the nurse who put Delilah in her mother's arms. Therefore, I was the nurse who cleaned her up. I may have added a little something to the bath water."

∽

"Jo, stop the car!"

Joanne slammed on the breaks. "What is it?"

Wanda slid forward and into the Camry's dashboard. The flashlight flew from her hands and bounced on the car's floor.

"Oops, sorry," Jo said, fighting off laughter.

"Don't worry about it, sweetie. I think I saw something. Back up a little. Slowly, I don't want to miss it."

Joanne did as asked.

"There!" Wanda shined the light down an alley. "You see that?"

"Where?" Jo asked.

Wanda lowered her left shoulder and scrunched down a bit in her seat so Jo could lean over her for a better view.

"Right there, bottom left. There are some bushes in the way, but that looks like the bumper to Archie's bus. And if I'm not mistaken, those look like florescent dancing bears on that bumper sticker."

"First off, I don't know how the hell you could see that with all the rain that's coming down. So, props for that. Second, what the hell are the dancing bears all about? And third, why in the world would they hide his car in the back alley of a church?"

"It's a bumper sticker Grateful Dead fans put on their cars. Archie is a Deadhead—it's what their fans call themselves. I've heard their music, and frankly, I don't get it. But that's neither here nor there. Thankfully, my eyesight is about the only thing that works as well as when I was a little girl."

"But why is the bus parked here?" Jo asked.

"You know, I've always gotten a strange feeling about this place whenever I go by it. I can't put my finger on it, either. It's like having mixed emotions about something. Like there's more to the place than meets the eye. You'd think you would get nothing but positive vibes, you know, the whole *holy place* thing. But not this place."

"I'm calling the others," Jo said.

Wanda nodded, still thinking about the church.

"That was Jo. They found Archie's bus. It's—"

"Over near the church. Not too far from Wanda's shop, right?"

Henry's eyes bugged. "How the fuck did you know that?"

"Earlier tonight, at Wanda's shop, I started to say I think I might know where they were... then you and I kinda got into it."

Henry wanted to kick himself in the ass. If he hadn't lost his temper with Byron, they could have saved a lot of wasted time.

"I know what's going through your mind right now, Henry, and just forget about it. Beating yourself up won't accomplish shit. Let's get over there right now."

"You're right. Let's go."

∾

"AT THE CHURCH? Okay, we'll see you there."

Archie turned to Penny. "That was Joanne. They found my bus at the church near Wanda's shop."

"At the church? That's weird."

He nodded. "It's probably the last place in the world I would have looked. Which is why it makes perfect sense."

∾

THE SIX OF them stood under an awning a few feet from the passenger side of Archie's bus, sheltered from the unending rain. Henry tried the door, found it locked, and pulled viciously at the handle.

"Henry," Byron said, "back up a bit. Everyone else, move away from the door."

Byron walked up to the door, tapped first the top of the frame, then the bottom. He nodded, took two steps back, and kicked at the doorknob for all he was worth. The left side of the door frame splintered. He stepped back again, gave it another kick, and the door flew open and slammed against the inner wall. It shook in its frame as it slowly swung back in their direction.

"My first B and E with a cop!" Jo said.

Byron smiled. "How'd I do?"

Jo gave him a thumbs up.

They entered, single file, into the building. Wanda took the lead.

The church was dimly lit by a row of votive candles at the front. Their soft glow was just enough to make out the dark outlines of two rows of pews stretching from front to back. The altar to the right of the candles was a mass of dark shadows. Jesus looked down from the cross, visible in silhouette underneath the candlelit reflection of the gold-flaked INRI plaque, watching silently from above as they approached.

"I always wondered what those letters meant," Jo said.

Henry followed her eyes. "The letters represent Latin words. It means *'Iesus Nazarenus, Rex Iudaeorum'* or, in English, *'Jesus the Nazarene, King of the Jews.'*

"Look at the big brain on you, Band-Aid boy!" Jo said.

Henry smiled. Jo licked her finger and tapped his forehead. Yet another gold star.

"There's a light on over there." Byron pointed to the right of the altar. He pulled the flashlight from his belt, turned it on, and led the way. The source of the light was a door at the far-right corner of the altar and down a short flight of three stairs. It was cracked open a fraction of an inch.

Byron descended the stairs, wrapped a hand around the wood just below the knob, and inched it open. The door creaked. He wanted to keep things as quiet as possible now, so he pushed the door open as fast as he could, squelching the creak, then held it just before it could bang into the paneling that lined the interior hallway. He was grateful for the plush red carpeting that lined the floor. Footsteps would not be a problem.

He shone the flashlight down the hallway. Doors lined each side in evenly spaced intervals. Three on the left and three on the right. He started down the hallway when Wanda whispered, "Not yet, Byron."

"Why not?" he whispered back.

"How many doors do you see?" Wanda asked.

"Six. Why?"

Wanda nodded. "That's what I thought. I have an idea. I want each of us to stand in front of one of the doors. When I nod, we all open our doors at the same time."

Byron looked at her like she'd lost a marble or two on the way in. "Why in the world would we do that?"

"Trust me. You'll see."

He looked to Henry and Joanne for help. None came. He looked to Penny, his last refuge. She just shrugged. He didn't bother trying with Archie. Byron shook his head, stood in front of the closest door to his right, and said, "I must be out of my mind." But he did what was asked of him, and a worm of excited anticipation crawled through him. He was a man at war with himself.

The rest of the crew of six took up position in front of their doors and trained their eyes on Wanda, waiting for her to nod. The hallway was in complete silence, save for the muted drone of raindrops tapping the building's roof. She made sure she had everyone's attention by looking each in the eye, or where she thought their eyes were—it was still mostly dark, aside from the chief's flashlight—then she gave them an exaggerated nod. Six doors were opened simultaneously, and then, to Wanda's left, a seventh door slid open where moments before there was only a wall at the end of the hallway.

Byron couldn't believe his eyes, and whispered, "What in the fuckin' wide world..."

Penny was far less surprised. "How did you know it was there, Wanda?"

"Just another thing I have to thank Mercy for when I see her again. I don't really know how long ago our friend fuckface went through this door, but his hand prints are all over this wall. I can still see traces of his aura. When I saw six doors lining the hallway, then the hand prints, I came up with the number seven. In numerology, seven stands for truth and perfection, the number three stands for heaven, and the number four stands for earth. Which, symbolically, is what a church is. I just put two and two together, so to speak. And I'd bet my life this is where they're keeping Delilah. It's protected by dark magic. No one in the church is probably even aware this exists."

Henry was elated and fought off the urge to lick his finger and tap a gold star on Wanda's forehead. Jo saw the look in his eyes, cracked a crooked smile, and shook her head.

"Byron, I think you should take the lead, since you're the only one armed," Wanda said.

Still a bit stunned by the secret door, he said nothing and led the way.

The phantom door opened to a courtyard. Trees lined the flagstone pathway; its stones appeared a shiny yellow from the dim lamplight and the fine sheen of rain. Their branches formed a makeshift natural tunnel, providing some protection from the downpour. Wanda counted the trees as she passed them. Six on the right side and seven on the left. Thirteen. *No coincidence.*

At the end of the flagstone path was a door to a structure Wanda vaguely recognized. "Archie, this place looks awfully familiar to me."

He stepped forward, stood next to Wanda, and studied the entrance. He felt the same thing. "Yes, it does. But I've no idea why."

Byron tried the latch knob on the door. It clicked, and he pulled the door open without resistance. He was immediately on high alert.

"That seemed awful easy," said Henry.

"Yep," Byron said as he pulled his gun from its holster. "Stay back a bit from me. If there's trouble, I don't want any of you getting hurt."

Joanne said, "It might not be the shooting kind of trouble, Chief. I think I should be close behind. Don't you?"

Visions of blazing green eyes and robes catching fire danced in Byron's head. "Okay, just hang back a little. The rest of you fall in behind Joanne."

No one argued.

They passed through the doorway and down granite steps so worn by time they were almost a slope. It curved slightly to the right at the bottom, enough to keep the inner door hidden almost until they reached it. A small, square window with black, iron bars covering it leaked soft, yellow light into the passage. The door was cracked open. Another all-too-convenient situation.

Byron pulled the door slowly open, its hinges creaking with every inch it moved. With his gun at his side and pointed toward the ceiling, he leaned cautiously over the threshold. Candelabras sat at each end of the room, burning silently in the gloom. It was empty.

"You all need to wait here. Let me clear the place, then we can fan out and search it."

Everyone nodded in agreement.

He came back five agonizing minutes later and ushered them all inside. It wasn't a huge place—three rooms in total—but old places like this had a lot of hiding spots. Byron wanted to be sure there wouldn't be any surprises. *There's been enough of those tonight already.*

Archie and Wanda began a thorough search of the main room, Henry and Jo took one bedroom, and Penny and Byron searched another. It didn't take long.

"Look at this, Arch," Wanda said.

Archie joined Wanda from the opposite side of the room. In a dark corner, on an antique dresser, was another effigy of Wanda. It was similar to the one Henry and Joanne had found hanging from their door the day before—with one big difference. Around its neck was a noose of a different color. It was made from what appeared to be long, red hair. A card sat in front of it, folded tent-like with Wanda's name scrawled across its front in blood. The letters leached toward the bottom of the card and stained the top of the dresser.

"Don't touch that!" Byron yelled from across the room. He made his way toward them, pulling latex gloves from his pocket and snapping them on.

"I need to see what it says," Wanda complained.

"I'll read it to you. I don't want you contaminating it. There's been a kidnapping tonight here, too. This is a crime scene. When we catch these shitheads, I want to make sure I can nail them to the wall."

No one had even considered the legal side of things . It was a good point.

Byron pulled the card from the table, holding on to a clean edge. He found another clean spot on the back side and carefully pried it open. By the look on his face, the message made little sense to him. He read it, "Remember—you can count on it, sweetie!"

Wanda and Archie locked eyes. She was about to say something to him when Henry and Jo burst from one of the bedrooms. "There's a hidden room in the back. There's an empty crib in it."

Penny was the last to return. She came out of the other bedroom holding a black cloak. It was burnt up one side.

In a span of ten minutes, from the time they'd entered the room to the moment Penny had emerged with the cloak, everything Archie had been piecing together slammed home at once.

CHAPTER 26

NOW YOUSE CAN'T LEAVE!

"So, let's think about this," Byron said. "We know the baby has been here—the crib is pretty self-explanatory. We've got the burnt cloak from fuckface, and now you're telling me your ex-girlfriend is involved in this. Is that right, Archie?"

"Yes. I'd recognize that hair anywhere. And with Wanda filling in the blank on what was written in the note, I'd say there's little doubt she's involved. But I couldn't, for the life of me, tell you why."

Byron asked, "Can you describe her, Arch?"

"Sure. She's about five eleven, longish red hair, very pretty. And she has a mole above her lip, on the right side of her face. Oh, and she always has black nail polish on her fingernails, and her right thumb almost always has a gold pentacle set into the polish."

Henry had been staring at the floor, lost in thought. His head snapped up. "I know her!"

Byron was surprised. "You do?"

He nodded emphatically. "When Delilah was taken from the room to be cleaned up the other day, one nurse took her away. That one was kinda short and stout. She had blonde, curly hair sticking out from under her cap. The nurse who returned Delilah was much taller. I noticed strands of dark red hair poking from under the cap. And I saw the pentacle on her right thumb. This is Salem, though. I didn't give it a second thought. Mondra was there! Anything could have been done from the time Delilah was out of the room until she brought her back."

Jo was pacing back and forth now. "Let's go."

"What? Go where?" Henry asked.

"To the Emporium," Wanda said.

"The Emporium? You think that's where they took her?" Byron asked.

"Of course, that's where they took her," said Wanda. "The last thing she said to me the night I broke the spell on Archie is exactly what's on that note. There's nothing else it could mean."

"The room is protected, though. How does it make any sense they would be there?" Archie countered.

"Right before we left the safe room tonight, I got the feeling I needed to leave the door open. I told Jo as much right before we left. I don't know the reason. I just went with what I was feeling. When I willingly leave that door open, anyone can enter the room."

"Why would you do that?" Byron asked.

"If I could give you a concrete answer on that one, I'd probably play Mega-Millions on a regular basis, Chief. All I can tell you is when I've relied on intuition in the past, it's never let me down. I have to trust it, even when every ounce of my being screams it isn't logical."

"But they've got the upper hand now. How does that make any sense?" Henry asked.

"No, they don't," Jo said.

"How do you figure?" Byron asked.

Jo said, "It's simple. Wanda was the one that, in effect, broke the seal. She allowed them in. When we go back there, it's gonna be like that scene from *A Bronx Tale*. You remember what Chazz Palminteri said to the bikers in the bar scene when they refused to leave?"

"I remember that movie," Penny said. "I forget the line, though."

Henry did his best Chazz, "Now youse can't leave."

Wanda snapped her fingers and pointed at him. She was smiling.

"There's still something I don't understand. But there's also something you all need to hear," Byron said.

"What's that, By?" Penny asked.

"Henry and I had a discussion in the car, right before we got here. It's a theory I have about what happened to you all on the morning of Halloween."

Byron looked to Henry for permission—he knew what he was about to say would probably send Joanne off the deep end. But say it, he must. Henry gave him a slight nod.

"I think it's possible—unlikely, but possible—that when Henry thought he'd killed Inanis, or Solomon, or whatever you want to call him, there might have been a way out for him. Or, more exactly, a place for him to hide and survive."

"I'm not sure I follow," Joanne said.

Wanda closed her eyes, her head hanging down. "I think I know where this is going. And I have to agree. It makes sense considering current events."

"What?" Jo said. The look on her face said she suspected

the answer. The question supported the denial her mind clung to. Verbal confirmation would pull her fingers from the cliff.

"Inanis attached to Delilah as she passed," Wanda said. "Byron suspects, and I agree, he is, somehow, hiding inside your baby, Jo."

Jo's eyes shifted from Wanda to Byron to Henry, and then back to Wanda. "And what proof, exactly, is there of this?"

Henry said, "Jo. Delilah has been coughing her brains out since we brought her to Wanda's shop. Remember the first spot in the room we brought her to? It was right in the middle, inside the circle of salt and near the pentacle. Inanis can't be near any of that without at least some reaction."

"Or, call me crazy, she could just be sick, Henry."

"Yes. And, I can't believe I'm saying this. I hope to God that's the case, baby. But then you have all this other shit going on with the hoodie, Mondra, and whoever else may be involved. *Mondra* was the one who handled her last at the hospital. She could have done anything to her. We *know* what she did to Archie. It's not much of a stretch."

Jo shook her head, not ready to concede the point. "Byron, you said there was still something you don't understand. What was it?"

Byron closed one eye and rubbed the back of his neck. "Well, there's another part to this that we're all forgetting about. And I still, for the life of me, can't figure out how it fits into any of this... the pineal glands. I just don't see how all this goes with the baby being kidnapped."

Archie cleared his throat. "I have a theory on that."

He was sitting on the couch in front of the coffee table, facing the dying fire. No one realized he had even moved from the circle in which the current conversation was taking place. In his hand was one of the two cups that had been on the table since they'd arrived. No one noticed them in the rush to look for Delilah. Archie swirled the cup in his left hand, staring into it.

"There appears to be some kind of residue in both cups. It smells pretty bad, actually." Wanda had made her way over to the couch and was sitting next to him. He handed her the cup. Wanda took a whiff and retched. Byron motioned for Wanda to hand him the cup. He sniffed and gagged.

"What do you think it is?" he asked Archie.

"Well, to me, it smells a lot like human remains."

"You think it has something to do with the pineal glands, don't you?" Byron asked.

Archie nodded. "I do."

"So, you think they drank them as, what? Some kind of potion? A spell?" Byron asked.

"Maybe, maybe not. But that's not what has me worried. If they are using the pineals of others for some kind of personal gain, or their own welfare... well, I've heard of stranger things. I know that sounds callous, and the fact that people are dying because of these bastards is not lost on me, Chief."

"But that's not what you're thinking about," Byron said. "So, I'm almost afraid to ask at this point—what do you think is going on, Arch?"

He gathered his thoughts, then dove in. "One of the unique things about the pineal gland is its involvement in your dreams. For the sake of time, I won't go into all the biology. Dreams are the playground of the psyche. Most take place within the mind, but some don't. The ones that *don't*... take place on the astral plane. The astral plane, some say, is a place where both the living and the dead can occupy the same plane at the same time. If you've ever had a dream of a loved one after they've passed—an extremely vivid one, as if you felt you could reach out and touch them, or you hugged them and it felt *so real*—that dream has taken place in the astral realm. You follow?"

Byron nodded. Penny noticed not a trace of skepticism on his face. It warmed her, despite all that was going on.

Archie continued, "Well, if you're right about Inanis hiding within my granddaughter, they may have found a way to get him out."

Wanda joined in, "Let's say you're right about this. Where are they trying to move him to? And how?"

"That's where the hoodie comes in. I think the concoction in this mug was for him. I think they've been harvesting the pineals from living human beings to sustain that bastard. And I think it's the only way they can continue to use him on both sides of the astral plane."

"But for what purpose?" Joanne asked.

"I think he's a sacrifice," said Archie. "I think the *Order Immortalis* has had a backup plan in case something like what happened last Halloween ever happened to their 'fearless' leader. Whoever, or whatever, the hoodie is, I think he's unaware of his status as a vessel. And Mondra is using him to bring back Inanis."

"That still leaves one very important question," Henry said. "Who the hell is this hooded guy?"

"I've been thinking hard on that, Henry," Wanda said, "and I come up with nothing. Same thing when it comes to Mondra. Most of the enemies of the *Foedere In Luna* I can account for. Solomon, obviously, because he never actually had to reincarnate from that time. And then there was

Leonard Shrumm—he made it through four hundred years with Inanis and then got two in the hat."

"Two in the hat? What's that mean?" Byron asked.

"It's an old mobster term," said Wanda. "It means put two bullets in someone's head to make sure they're dead."

"New one on me," said Byron.

"Anyway, as I was saying, all of us in this room were part of the League of the Moon back then. They considered me the organizer. Henry, who was Madeleine back then, was the spiritual leader. Joanne was Madeleine's husband, David. Penny, back in that time, was named Matilda Sutton—"

Byron's eyes shot up in surprise.

"We can talk about that later, By," Penny said. Crimson colored her cheeks. That conversation was going to be interesting.

Wanda continued, "So, we have three souls that are unaccounted for in this time frame when compared to sixteen ninety-two."

"Three?" Henry asked.

Wanda nodded. "Mondra, fuckface, and Mercy."

"I thought you said you thought Mercy was on our side. You've changed your mind?" Joanne asked.

"No. I didn't say I thought she was with them, I just said she's part of the ones in *this* time frame I can't account for from the last."

"What about Archie?" Byron asked.

"We've been investigating who I used to be. Wanda and I have recently been working on that in regression therapy. We still haven't figured it out yet."

"Okay, so what do we do next?" asked Penny.

"We kick them out of the bar," Jo said.

CHAPTER 27
DAWNING DARK

"Raul, this is Byron. I want you to head over to Wanda's Wicca'd Emporium on Essex. Park as far from the building as you can, but close enough so you can keep an eye on the back parking lot. Make sure you approach without any lights, including your headlights"

"Okay, Chief. What's going on?"

"Right now, it's on a need-to-know basis. There are people in there at the moment that I *need to know* if they leave the premises. I'll fill you in later on the deets. Copy?"

"Ten-four." Raul hung up.

"No more walkie-talkies, Chief?" Henry asked.

"We still got two-ways in the cruisers. I just don't think this is the kind of thing the rest of my guys need to hear about right now."

"Good point," Henry said.

"They're not going anywhere, Byron," Wanda said.

He nodded in agreement. "I know, but humor me. I'm an old cop dealing with some heavy new shit here. I just like to have a little back-up. Can't hurt, right?"

"True enough," Wanda said.

Byron looked around the room, scanning for threats before they made their exit. Nothing appeared, to his eyes, out of the ordinary. He drew his gun and started for the door.

Joanne put a hand on his arm. "Not this time, Chief."

"Jo, I need to protect all of us on the way out, so just—"

"I have to agree with Jo, Chief," Henry said.

"Have you all lost your minds?" Byron asked.

"They're right, Byron," Penny said.

"About what?"

"Don't you think it's just a little strange how easy it was for us to enter this place, Byron?" Wanda asked.

"In some spots, yeah. But I *did* have to break the door down, and what about the seven doors? I wouldn't exactly call that a welcome mat."

"They knew we would find it. Granted, it wasn't a neon sign. But, where magic is concerned, it might as well have been. That last door could have only been found by a witch," said Wanda. "They've probably come and gone from this room as they've pleased for who knows how long. Yet the business of this church goes on as if this room doesn't exist."

He looked from one face to the next, settling on Penny's last.

"I have to agree with them, honey. They may have made it easy on us to enter this place, but everything they've done up to this point has forced us into what *they* want us to do."

"I'm not following the logic here," Byron said.

"They may know we're coming to them, but they don't know *exactly* when, how, or how many," Henry said.

"So?" Byron countered.

"Well, if you were in their shoes, wouldn't you want at

least a heads-up things were about to go down?" Henry asked.

"I guess. But the whole point of drawing you from the Emporium was so they could take it over. Or am I mistaken?"

"No, you're partially right," said Wanda, "but it was my decision to leave the door unguarded. They *might have* relied on that decision to get inside, though it's more likely they planned to *force* their way in when they knew we'd stop at nothing to find Delilah. That's why the hoodie was scouting out my shop. Anyway, *my decision* to leave that door open wasn't so they could get in."

Now everyone in the room looked confused. All of them had assumed Wanda had left it open in order to trap Mondra and her crew.

"Do you remember what I said just before we left, Jo?" Wanda asked.

"You said—'don't lock it, Jo.'"

"After that," said Wanda.

Jo thought about it for a few seconds, then her eyes opened wide. "You said, 'Something we need is coming.'"

Wanda closed her eyes, smiled, and nodded.

"Mercy is there, isn't she?" Jo asked.

"She is," Wanda said.

"But you still don't know if she's with them or with us."

"I'm pretty sure she's with us."

"How can you know for sure?" Archie asked.

Wanda smirked. "It just rings true."

Archie cocked his head. His friendship with Wanda went back many years in this lifetime. He knew that smirk. It meant she knew something the rest of them didn't, and it was her way of letting him know that.

Mercy had heard enough. She had a rough understanding of what these people meant to do, and she intended to stop them. But she was trapped in the dark, sigil-covered hallway. The door to the inside of the store was locked, and another trip under the beaded doorway was not an option. That was when Mercy remembered the cell phone in her front pocket. She prayed to whoever she thought might listen that it hadn't gotten too wet to work.

She got up from the floor, tip-toed to the other end of the hall, near the locked door, and turned the power on. As the screen lit up, she flattened her hand over the speaker, drowning out the AT&T jingle that played whenever she restarted her phone. It was muted but still audible. Mercy held her breath, sure that someone from the safe room had heard it. After a breathless eternity passed, she finally felt safe. No one had been drawn to the hallway by the noise.

Turning her back to the beaded-door-end of the hallway, she opened the phone's flashlight app. Mercy smiled at the thought of smacking flashlight guy in the face with her phone. Maybe if all went well, she would. But revenge could wait. Right now, she set the app to its dimmest setting and aimed it at the ceiling. Nothing of value rested above her head, but it didn't take long to find what she was looking for.

Seven feet from where she stood was the pull-down door to the attic. Tucking the cell phone back into her front pocket, she knelt down and inched the zipper down on first her left boot, then the right, and placed them against the wall. Her ankle socks glowed softly in the sparse light thrown from the end of the hallway. They were the only things she could see with her own eyes other than the sigils that lined the hallway's walls. But they didn't throw the light needed to see in the earthly dark.

Mercy leaped in the air and snagged the chain hanging from the attic door. When she landed, she did so on her toes. *That fucking hurts!* But it was just enough to keep the door from being pulled too quickly downward, which would have caused it to squeal out her location.

With the chain in hand, she lowered herself toward the floor at a snail's pace; the door mimicking her descent. Once her feet were flat on the floor, she grabbed the handle inset into the door's frame, unfolded it as if she were handling a Vatican relic, and after what seemed to take forever, rested the bottom of the ladder on the hallway floor.

Mercy retrieved her boots, placed her weight on the attic ladder, testing it for squeaks, and thanked whoever was watching over her tonight that Wanda was meticulous about the maintenance of her shop—the ladder was silent.

She climbed without sound to the top, hauled the ladder up at a glacial pace, and closed herself in. Leaving her boots behind, she pulled the phone from her pocket and made her way toward the corner of the attic directly above the bar. Once there, she assumed the lotus position, calmed her mind, and thought about what might come next.

"They should have been here by now," Mondra said. "

I told you not to underestimate them. Look what happened to the last one that did," Zachary warned.

"What's the problem?" Biltmore asked.

"No problem," said Mondra. "It's a fucking monsoon out there tonight. It's no surprise things might get delayed. They'll be here. They don't have a choice."

Biltmore nodded, but the look on his face suggested to Mondra he was beginning to doubt her.

"Don't worry, Darren. You'll get what's been promised to you. And he will, too." Mondra nodded to Biltmore's protégé. "The *Order Immortalis* keeps its word." The lie slipped from her lips so smoothly she was beginning to believe it herself.

There was a time in her life when Mondra would not have been able to lie with the ease she did now. But that was long ago. And she was, for all intents and purposes, a different person. Her father had driven her to it.

Growing up in the Murphy household had taken its toll on all the Murphy children. Irving Murphy was strict. His years in the military were few, but they had left their impact on his life. Being responsible for a platoon of men in Vietnam was an important role. Running your *family* like that platoon was a recipe for disaster. Add booze and bad memories to the mix...

Rhymendara's mother was a strong but quiet woman. She'd met Irving at an officer's dance during the height of the war. It was a million-to-one shot the two would meet.

Minadora was a Romanian exchange student working part time at the bar where the party took place. She was carrying a tray of empty champagne flutes toward the kitchen when Irving, in full storytelling mode in front of a group of other officers, swung his hands up in a demonstrative display and sent the tray resting on Minadora's splayed fingers flying. Thirteen delicate glass flutes crashed to the floor, rendering the entire hall momentarily silent. Mortified, she apologized profusely to anyone that would listen, then set about cleaning up the shattered flutes. Irving felt terrible and immediately got down on all fours to help retrieve the shattered glass. Tears of embarrassment formed in the corners of Minadora's eyes, and Murphy felt utterly responsible for them. He made it his mission to make her laugh.

It was, at one time, a gift he'd had—making people laugh. And that night, he'd used that gift to perfection. By the time they'd cleaned the glass from the floor, Minadora was smiling warmly at the redheaded crew-cut soldier. When he'd offered to buy her a drink after her shift ended, she'd accepted. They'd talked until the moon got tired and yielded to morning sun. They were inseparable from that day on.

When the war ended, and Murphy was swept away, Minadora followed him back to the United States. They married almost upon arrival and settled back in his hometown of Salem. Minadora was already pregnant six months with Roger, but it barely showed. When the seventh month rolled around, she went into premature labor. Complications necessitated the baby stay at the hospital until he could breathe on his own.

Irving and Mina, as he called her now, made nightly trips to the nursery to check on little Roger. One night, Mina decided she would try to speed up the recovery of her son with a remedy from the "old country." It was a spell handed down from her mother, who'd gotten it from *her* mother, and so on, through the ages.

Mina came from a long line of witches, a fact she never felt comfortable revealing to Irving when they'd first met—she was unsure how he'd handle witchcraft. But her baby was sick, and she decided she didn't really care if he liked it or not.

As Irving talked with their doctor just a few feet away and behind her, Mina removed a blue vial from her purse. She pulled the cork stopper from its top. It made a soft popping sound, and she moistened the tip of her finger with a few drops of the concoction she'd put together the night before, at her hidden altar in the attic at home. She gently applied the oil to her baby's forehead and, as quietly as she could, recited the incantation for her spell. Despite her caution, she'd caught Irving's attention.

"What the hell are you doing?" Irving asked.

"I'm healing our son."

"What's that?" Irving pointed to the vial.

"It's a healing potion," she said, her chin raised in defiance.

"Is that something from the pharmacy?" He looked confused.

"I made it."

He tilted his head to the left. "What do you mean you made it?"

"It's an old remedy, handed down from generations of women in my family."

Irving looked from his wife to the doctor and back to his wife. His face was crimson from embarrassment. The doctor sensed the tension and excused himself.

"Is this some sort of witchcraft crap?

"It's not crap! It works."

Irving was looking at his tall, blonde, beautiful Romanian wife with new eyes. He wasn't sure he liked what he was seeing.

"I will not have my children being raised with witchcraft. They are going to be Roman Catholics. Do you understand me?"

"There's room for both. Why does it have to be one or the other?" Mina asked.

"No! They're not compatible. One is the truth. The other is evil. I will not have it!"

Mina put the vial back in her purse, closed it, and put her hands on her hips. She said nothing more on the subject, but she had no intention of doing as she was told. Irving took a lot of cold showers for the next few years.

Eventually, the relationship thawed. Three and a half years later, Rhymendara was born. It was a flawless birth—a breeze compared to Roger's. Mina had made sure it would be. Of course, she'd never stopped practicing her craft.

Though the altar she'd hidden in the attic had been dismantled and trashed by Irving, she'd set up another one, hidden in plain sight. Her living room was decorated in such a way that the entire room served as an altar now. She'd infused the coffee table with spells, carving a large pentacle on its underside, and then concealed it with a fine layer of brown cloth. Candle holders sat at both ends of the coffee table. Irving had even complimented her about them—she'd ordered them from their church, after all. This was not a problem for Mina. She believed in higher powers that were all-inclusive, so the vessel for the candles, to her, meant little. A small potted plant sat in the middle of the coffee table, in what appeared to be a metallic, gold-flaked stand. The plant was easily removed, and the stand served as her incense burner and cauldron. Dragon's blood cones sat in the small drawer on its side. The dagger awarded her husband during the war by his peers served as her athame.

During her pregnancy with Rhymendara, Mina would use the afternoons her husband was at work to perform the rituals she deemed necessary to ensure her daughter's birth would go well. She would have preferred to perform them at night, but this wasn't possible. Irving's drinking had progressed to a point where it was better to keep the peace during the evenings.

Despite the advance of Irving's alcoholism, the next few years were quiet ones. Roger and Rhymendara were obedient children, but the two of them were almost mirror images of their parents when it came to personalities. Roger was sullen where Rhymendara was vivacious. He was pessimistic where his sister found the good in things. And Roger believed in Heaven and Hell, and all the rigidity of his father's beliefs. Rhymendara believed in the things her mother believed, but she had to keep it to herself and present the image of a practicing Roman Catholic. For a girl of seven, it was confusing. And carrying on in this fashion for years warped her personality.

By the time she was sixteen, Rhymendara had turned inward. The breezy days of her childhood were long forgotten. Resentment of her father for imposing his beliefs on her, and anger at her mother for refusing to confront him and bring their beliefs into the open had turned her bitter. That bitterness cut both ways.

Rhymendara saw the only way she could truly be free was to rebel. She began dressing in black and hanging out with friends neither of her parents would approve. She took joy in their disapproval. It fueled her.

By the time she was sixteen, she had discovered the darker side of life and had given herself to it with abandon. She ignored curfews set by her father, staying out all night sometimes. On days she did this, she would arrive in the family kitchen in the morning, plop herself at the table, and watch as the rest of the family got ready for their day.

For a time, Irving and Mina had decided ignoring her was the best approach. They reasoned maybe she would grow out of it. This proved to be a poor strategy. Things escalated.

One morning, Irving was suffering through a terrible hangover. Rhymendara had taken up her position at the breakfast table. Her passive-aggressive morning ritual was underway. Irving had finally had enough. He told her to leave the house. She told him to go fuck himself. All hell broke loose. The shouting back and forth lasted several minutes.

In that short amount of time, however, bonds broke. The things we say to each other in the heat of the moment, though meant for temporary victory, can forge chasms of separation lasting a lifetime. This happened between Rhymendara and her parents on that day. Her father removed her bodily from their home, she never went back. And because Mina, cowed by years of supplication to her husband's will, failed to defend her daughter, she never spoke to her mother again.

Later that night, something in Rhymendara broke forever. She called Lucia, her best friend, and asked if she could crash at her place. Lucia told her it was no problem, but she probably wouldn't be getting much sleep if that's what she intended. Rhymendara asked why.

"It's going to be the party to end all parties, girl! It's my sixteenth birthday!"

Rhymendara was thrilled! She told Lucia she couldn't wait to get there and get ready for it. She filled her friend in what had happened that morning with her parents.

"Your dad's a total dick, Rhy! Fuck that asshole! And your mom? I can't believe she didn't stand up for you. Fuck her, too! Get your ass over here right now. *I* got some weed, and *you* need to mellow out."

"On my way. And thanks, Luc!"

"Mi casa, su casa!"

Lucia was right, it was the party to end all parties. Lucia's parents were nowhere to be found, and it seemed half the town had shown up. Rhymendara was in awe of the place. Though the amount of people at the party was staggering, the property was more than adequate to accommodate everyone—with room to spare. There were people by the pool, across the spacious, manicured yard, near the greenhouse, inside the greenhouse, down by the dock, on the huge boat tied to the dock, inside the huge boat—everywhere.

This impressed her so much she vowed to herself this was going to be her goal in life. She would have the things she wanted, when she wanted them. And she was willing to do whatever she needed to get what she wanted.

As she took in the surrounding sights, a young man had walked up beside her, offering her a beer. She accepted. They talked and drank. He was funny, and she thought he was cute. A little short and stocky for her taste, but cute.

One thing led to another and they found themselves alone in the boathouse. It was just about the only place on the entire property uninhabited by party-goers.

A ladder led up to the loft area of the boathouse. He looked at the ladder, then back at her. Rhymendara smiled and led the way. She got to the top quickly. He was a bit more drunk and his coordination failed him. He slipped back down the ladder, cursed, and started back up again. When he got to the top, Rhymendara was naked and standing in front of the window. She stood sideways, her curvy silhouette cut through the light and through his drunken fog like a sexual talisman. He went to her.

That night proved to be the night that changed her life forever. Gone was the lighthearted girl who looked forward to the afternoons with her mother, learning about the witchcraft passed down through countless generations of women in her family. Gone was the girl who thought pleasing her father was the way to a peaceful life. Gone was the girl who held out hope her mother would stand up to her father and defend their faith. Gone was the girl who once had concern for the feelings of others. She didn't believe in the goodness of others anymore. Everyone was out for themselves; she'd seen too much evidence to believe otherwise.

The boy climbed on top of her, and she let him have her. Rhymendara, after the initial pain of losing her virginity, found she really liked sex. But, more important than that, over the next few months, she realized her looks and men's desires could be a potent combination. It was a lesson she never forgot, and it was a means to get the things she wanted.

From that day to now, only two things had eaten away at her abandoned conscience. She never found out the name of the boy who had taken her virginity, or where the daughter she had given up for adoption from their one night of passion had ended up.

Rhymendara wanted to erase her past completely. On her eighteenth birthday she changed both her first and last names. Mondra never contacted her parents after that day.

One morning, she read about her father's death in the obituary column. He died of "natural causes." Liver failure was the first thing that came to mind. Her mother had divorced him well before that, of course. Mina had changed her last name back to her Romanian maiden name—Sticla. "Rot in hell, you spineless bitch."

CHAPTER 28
CHANGE THAT TUNE

"There has to be another way out of here," said Wanda.

"I don't know. The place is pretty small and we've been through all the rooms already," Jo said.

"For the love of God, let's just go back out the way we came," said Byron.

Archie cleared his throat and said, "I've got a better idea. It'll kill two birds with one stone, too."

"I'm all ears, Arch," Byron said.

"You're not gonna like this too much, Byron, but I think you need to give your gun to Joanne, let her take it into the courtyard, and she can see if the way out is safe—or at least not some kind of setup to give Mondra advanced warning we're coming."

Byron had been shaking his head from side to side since the word *gun* had left Archie's lips. "Are you out of your fucking mind, Archie? I can't hand my gun over to a civilian. First off, I don't even know if she's ever shot a gun in her life."

"I have," Jo said.

"Good for you," Byron said. "And I'm pretty sure you're a good shot, too. That, however, is neither here nor there. And second, I ain't about to lose my job and be brought up on charges if something happens out there and everything goes to shit. So, no. I will not be giving my gun to Joanne."

"So, both of you go into the courtyard," Wanda said.

Byron and Jo looked at each other. The logic was hard to argue with, and Byron wanted to get things moving. Jo was thinking the same thing. Without a word, she headed for the door first—Byron close on her heels.

As they walked through the door to the sloped staircase, Byron said, "I think I should take the lead, Jo, since I'm armed."

"You remember what happened out there with Delilah and the hoodie?"

"Don't remind me."

"In here, I think you either let me take the lead, or we head out side by side, because that"—Jo pointed to his gun—"is probably going to be useless."

Byron nodded. "Okay, side by side. But I think I'll keep the gun out and ready just the same."

Jo shrugged. "Suit yourself."

They entered the courtyard together. Rain continued to pound down, slowed a little by the natural tunnel formed by the canopy of thirteen trees—their branches looked like black fingers ready to rip Jo and Byron to pieces if they made one false move. Lightning flashed and the trunks of the trees reminded Byron of the hooded entity. Thirteen copies of a faceless enemy he didn't understand. He would never in a million years admit it out loud, but he was glad Wanda had suggested Joanne go with him—as an armed stranger in a new world where guns were not the ultimate arbiter of law and order, he felt safer.

Suddenly, Jo stopped. Byron was on high alert now. He raised the gun in his right hand, cupping his left underneath the right, and turned slightly sideways, assuming a shooting position.

"There. That's why I had to come out."

Byron followed Joanne's eyes. All he saw was the shiny yellow reflection of the flagstones winding into the darkness at the other end of the courtyard. They reminded him of teeth.

"What am I supposed to be seeing, exactly?" he whispered.

"You can't see that? The spot where we came in?"

"Nope."

This surprised Jo. To her, it appeared clear as day. "Take my hand, Chief."

"I'm a big boy, Jo. I'm nervous, but I ain't *that* nervous."

She rolled her eyes. "No, ya big dope. I want you to take my hand so I can show you something."

Byron kept his eyes and gun aimed in the direction of the winding path. He dropped his left hand and Jo took it in hers. Slowly, like an old console TV from the 1970s, the ones where it took the screen some time to warm up, the end of the path glowed. It was a pale, pulsating blue light that grew more intense the longer Byron held on to Jo's hand.

"Ho-ly shit! What the hell is that?" Byron asked.

"I'm not sure exactly, but if I had to guess, I'd say Wanda's hit the nail on the head again. If we tried to go back through the way we came, they would know we've already been here, and we were on the way back."

"How d'you do that?"

"Let's go back inside. I'll tell you when I tell them."

Jo and Byron entered the room and shook the rain from their clothes.

"Well, what did you see?" Wanda asked Joanne.

"Another episode of *Mercy Vision*. You were right. There's definitely a barrier up to mark our leaving. There's got to be more to it than just warning them we're on our way back. As a matter of fact, I really think the idea doesn't stand up."

"How so?" Henry asked.

"Well"—Jo turned to Penny—"you said earlier you saw something similar on the mausoleum door, right?" Jo asked.

"Yes. And I knew right away that I'd compromised myself, too."

Jo was nodding. "So, he used it to mark you, or track backwards to you. He *needed* to know who you were. He wanted to account for everyone, no surprises. Well, this whole thing—it's set up to divide us from the start, but not in the way we thought. He's drawing us out and sizing us up. Think about it. First, we have the threat against Delilah back at our apartment. They had to know the first thing we would do was bring it to Wanda's attention. What's the next thing that happens? The hoodie shows up at Wanda's shop later that same night, seeming to surveil the place. But I don't think that's all he was doing."

"You don't?" Wanda asked.

"No. He knew Mercy was working there that night. And I think he knew enough about your routine, Wanda, to know you were in the back of the shop. It's where you go every night after work for tea—like clockwork. Mondra, or someone she sent, could have been checking the place out for a while just to confirm it. I think he was hoping Mercy would come outside and try to confront him so, like he eventually *did*, he could take her. What he didn't count on was how sensitive *you* were to a presence like *his*. He didn't expect you'd come to the front of the store. When you and Mercy touched hands, he knew it. And he knew he would be outmatched. That's why the chickenshit took off like a bat outta hell. That entire business afterward, when Henry went after him in the astral plane, had to be a reaction to failing the first time."

Jo was on a roll now. No one said a word. "But the two of you touching hands was definitely the last thing he wanted. He knows what Mercy's capable of because he was *there* when she died."

Wanda's eyes lit up. And she couldn't believe she'd not thought of it already.

"Wait a minute," Henry said, "how in the world would the hoodie know to be there when Mercy died? Or that she was going to die at all?"

Archie said, "He must have been following her for a long time, waiting for whatever chance he'd get to influence Mercy. And, also, he must know something about her past. Either in this life, or the last one."

"Then he's one step ahead of us there. I still don't know who she used to be," Wanda said.

Jo continued, "So it's safe to assume he knows her, knows what she's capable of, and knows who she used to be. And the barrier out in the courtyard is his way of sizing up what's coming at him, Mondra, and whoever else is at the Emporium. He needs to know who Mercy has *touched*. And that barrier will tell him."

Something occurred to Byron then. "Jo, when he was in front of the Explorer tonight, did you see where he came from?"

"No. It was like he'd appeared out of thin air. And you saw him first, anyway," said Jo.

He turned to Archie. "Do you think that's how this business with the pineal glands works? He can just be on one side, then *BAM!* He's able to pop out of thin air?"

Archie looked skeptical. "I doubt it's that easy. Why?"

"Well, that part of town, there's an empty lot on either side of the building where Jo chased after him. And nothing but woods on the other side. That building, I know for a fact, is under renovation. It's sealed up tighter than a butthole on ice."

"What are you getting at, Chief?" Henry asked.

"I think I know how he's getting around town, when he's on this side of whatever the other thing is, the 'astro' plane—"

Wanda smiled. "—*astral*, Chief."

"Yeah, that. I think he keeps himself hidden underground. There are tunnels that run underneath this entire town. And I'll bet a year's worth of paychecks there's another way out of here. We just missed it on the first pass. Let's check every crack of this place again. Two to a room, until we find something."

Everyone moved without saying another word. Byron and Penny took Mondra's room, Archie and Wanda took the main room, and Jo and Henry started in on the crib room. Less than five minutes later, Henry said, "Found something!"

All six of them crowded into the crib room. Henry pointed to the edge of the circular throw rug. "There's a smudge of dirt here. It ends where the rug begins, but it's not on the rug itself."

Joanne picked up the crib and hurled it into a corner. Henry pulled at the rug, which stuck a little in the drying dirt. There was a brief ripping sound as some fibers from the rug pulled free from the dirt caked underneath it. A black iron ring sat inset into a small wooden hatch on the floor. Henry pulled on the ring and the hatch creaked open. He stuck his head over the edge and peered down into the hole. A rust-flaked ladder disappeared into the blackness below.

"This thing clear of any kind of trap, Jo?" Byron asked.

Jo peered down into the hole. "I don't see anything."

"Okay," Byron said, "which of you has come into contact with Ms. Glass?"

Wanda, Jo, and Henry raised their hands.

"What about you Arch?"

"I took her from the Emporium, but we never actually, physically touched each other."

That left only Penny. He knew she hadn't come into contact with Mercy.

"What are you thinking about, Byron?" Wanda asked.

Byron chewed on his left thumbnail and held up his right index finger, asking for a moment, collecting his thoughts.

"Henry, you said Mercy touched you?" Byron asked.

Henry nodded at the chief. "We shook hands the day I met her."

"And what's your thing?"

"I can travel the astral plane pretty much at will. I usually have someone bring me down to the level I can leave my body through hypnosis—usually Archie or Wanda. Jo helps me get there at home sometimes. Lately, I've been practicing on my own. I'm getting pretty good at it. I'm not sure what effect shaking hands with Mercy will have on that, but I'm guessing it can't hurt."

"Okay, and Wanda—what happened to you?"

That surprised Wanda. She had assumed Penny had told him all about what happened between Mercy and herself.

"I didn't have the chance to bring it up, Wanda. And, to be honest, I wasn't sure he would have believed it, anyway," Penny said.

Byron smiled at Penny. "You're right, baby. At least, you would have been a few hours ago. Now, I'd have to say I'm all-in."

"I could see through her eyes," Wanda said, "but it really was just an enhancement of something I'm already skilled at, which is seeing and reading the auras surrounding people."

"What does that mean, exactly?" Byron seemed genuinely curious.

"The aura is an energy field that emanates from your body. It can show a lot of different things: physical health, disease, emotional states—good or bad, loving or hateful—and that's just the tip of the iceberg. It's part of how I knew you'd hurt yourself recently. I fudged just a little to get you up on the Reiki table." She winked at him.

He smiled. "That's cheating!"

"If you ain't cheatin' you ain't tryin'!" Wanda smiled.

"Touché." Byron winked back. Now that he knew what all of them were capable of, he clapped his hands together. "Okay, this is what we're going to do."

Everyone gathered in a circle and listened to Chief Byron Miller lay out his battle plan. When he finished, everybody knew their role. By the time they left the room, no one doubted the chief had changed his tune on matters spiritual.

CHAPTER 29
ON THE MOVE

Joanne wasn't sure how long the residual effects of touching Mercy would last, but she hoped it had a really long shelf life. The things she saw astounded her. Spirits of every stripe roamed the tunnels under Salem. Men and women dressed in clothing from several eras passed through walls, dropped from ceilings, and rose from the tunnel floors. They carried on silent conversations. Some walked hand in hand. Others argued. A small group gathered, listening to a man on a soapbox making an impassioned plea about God knew what.

All the entities in the tunnel gave off the same mellow blue glow as the door in the courtyard. Most were benign—the majority, it seemed—others were not. Those others noticed her. They would make their approach and Joanne would stare them down. The message in her eyes was crystal clear—back off!

Ten minutes had passed from the time she'd left the crib room in the church's hideaway to her arrival at the ladder. Jo looked up the ladder's length to the top. A sliver of LED light shone down from the opening of the shaft. She grabbed one rung and began her climb to the top.

Unlike Mercy, who'd struggled mightily to remove the heavy iron cover, Jo flashed a hand skyward and blew the cover from its spot with a mild blast of energy from her hand. The cover flipped twice in the air and crashed to the ground. The sound was loud, despite the falling rain. Loud enough to possibly be heard by the temporary occupants of Wanda's Wicca'd Emporium. And she couldn't give a rat's ass.

Byron thought sending Jo through first was the best, safest, and—if the magical shit hit the magical fan—most prudent first line of attack. To the best of his knowledge, the hoodie was the only one in Mondra's crew to have had contact with Mercy. If the history of the past two days was any indication, they would be better off having Jo handle him if he were guarding the place from the outside. Luckily for him, he wasn't.

Jo lifted herself from the hole in the street, made her way to the front door of Wanda's shop, and checked to make sure it was still locked. It was. She wanted to guarantee they didn't have an escape route.

∾

"Anything?" Mondra asked.

"Nothing so far," Zachary replied.

"They should have left by now. What the fuck is taking so long?" Biltmore asked.

"If I had to guess, they've probably just found the note," said Mondra. "They know for sure it's from us and they're confirming what they've probably suspected all along—that we've come here to face them. Don't worry so much, Darren. It's all going the way we want. The minute they go back through the courtyard, we'll know. And we'll be able to control the situation a hell of a lot better, too. Have your little helper look outside if you're worried."

Biltmore looked at the young man. He didn't have to say a word. He watched as the kid pulled the red hoodie up over his head and went out through the back and into the storm.

∽

Byron answered his cell phone, "Chief Miller."

"Someone just came out through the back door, Chief. Hard to tell from here, but it looks like a male, about six two. Red windbreaker, hood up. He's just standing in the lot behind the building. Looks like he's waiting for someone or something. You want me to do anything?"

"No. Just keep an eye on him, Raul."

"Wait, there's someone coming around the corner. Female, about five six, five seven."

"That's Joanne Trank. Henry's wife. I sent her there."

"It's like she appeared out of thin air. I never saw another car coming or anything."

"She just got there through the tunnels, Raul."

"Umm, okay. That's strange, Chief. Any chance you can tell me why?"

"Not now. Just monitor the situation. I'll fill you in later. Oh, and Raul?"

"Yeah?"

"If you see anything... out of the ordinary. Keep it on the down-low. And by out of the ordinary, I'm talking last-year-in-the-library out of the ordinary. *Comprende*?"

"Shit. Yeah, big time."

Byron tapped the cell phone, cutting the connection. Wanda was in the passenger seat next to him and Archie rode in the back seat of his own VW microbus. They'd come from the tunnels right outside the church, avoiding the portal. The manhole cover was a bitch, but Byron managed to get it off. He had the sore shoulders to prove it, too.

"You think red hoodie will be a problem for Joanne?" Byron asked Wanda.

Both Wanda and Archie laughed at the same time. Byron smiled, keeping his eyes on the road. "Me neither."

"How did you know they'd send someone out to check for us?" Archie asked.

"I just had a feeling. Intuition. You guys are rubbing off on me. But I thought it would be your buddy, fuckface," said Byron. "There's another reason, too. We've messed up their schedule. Done things they weren't counting on. Not going through that blue, whatever you call it—"

"Portal," said Wanda.

"Yeah, I think that's gonna freak them out," said Byron. "It's the one thing you can count on when you're dealing with criminals—magical or otherwise. They're stupid."

Neither Archie nor Wanda said anything to that. It was a hard point to argue against.

HENRY AND PENNY had stayed behind. It was Wanda's idea. She had suggested a slight alteration to Byron's plan. They could best be used for their ability to travel the astral plane; something which didn't require them to be at the Emporium at all. And, should fuckface decide to flee to the other side to save his own ass, they would be waiting. No quarter would be given tonight.

Henry was stretched out on the sofa in the main room. Penny was on the floor in Mondra's room—the idea of lying on the bed in there made her gag. Both were deep in meditation and ready to leave their bodies if the time came.

IN THE AREA Mercy had settled, there was a small, vented opening looking out over the parking lot. When she heard the back door to Wanda's safe room being opened, she rotated around, got on her knees, and peered through the vents. She couldn't believe her eyes. One of Dr. Love's favorite students stood in the parking lot, seeming to keep an eye out for the return of the members of the League of the Moon.

Something other than his face seemed familiar. His clothes! He was wearing a red-hooded rain jacket. When Mr. Flashlight had gotten into the driver's seat of Archie's bus, she'd barely had time to register anything but the color of his clothes. She never saw a face. Together, they sent an instant jolt of recognition through her—sadness, then anger trailed close behind.

She'd always liked Aaron Hendricks. He seemed like a nice guy. The kind of guy she could've seen herself getting to know. Too bad he was going to end up either jailed or dead by the end of the night. She thought about Joanne and her baby, and she mentally placed her bets on option two.

This was the thought going through her head at the exact time Joanne rounded the corner. Aaron had his back to Joanne, shielding his eyes from the rain with his right hand

and shining his flashlight toward the back of the parking lot. Everything about Joanne's posture suggested attack.

As if sensing Mercy's gaze, Jo looked up and directly at the vents. Her eyes glowed emerald green, lighting up the raindrops falling in front of her and painting the puddles of the parking lot all around her. Mercy could feel the energy radiating from them, and it felt familiar. There was a connection with Joanne, and in that moment, Mercy realized it was exactly the same feeling she'd gotten from Wanda the night before. And from Henry, too.

With a sinking feeling, she realized there was one other with the capacity for magic who'd also touched her, and he was downstairs right now. She wasn't sure if Joanne knew exactly what she was walking into, and she knew the hooded entity and the dark witch awaited her inside. *Where is the rest of the League?*

Mercy almost made a move to leave and help Joanne when Jo spoke. Mercy stayed to listen.

"Strange time to be out for a stroll, don't you think?" Jo said, low and quiet.

Aaron whipped around, training the flashlight on Joanne. He was about to say something when Jo put her index finger to her lips.

"Make a sound, and I'll drop you where you stand."

The young man's lips clamped together as he took in the dangerous-looking witch with the glowing green eyes.

Jo pointed to a corner of the lot. "Over there. Now!"

He wavered, afraid of the consequences from Mondra, Darren, and the psycho in the hood. Mercy could almost hear the debate going on in his head. It didn't take too long. Aaron turned around and did as told. Mercy breathed a sigh of relief. Happy, for now, she didn't have to reveal her whereabouts to the occupants one floor below. But she would have to move soon.

~

Raul was fifty yards from the parking lot when he saw Joanne entering it. The wipers were working overtime to keep up with the rain. He lifted the binoculars from the passenger seat to get a better view of the situation unfolding before him.

What he saw jolted him so badly they slipped a little from his hands. He righted the binoculars, brought them to his eyes, and sharpened their focus. *Her eyes! What in the hell?* It was something he would never forget, much like the night at the library. Rattled and barely holding it together, he remembered his cell phone and called the chief.

"Miller" was the response.

"Chief!" Raul sounded frantic. "It's last-year-in-the-library time again! I don't know how, exactly, to explain this to you, but that Trank lady... there's something really, really strange going on here. Her eyes—"

"Lit up green like a traffic signal, Raul?" Byron asked.

Raul held the phone away from himself, staring at it like he'd never seen a cell phone before. He brought it back to his ear. "How d'you know that, Chief?"

"I'll fill you in later. What's happening right now?"

"She's got some guy cornered in the lot. I'm not feeling too good about his health right now. Not the way she's looking at him."

"Hang tight, we're about a block away. When you see me pull into the lot, follow me in. Keep your lights off. Copy?"

"Copy," said Raul.

Less than a minute later Raul watched as a VW microbus swung, lights off, into the Emporium parking lot and pulled up next to the Trank lady. He put the cruiser in drive and headed up Essex Street, pulled into the lot and alongside the VW, and killed the engine.

Raul watched as the chief got out of the bus, gun raised, and pointed at the man in the red hoodie. He did the same, following closely behind Byron and then positioning himself off to the side. Red hoodie raised both hands.

Archie and Wanda were watching it all unfold from the VW.

"Oh my God, I know that kid! That's one of my students, Aaron Hendricks. He's flashlight guy!"

"The one that hit you tonight?" Wanda asked.

"Yes. What the hell is he doing mixed up with this crowd?"

Before Wanda could stop him, Archie got out of the bus and approached Hendricks. "Aaron?"

Hendricks, arms raised in surrender, looked toward Archie. His eyes went wide with recognition, then closed in shame.

"What's going on here, Aaron?" asked Archie.

"I swear I didn't want it to go this way, professor. They left me no choice. My mother is sick, and they promised me they could save her."

"Who promised you?" asked Archie. "Mondra Tibbets?"

Hendricks nodded toward the Emporium's back door. "Her and Dr. Biltmore. And that psycho in the hood."

"Biltmore? DB? What's he got to do with this?"

"He approached me the other day, after your lecture about the shapeshifter. He said he slipped into your class with the redhead. They were watching from the back row, up by the doors."

So, it was *Mondra's* anger he'd felt coming from the back of the room when he'd told the class about Chesrule's fate. He'd assumed it was one of his students who'd gotten mixed up with the *Order Immortalis*. He asked, "What did they tell you they could do for your mother?"

"They said if I helped them, they could heal my mother. Make her good as new again. They said they could even make her and me immortal, if we wanted. It sounded too good to be true."

Archie closed his eyes and hung his head in resignation. "That's because it is, Aaron."

Hendricks shook his head from side to side. "No! It's real! My mother is healed, and she looks twenty or thirty years younger now."

Archie's head still hung down as he spoke. "Is that why you had all those questions about the pineal and meditation during my lecture, Aaron? Did they tell you they could heal her if they could harvest pineal glands? Perhaps they brewed a special tea for her?"

"Yes. And it worked. But that's not all they told me. The other stuff had to do with you. And they threatened to take it all back, and worse, if I didn't help them."

"What did they say about me?"

"They said the baby in the room was your granddaughter. And they needed to get her to get to you."

"Why didn't they just come after me instead of my grandchild? It's not like I've gone into hiding," Archie said.

"I asked them the same question. I really didn't want to do any of this, professor, but they really left me no choice."

Archie's patience was wearing thin. In a hushed tone, he said, "Answer the fucking question, Aaron!"

"They said they put some kind of curse on the kid. The redhead said she still had some of your hair from the time you were together. She's bound to you now. The only way for it to be removed is for you to surrender yourself to them. The longer you wait, the worse off it is for the baby. She said if you wait too long, the kid will get sick and die. And she said every time you get closer to the baby, the curse accelerates. She said something about someone named Inanis—about bringing her master forth from the child."

"Leaving me no choice," Archie said, more to himself than to Aaron. "That's why the baby has been coughing all night any time I get near. I thought it was the hooded entity causing the coughing fits. But it's not. It's me."

Joanne made a move toward Aaron like she was about to kill him. Archie stepped in front of her. "Don't, Joanne."

Jo stared daggers at Aaron. He could feel his balls shrivel as the emerald green eyes bore a hole through him.

Byron and Raul had kept their guns trained on Hendricks the entire time. Byron made a motion with his head and Raul holstered his gun, took the cuffs from his belt, and pulled Aaron's hands behind his back and cuffed him up. He escorted Hendricks to his cruiser and deposited him in the back seat.

Wanda had been listening through the open window from the back of the VW. She watched with sadness as Archie, slump-shouldered, made his way toward her, with Joanne following close behind. Byron and Raul hung back but within earshot.

"I have to go in there. I have to give them what they want," said Archie.

Wanda said nothing, just nodded. There was nothing she could do at the moment to counter the curse Mondra had put on Delilah. When Henry figured out Mondra was the nurse who'd handled his baby, Wanda knew there was a curse. And she was pretty damned sure Byron's theory about Inanis attaching himself to Delilah as she lay dying on the Emporium floor last Halloween was spot on. She was one hundred percent certain she could remove the demon and be rid of him forever. And she'd been positive the hooded entity was about to be the body Inanis would inhabit. What she'd underestimated, what they'd all underestimated, was how twisted and vindictive Mondra could be. There could be no simple exorcism now. Archie might have to die, so Delilah could live.

CHAPTER 30
DECEIVED AND DECIDED

Mercy watched the two cops put Aaron in the back of the cruiser. The crowd at the rear of the parking lot was too far away to hear what was being said. Judging from the body language, it looked like Aaron told Archie something that deflated his entire being—and pissed Joanne off to no end.

The smaller cop got back in the front seat of his cruiser, keeping his prisoner company. The bigger one got back in the bus; he was in the driver's seat. Archie joined him in the front and Joanne hopped in the back, next to Wanda. Mercy pondered what the entire scene might be about.

She thought about Aaron and rubbed the spot on the side of her head where the flashlight had connected. Why had he attacked Archie, then kidnapped her? What did he stand to gain? Questions she had no earthly way to answer, or so it seemed. But there were definite connections.

She thought about the lecture Archie had given about the dark entity and the dog. He'd mentioned his son killing it. And then she'd felt that terrible streak of anger envelop the room for a moment. Archie had felt it, too. She was sure of it.

Did that anger emanate from Aaron? Possibly, but she didn't think so. It seemed too powerful and laced with menace to be from Aaron. And Aaron had some new friends now, didn't he?

The redheaded witch and Dr. Biltmore were running this show. That was obvious. They were in the lecture hall that day; she knew now. Biltmore didn't come off to her as someone exactly filled with magical ability. But the red witch, she gave off that vibe in *waves*! Even now, in this stuffy crawlspace above Wanda's shop, she could feel her energy.

Whatever she was, and whatever she was up to, it had an evil, selfish undercurrent to it. And whatever her underlying reasons were, Mercy was pretty damned sure the red witch had kept the ultimate end game to herself.

Mercy knew, as did most of the students at the U, Biltmore and Archie were rivals. There were rumors about the feud between the two. Some of them were hard to believe: like that the two were lovers at one time and had parted ways; or estranged brothers from another mother; or they were rivals for the affection of the same woman. Actually, now that she thought of it, none of them were all that farfetched. But that last one, it had the ring of truth. The fact the red witch and Biltmore were together in the room below her put the truth to the lie. And Archie being attacked only bolstered her intuitive feeling there was a love angle at the bottom of this.

It made her wonder if maybe Archie and the red witch had been together in the past. It would explain a lot.

What made little sense was the baby. Why would Biltmore, the hoodie, and the red witch need the baby?

Just a few short hours ago, she'd been in the room with the members of the League of the Moon when the hoodie had tried to connect with either herself or the child. Henry and Joanne's child. She wanted to kick herself. If she'd had more time with the League members earlier tonight, she would have eventually made the connection she now saw shining like a Times Square billboard in her mind.

This was the connection as she saw it; Archie's son had killed the demon, well two demons, a servant and a master—something the red witch seemed quite angry about. The witch had recruited Biltmore to help her (which meant the witch knew who Biltmore was, and about his feud with Archie) so yes, she had a history with Archie! Maybe she was in love with him once? Maybe during their time together, they had discussed the feud between himself and Biltmore at the end of a long day?

But why did Henry killing the two demons anger her so much? The answer was obvious. The witch and the hooded entity were connected to the demons somehow. And the birth of Henry and Joanne's daughter related to their deaths. Otherwise, why would the witch need the child? The answer, as she saw it, was the baby was a bartering chip being used to lure Archie—Henry's father—to the Emporium.

Mercy had gotten to know Wanda pretty well in the months she'd been working for her. Wanda was afraid of nothing, yet remained outside. Same with Joanne. Even the cops lingered outside. So why hadn't they gone in and arrested the red witch and Biltmore when they hadn't hesitated to arrest Aaron Hendricks? There was only one conclusion Mercy could come to: they couldn't.

Mondra had done something with the baby, preventing them from simply arresting her and ending the situation. Mercy knew in her heart, considering the evidence her mind had churned through, that there was a binding curse on the child. And, judging by the body language she'd observed in Archie, he blamed himself—confirming what Mercy suspected—this had to do with Archie and Mondra's relationship.

Had the night gone the way it should have, things would be different. But it hadn't, and that seemed an awfully funny coincidence to Mercy. Which meant the attack in the Emporium earlier tonight by the hoodie from the astral plane had been designed to remove her from the situation. And the fact the hoodie had not just killed Mercy when he had the chance spoke volumes. It meant they'd had plans for her. It meant they knew about her abilities.

The thought depressed her to no end. It meant the near-death experience she'd gone through hadn't been the wonderful gift she'd assumed it was. And it meant they'd planned to use her against the League all along. Armed with these new facts, Mercy knelt down on the board that stretched across the length of the attic crawlspace and made for the folding attic ladder. It was time to do something.

∽

"We have to go in there now!" Jo said.

"Honey, I don't have any children of my own. So, I won't pretend I know what you're going through. All I can say is if you go bursting in there now, you'll do more harm than good. There's a binding curse on Delilah, and we both know what that means."

Archie had been silent since entering the VW. He was ashamed and embarrassed. Someone he used to be involved with was responsible for all the trouble that had come upon his son, his daughter-in-law, and his grandchild.

He was silently stewing in his seat about his naivety with Mondra and the emotional wreckage it was causing those he loved. Wanda had been first threatened and then stalked. His son's living space had been invaded, and a threat posted *on his front fucking door*! Mercy had been set up and unjustly accused of having something to do with Delilah's condition. His sister had been followed and then attacked. They had turned a student he held in high esteem into a patsy and he was now likely going to jail. It was more than he could bear. Without a word of warning, he yanked the door handle on the passenger's side, leaped from his seat, and bolted across the parking lot of Wanda's Wicca'd Emporium. He ran through the rain as fast as his legs would carry him, ignoring the cries of those he loved imploring him to stop. Archie almost crashed into the door as he skidded to a stop in front of it, yanked it open, and walked toward whatever destiny awaited him.

CHAPTER 31
THE LIGHT AND THE GLASS

"Well, I can honestly say I didn't see that one coming," said Byron.

"You and me both, honey," was Wanda's reply.

Joanne was as stunned by Archie's bold move as the other two. And every fiber of her being wanted to burst into that room and join him. When she had calmed, she realized Wanda was right about just flying off the handle and committing a full-frontal assault. The only thing it would accomplish was harming Delilah. So now they had to wait.

Jo was hoping Archie could figure out a way to put an end to this without causing harm to himself or the baby. But if Wanda was right, she couldn't see how that was possible. Then again, what happened last year with Inanis also seemed, at one time, an impossibility.

"I'll be right back," Byron said to Jo and Wanda. He got out of the driver's side of the VW and got in the backseat of Raul's cruiser.

"Raul, could you give me a minute with our new friend?"

"You got it, Chief."

Raul exited with his umbrella and made his way over to the VW. He chose the driver's seat, just in case the need to move the vehicle arose. You never knew.

Byron turned to face Hendricks.

"Aaron... do you realize the mountain of shit you're in right now?"

Aaron nodded. He seemed far away and removed from the situation. This didn't sit well with Byron.

"Hey, dipshit! I'm talking to you. You better look at me and pay real close fuckin' attention. You copy?"

Aaron's head snapped in Byron's direction. The kid was obviously terrified and confused, and part of Byron pitied him. It was a very small part. There were lives at stake, and this piece of shit played a part in putting them there.

"Now that I've got your attention, we're gonna have a chat, Aaron. You're gonna answer every question I ask you. You're gonna tell me the truth. If I even get the faintest whiff you're not being straight with me, you're gonna be someone's new girlfriend at the 'graybar' hotel for a long time. You pickin' up what I'm puttin' down, Aaron?"

Aaron nodded vigorously.

"You have a chance to put things right for yourself, which, to be quite honest, I couldn't care less about, but you can also help save that baby in there... and your professor, too. I care a whole lot about both of them. So, believe me when I tell you, you better shoot straight with me. Now, spill it. Everything you've seen and everything you know. Now!"

For the next ten minutes, Chief Byron Miller interviewed his suspect. He wrung every detail from Aaron about what he had seen in his time with Mondra, Biltmore, and Mr. Fuckface.

Byron wasn't expecting to learn a lot, and much like a prospector panning for gold, most of what passed through the pan was useless dirt. But that's why prospectors did what they did. Sometimes you found a little nugget in that pile of useless dirt. When Aaron finished, Byron had his nugget.

∼

Archie let the door slam behind him. The room was dark but brighter than the stormy night outside, so it still took his eyes a second to adjust. When they did, Mondra came into clear focus. She smiled at him. He did not return it. He began toward the middle of the room, but Mondra held up her hand.

"Why don't you stay where you are for now, Archie."

It was a command, not a request. Archie halted.

"What do you want, Mondra?" Archie asked.

"You don't know?" She looked legitimately surprised.

Archie folded his arms across his chest. "No. I don't. Why don't you fill me in."

She shook her head in disapproval, like Archie was a poor student who'd misunderstood his assignment.

"You always were about a step or two behind," Biltmore said as he stepped out from behind Mondra. Archie stared daggers at him.

"What's the matter, Love, surprised to see me?"

"No. Quite to the contrary, DB. You've always been a gullible bastard. So, it's no surprise you ended up with Mondra pulling your strings. What I am curious about is how the two of you ended up together."

Mondra said, "Who's gullible now, Archie? You don't

think I filed away all those nights you bitched to me about the battles you had with the physics department? And Darren in particular? You don't think I'm clever enough to use them to get what I want?"

Biltmore snapped his head in Mondra's direction when she uttered the word "used."

She turned to him. "Come now, Darren. You knew the arrangement was temporary. Don't be so sensitive."

His face turned crimson. It was true, but it didn't mean he had to like it. He'd fallen for Mondra, hard. And he believed it with every ounce of his being. He was completely unaware of the literal spell she'd cast on him.

The hatred and jealousy he'd harbored for Archie had only made it easier for her to manipulate him. Being a gorgeous redhead hadn't hurt all that much, either. *Lessons learned from an early age and well played*, she thought to herself. *Consequences be damned*.

"Oh, I know you're clever, Mondra," said Archie, "but you seem to have forgotten one enormous detail. Care to know what it is?"

She cocked her left eyebrow, looking curious and amused, but not in the least worried. This was exactly the opposite of what Archie was hoping for, but he had to play the hand he had in front of him.

"You're in Wanda's shop now. I know you think this is the way you wanted it to go, but trust me when I tell you, it isn't."

"Oh? And why is that?"

Archie smiled. "Such a short memory. We know why you're here. And we know why you kidnapped Delilah. But you're forgetting something. He lost his battle here last Halloween. He employed the very same strategy you're using here today. Inanis thought he could trap the League of the Moon on our own territory, and he paid with his very existence. Well, almost. I know he's trapped inside Delilah. And I know you've used something from my past to bind her to me. To force me here against my will and help you release him."

"I'm not forgetting anything, Arch. I never do."

As if on cue, Delilah coughed.

Mercy lowered herself from the attic without unfolding the ladder. She didn't want to make the slightest sound. Too much was at stake now to slip up. She dangled from the opening, hanging as far down as her arms would allow her, then dropped to the hallway floor, her socks dampening the sound.

Moving to the side of the hallway, her back to the wall, Mercy inched her way toward the beaded doorway and listened. She could hear the red witch in conversation with Dr. Love, and it didn't sound like they were reminiscing about the good old days.

As she strained to catch every syllable of the conversation, the hooded entity (who'd been patiently awaiting her return from the attic) crept up behind her, touched Mercy's shoulder, and caught her as her body went limp. He carried her into the safe room and placed her in the center pentacle. Mondra looked down at her, then up at Archie. She smiled.

Byron returned to the VW, getting in on the passenger's side. "I just pried a very interesting tidbit from Aaron." He told everyone in the car what it was.

"You gotta be shitting me," said Joanne.

"So Mondra's last name isn't Tibbets?" asked Wanda.

Byron shook his head. "No. It used to be Murphy. But her mother's maiden name is what's important. It's Sticla. Do you know what that translates to from Romanian to English?"

Both Joanne and Wanda shook their heads from side to side.

"Glass," Byron said.

Henry and Penny remained deep in meditation. Each had one foot in this world and the other in the astral plane. Henry, thanks to the augmentation of his ability through Mercy's touch, could monitor the Emporium from the inside as well as the out. Penny remained at the ready in the area of the church, pulling double duty identical to Henry's. The hooded entity would have no safe place to return should he attempt to flee.

When the entity had grabbed Mercy from behind in the Emporium hallway, however, no amount of extra boost from Mercy would allow Henry to stop what was happening. He watched in horror as the hoodie crept up behind her, touched her, and scooped her away and into the safe room.

After an internal debate, Henry decided there was no good reason to remain where he was. He dropped from the astral plane, rose from the depths of his meditative state, and prepared to leave for Wanda's shop. The others needed to know before they made a move against Mondra. Calling them from his cell phone was out of the question; he couldn't be sure where everyone would be when he got there, or if a ringing phone would give away someone's position if things had changed.

He made his way to the room where Penny lay. Quietly, without startling her out of meditation, he informed Penny he was leaving. Her nod was almost imperceptible.

That done, he went to the crib room, climbed down the ladder, and took off into the tunnels leading to Essex Street. It took him less than ten minutes to get there. Henry ran around the corner of the building and into the parking lot.

"Freeze!"

Henry froze. He was staring at a squat Latino police officer, pointing a gun at him over the top of the VW's driver's side door.

"It's okay, Raul. He's with us," Byron said, inwardly pleased at Raul's vigilance.

When Henry's heart slowed again, he approached the VW, getting in on the side behind Raul and cramming Joanne up against Wanda.

"What's the matter, sweetie?" Wanda asked.

"They've got Mercy. I saw from the other side. Fuckface crept up behind her and did something that put her out cold. It looked like Mercy was planning something when he got to her."

Everyone was quiet after that. The silence emblematic of the desperate situation.

After a time, Joanne said, "Well, your gut feeling on Mercy coming back was dead-on, Wanda. But it looks like the situation just got a hell of a lot worse."

"It's not gonna get any better when Mercy finds out Mondra is her mother," Wanda said.

Henry's eyes bugged. "What?!"

Wanda nodded. The gravity of the situation writ large on her face. "Byron just pried that nugget from flashlight guy." Wanda pointed to the occupant in the back of the cruiser. Henry hadn't noticed him upon his arrival at the parking lot. A gun in your face will cause you to miss some detail.

What he did notice, after the shock about Mercy and Mondra had worn off, was Archie's absence. He said so.

"He took off like a bat outta hell and ran into Wanda's shop," said Byron.

"Why would he do something like that?" Henry asked.

Wanda answered, "Knowing your father, he undoubtedly shoulders the blame for all that's happened. He likely feels responsible for Mondra and thinks he can somehow fix it. He's always been too trusting and forgiving. It's an admirable trait, but it's one that can land you in a lot of hot water, too."

Henry nodded. He'd only discovered Archie was his biological father less than a year ago, but he knew him well enough and was not surprised he'd gone into the lion's den —possibly to sacrifice his life for his granddaughter.

Henry considered himself the de facto leader of the League of the Moon now. Wanda was the conscience and the organizer. But she'd made it perfectly clear to him he was their leader during the events of last October, taking back the mantle Madeleine had held when the *Foedere In Luna* were together in their last incarnation. He felt the time to assert that leadership was now.

"I'm going in," Henry said.

Wanda nodded. Byron frowned. Though his plan had

succeeded up to this point, Byron knew the adage about a battle plan always being perfect until they fired the first shot applied here.

Getting the nugget of info from Hendricks had been huge, making his plan a success. In the end, he knew his part (as far as the planning went) was over. But there were crimes committed here tonight, and he would make damned sure Hendricks wasn't the only one who left here in cuffs.

"Let's go, Jo," Henry said.

Jo didn't say a word. She sprang from the seat and followed Henry out of the VW.

"I'll be right behind both of you," Wanda said.

Henry nodded. Jo never looked back. They strode toward the safe room door. Wanda turned to Byron. "I wonder if you could check something out for me, Byron?"

"Sure. What did you have in mind?"

When she told him, Byron gained a new level of admiration for Wanda. They exited the VW and went over to the cruiser, leaving Raul alone with his thoughts.

CHAPTER 32
ARCHIE GAMBLES

Henry took in the scene inside Wanda's safe room. *Safe no more* was his first thought, hoping he was wrong.

Delilah was in the middle of the room in a carrier and on the Reiki table to Mondra's right. Mercy lay unconscious on Mondra's left. The Biltmore guy, Henry noticed, stood behind Mondra, seeming unsure of himself and lost in thought. *Regrets?* Henry wondered. The hooded entity was nowhere to be seen, but his presence hung in the air like the stink of a long-departed skunk.

The room was dark, lit only by the candles that seemed to burn in perpetuity at the four compass points of the safe room. Plenty of shadows for the creep in the hood to find refuge. Henry, Jo, and Archie remained outside the furthest circle from the middle—not for fear of Mondra, but for the safety and health of Delilah. The curse was speeding up simply from the presence of Archie. He didn't want to increase Mondra's advantage by moving closer. At least not yet.

Jo stared at Mondra. Hate radiated toward the red witch with every breath she took.

"I'm taking back my daughter. Now."

Mondra cocked an eyebrow. "That's not possible at the moment, dear. But I'll let you look at her. She's perfectly fine, for now. Should you decide to take matters in your own hands and flee with the child, she won't last the night. If I get what I want, she'll be one hundred percent fine."

Jo didn't hesitate. She walked to the middle of the room, bent down, and looked over every square millimeter of Delilah. Aside from the occasional light cough, she was fine. When Jo finished checking over Delilah, she stood face to face with Mondra.

"No matter what happens after tonight, you're gonna regret ever having crossed paths with me. I promise you that."

"Finished?" was Mondra's reply.

"Just getting started, red."

It was an act of unbearable restraint for Jo to return to the outer ring and rejoin Archie and Henry.

Mondra asked, "Where's Wanda, Archie?"

Archie refused to answer at first. He was well aware Wanda was still outside with Byron and Raul, and he, too, was curious why she hadn't come in with Henry and Joanne. Archie thought one of them might offer something about Wanda. When neither did, he simply said, "Outside. In my bus."

This seemed to make Mondra edgy. It was a small thing, but noticeable *and* notable. It gave the three of them hope.

Mercy stirred on the floor. Mondra looked down at her, then up at the members of the League of the Moon. "Look who's awake! And at just the right time. Darren, help her up. Please."

Biltmore did as he was told. Mondra went over to the bar, maintaining eye contact with the League, and returned with one of the stools. She placed it behind Mercy, who was being steadied by Biltmore, and they both eased the dazed young woman onto it.

Henry and Jo exchanged a quick, worried glance. It was not lost on either of them that Mondra had now come in contact with Mercy. Whatever powers the red witch had, they were—more than likely—much more intense.

Mercy rubbed both temples, trying to focus. "Where am I? And what was the number of the bus that hit me?"

Mondra said, "You're in Wanda's little shop, Mercy. And we are so glad you could make it!"

Mercy's head cleared quickly at the sound of Mondra's voice. She started to rise.

Biltmore held her down on the stool by the shoulders. She struggled a bit, and the professor almost lost his grip, but he kept her seated. "What the hell do you want with me?" Mercy asked.

"We're going to have a little ceremony here tonight, dear. And you get the chance to be a hero to everyone! Isn't that great?" Mondra asked.

"You think I'm going to help you? You're out of your redheaded fucking mind, lady."

"Uh-uh-uh. That's not what we're looking for at all. You wouldn't want anything to happen to this beautiful little girl over here in this carrier, would you?"

Mondra moved to the far side of the Reiki table, putting it between herself and Mercy. She waved a hand over the carrier as she spoke, like a product model from a game show. Jo badly wanted to punch a hole through her skull.

Mercy tilted her head, pretending not to understand the connection to her being in the circle with Mondra and Delilah.

"I see you're a tad confused," said Mondra, extending her bottom lip in a mock pout. "Let me clear things up for you. There is a curse on this child."

Mercy played dumb, trying to see if Mondra would hang herself with her own words. It was a long shot, but you never knew.

Mondra continued, "What you are going to do is hold my hand during the ceremony. I need the power you've gained from the other side to remove the binding and complete the transformation. It cannot happen without your help. I'm strong. Stronger than most any witch. However, the curse I've set on the child requires the help of one who's left this world. And do you know why that is?"

She asked this in the tone of an obnoxious professor lecturing to a classroom full of neophytes.

Mercy rolled her eyes. "Is there a point coming somewhere soon?"

Mondra glared at her. Mercy had pricked her narcissistic bubble. Jo wanted to kiss her.

"The reason," Mondra continued, "is twofold. First, the soul trapped in this body needs a conduit to bring it forth. The second, we know what you're capable of. Zachary, or, as Wanda likes to refer to him, 'fuckface,' witnessed the power you displayed earlier, from outside. We are going to make use of it tonight."

At the mention of Wanda's pet name for Zachary Villitz,

Jo and Henry both drew in a sharp breath. How could she know about the doll and the nickname?

Mondra laughed. "Relax, you two. It was written on the doll behind the bar. I'm good. But I'm not *that* good. Now, where was I? Oh, yes. Zachary has been kept alive, as you've undoubtedly figured out by now, by the generous donations of living pineal gland donors."

"You mean the innocents he murdered?" Archie asked.

Mondra waved him off. "There are larger things at work here, Archie. You never could see the big picture. But you will."

Zachary Villitz materialized from the gloom, taking his place to Mondra's left and grasping her hand. Mondra made her way to the side of the table nearest Mercy, reaching for Mercy's left hand. She resisted, keeping her hands at her side, looking at Mondra's hand like it was a cobra. Biltmore grabbed Mercy's elbow, forcing her hand into Mondra's.

"Archibald? Care to join us?" Mondra asked.

"As if I had a choice" was his reply.

Archie turned a sad smile on Joanne and Henry. Henry started to speak, but Archie held up a hand. "Let's leave it for later, Henry. I don't know what's about to happen, but that's the point. Saying any kind of goodbye now is tantamount to admitting defeat. I won't give that psycho bitch the satisfaction." Instead, he hugged Henry.

He turned to Joanne, seeing the tears in her eyes. Tears born of frustration and sadness. He put a hand up to each cheek and wiped them gently away with his thumbs. "My wonderful daughter-in-law. You're the strongest woman I know. Stay that way... and be ready." Archie winked.

Jo thought that was an odd thing to say at a time like this, and she took it as a sign Archie knew something she didn't. For the first time tonight, the dying embers of hope glowed anew. If Archie thought she needed to be ready for something... anything, she would.

Archie turned toward Mondra, his shoulders raising as he breathed in deep, and dropping as he let it out. Though scared out of his mind, he never let it show. He strode to the inner circle, false bravado hanging on him like high-quality costume jewelry. He didn't need to be told what to do next.

Mondra stood at the head of the Reiki table. Mercy was to her right and currently standing after an angry prompt from Biltmore. Zachary was to her left. All three were holding hands. Archie was expected to complete the circle. He did. Mercy's right hand was damp, he noticed. The poor girl was, much like himself, terrified but putting on a brave face. Zachary's hand was ice cold—*a living corpse.*

Archie glanced at Mondra's left hand. Until now, he hadn't noticed the red ribbon wrapped around her wrist. It looked moistened with water or oil, and it ran down the fingers of her left hand and into Zachary's. Something about the way she'd tied it rang a distant bell in his mind.

Three knots—one at the wrist, one about three inches below that, and then another, six inches further along, closing in a loop. He'd seen this somewhere before, but couldn't recall exactly where or when.

Zachary Villitz noticed it at the same time as Archie, and he seemed equally surprised. "What is this?" Zachary asked Mondra.

"It's part of your becoming. Part of the spell that will bring forth our master and join him with you. After all these centuries, your reward is at hand, Zachary!"

It was about to go down. Archie decided that for now, delay was all he had left. He remembered Wanda's comment from earlier, 'It just rings true.' He decided to play the last card in his hand.

"Mercy, I'm curious"—he tilted his head—"how did you end up back here tonight?"

Mondra glared at him. "Now is not the time for questions, Archie!"

Archie ignored her. "Mercy?"

Mercy wasn't sure what he was getting at, but she knew to play along. "Well, after Aaron knocked me out, I was dragged into a crypt by him." She nodded her head in Zachary's direction. "When I got loose, I came here through the tunnels. Why?"

Archie's brow furrowed. Confused, he asked, "Are you *experienced* with the tunnels under Salem?"

She shook her head.

He continued, "It seems awfully unlikely you could have made it here successfully and not gotten lost. There are probably a thousand different paths you could've taken. Not to mention the power being out and having to travel through them in the pitch-black. How did you do it?"

"You know, that's the funny thing. He almost caught me down there." Again, she nodded at Zachary. "I heard a bell ringing, so I followed it. At just the right moment, someone pulled me into a space in the wall. It was a ghost or a spirit, but it was as solid as a live human being."

Archie nodded.

"Whoever or whatever that ghost was, she saved me just as the hoodie was passing by. And every time, just when I thought I was getting lost again, the bell would ring. The last time it did was right out front, under the manhole cover outside."

Archie noticed Mondra squirming. He'd hit a nerve.

Whatever it was about Mercy's arrival here, it was clearly not something Mondra wanted discussed in the open. So, he pressed on. "Obviously, someone needed you to make it here. Had to *guarantee* it happened, in fact. But I'm curious. If you and Mr. Villitz here are in this together, Mondra, then why not just tell Zachary where Mercy was and have him retrieve her? Why guide her here yourself? What are you hiding from him? Indeed, all of us, at this very moment? You wouldn't have a bell on you by any chance?"

Mondra seethed, but she couldn't reply. To do so would reveal her ultimate motive. What the hell Archie meant about some bell, she hadn't the foggiest idea. Mondra *knew* Mercy was her daughter and also knew she would escape Zachary and be drawn to her eventually. And now, while delaying what he thought was the inevitable, Archie had pieced it all together. He remembered where he'd seen the red bow and the succession of three knots. He knew what it meant, and he hoped he wasn't too late.

CHAPTER 33
SURPRISES AND SPELLS

Wanda and Byron sat in the front seat of the cruiser. Byron was on the phone with Shelly Morgan, one of his dispatchers. She was at home. Her shift was the day shift, but Byron knew she could access the information he needed from her home computer.

Wanda had suggested looking into Mercy's past. They knew Mondra was her mother, but it was strange that Mercy would still have the name Glass if she had been adopted. And stranger still, Mondra had rid herself of her own last name completely. Something wasn't adding up.

Byron listened, his eyes growing wide. He looked at Wanda, his mouth agape. "Are you sure, Shell?" He listened some more, then hung up the phone. Byron shook his head in disbelief.

"What is it, honey?" Wanda asked.

"Just when I thought this night couldn't get any weirder," Byron said, "it goes up another notch. Shelley just told me who Mercy's father is."

"Really? How could she get a hold of that if the state seals adoption records?" Wanda asked.

"Shelley has her ways. I've had her get me info in the past that would probably get me in some deep shit, were it known. But it's helped to put away some serious scumbags, so the risk is worth it."

"So, what's the earth-shattering news then?" Wanda asked.

"Hold on to your hat. Mercy was raised by Mondra's mother. Mondra must have had her, gave her up for adoption, obviously, and her mother somehow found out and made sure she adopted her. When she Americanized Mercy's last name, Mondra probably wouldn't have thought twice about it. I doubt she even knows, or cares, what Sticla means. And I'd bet dollars to donuts Mondra never found out because she left home and never talked to or saw her parents again. Which doesn't come to me as much of a surprise. Mondra doesn't seem the forgiving type."

"Well, that's certainly strange, but not exactly the bombshell I was expecting," said Wanda.

He was nodding. "I agree, not your everyday arrangement. The weird part, or, more accurately, stranger than all get-out, is who Mercy's father is."

Byron told her. Now it was Wanda's mouth hanging open.

∼

THE RIBBON, the ceremony—all of it—were exactly what happened to Archie when Mondra had put the spell on him the first time around. That night in his living room, she'd spiked his drink. A specialty of hers, it turned out. She'd waited by the fire, the ribbon secretly wrapped around her wrist in exactly the same fashion. The spell had been so powerful, and its reversal so traumatic, Archie had almost blocked all of it from his memory. Ironic, considering his profession, he thought to himself.

The stall for time had allowed him to figure out what was going on. It didn't, however, change the situation one iota. Delilah was still bound by the curse, and the curse still required Archie's participation to save her. But his questioning of Mercy's arrival as he stalled for time set other things in motion. Now those things couldn't be stopped. The genie was out of the bottle, so to speak.

"Yes, why not tell me where Mercy was?" Zachary asked Mondra.

"I didn't know where she was. He's twisting your mind. I know nothing about a fucking bell. Let's get this started!" Mondra demanded.

Zachary said, "You still haven't told us what the ribbon is for." He was working something out in whatever passed for a brain in a four-hundred-year-old. He looked from Mondra, to Mercy, then to Archie. Mondra saw the look on his face in the instant Zachary recognized what his true role was in the ceremony.

The hooded entity ripped his hands from the circle. "Liar!" he bellowed at Mondra.

Mondra grinned at him. There was zero humor in it.

"I never needed you here for this part, Zachary. It was really a matter of convenience. Now that you're here, you can't leave until the spell is complete. Try to if you don't believe me."

"You were never going to follow through and join me

with Inanis! You're going to join me with him!" Zachary screamed.

He pointed at Archie.

"Very good! You're a lot smarter than you look, Zachary. But your brains aren't what I'm after. You were a very handsome man back in 1692! And with the man who truly loves me inhabiting your body"—she nodded at Archie—"you'll be everything I've ever wanted. Everything I've always *deserved!*"

"You never *intended* to bring Inanis back, did you?" Archie asked.

"Yes and no," was her simple reply.

"What is going on here, then?" Archie asked.

Mondra shook her head. "Still a bit slow on the uptake, Archie. That's okay, we'll have a long time to work on things like that together. Inanis is indeed alive and well. And inside Delilah at this very moment. I am going to incorporate his essence into mine. You are going to be joined with Zachary. I will be the new leader of the *Order Immortalis*, with you by my side."

It was worse than Archie had imagined. He stared open-mouthed at Mondra, stupefied by her lunacy and rendered momentarily speechless by her thirst for power. "You're going to intentionally absorb a demon? Have you completely lost your mind?" Archie asked.

Mondra ignored him. "Darren, please take Zachary's place in the circle."

"What?" Biltmore looked terrified. Archie almost felt sympathy for the foolish bastard... almost. Lie down with dogs, get fleas.

"How could I have anything to offer in this—" Biltmore started.

"Do you really think I kept you around for your good looks, Darren? You've already drunk the same tea as Zachary, back at the church. There's a little bit of him brewed into it... which is now a little part of you. It'll do."

"But I—"

For the first time tonight, Mondra's eyes glowed red. Mercy's power had leached into her body. Her own power was growing. This seemed to motivate Darren to take his place in the circle. When he did, Mondra began her incantation:

> *"A soul from now, and one from then*
> *Passed through the never, then back again*
> *One that I love, one I desire*
> *And one from the void, joined by fire"*

Mondra's eyes were closed, her head thrown backward and facing the skylight, lost and consumed by the moment. A fine red mist drifted slowly down from the skylight above and toward the Reiki table. Mondra repeated the incantation, each repetition gaining in intensity with the thickening mist matching it. It coated the table, making a ring around the baby's carrier, then falling on the child directly.

Archie shuddered and his eyes bulged in fear as he beheld something only he could see. The room disappeared before him. All went black for a time, then he was falling down a dark well. It in no way resembled a water well other than the word "well."

In place of stacked stone were scenes from his life playing out to his left, while scenes from what he could only assume were Zachary Villitz's life played out on the right.

Memories, good and bad, from both sides meshed together and joined at the well's bottom. Images of two vastly different lives flew by him in a blur. When he reached the bottom, where the memories pooled together, there would be no turning back.

Mercy fought with all her might to break the circle—it was useless. Whatever chance she'd had of escaping Mondra's grasp, ironically, disappeared once she had touched hands with her. And she wasn't sure if interrupting the incantation in progress might do permanent harm to Archie, Delilah, Biltmore, or herself.

∼

Wanda and Byron exited the cruiser. Wanda headed for the Emporium's back door while Byron retrieved Raul from the VW.

"What's going on, Chief?" asked a wide-eyed Raul.

"We're going in, Raul."

Raul sprang from the bus and fell in behind Chief Miller.

The two cops dashed across the drenched parking lot and burst through the door right on Wanda's heels. Wanda was the first to reach Joanne and Henry. She tilted her head, motioning them toward a spot behind the bar. Wanda whispered to both of them the information Byron had ferreted out. Their mouths dropped open at the same time. Wanda winked at them. "You both know what to do."

Henry skirted around the right side of the bar, Jo took off from the left. They slowly circled to the opposite side of the room. Jo took position a few feet behind Mondra, Henry a few feet back from Biltmore. They stood at the ready.

Wanda made her way over to Byron, beckoned him to

lean down, and whispered her instructions to him. Chief Miller then told Raul what he wanted him to do. "I'll give you a nod, then you do it. Okay?"

"Okay. Seems kinda weird, but you 're the boss," said Raul.

Byron made his way in Archie's direction and sent Raul to stand opposite him, across the room and behind Mercy.

Henry, Jo, Byron, and Raul covered all four from behind and within the spell's range. Seven feet of gleaming obsidian floor stood between the four on the inside, at the pentacle's center, and the four on the outer ring.

Mondra was oblivious to all of this. Her head remained tilted to the skylight. Her voice picked up speed and urgency with each recitation of the spell's incantation. The red mist covered the Reiki table and spilled lazily to the floor, where it crawled over itself in soft, undulating clouds. Delilah was barely visible through the mist, and little puffs of red shot out from her carrier as she coughed into the cloud.

Archie spasmed as his essence poured from his body and into Zachary Villitz's. Zachary, removed from the circle and hiding in a dark corner of the safe room, felt his face becoming fully formed. The barely there visage of a few brief moments ago took on the fullness of life again.

Mercy's eyes, much like the night the hoodie visited Wanda's shop, rolled back to the whites. Her feet lifted from the ground. Those in the room who were magically inclined were surprised but unafraid. Raul, Byron, and Biltmore were all scared out of their minds by this fresh development, but each stood his ground. Biltmore really had little choice. Byron watched in awe, and Raul swallowed hard.

Wanda came out from behind the bar holding a glass Mason jar. In it was a powerful exorcism powder. Its ingredients were the herbs heliotrope, comfrey, angelica, and peony, and it was shot through with dragon's blood essential oil. She had used it in the past, sprinkling it in places that called for protection and purification. And this situation seemed to fit the bill.

She entered the circle, popped the jar's top, and sprinkled it between the circle containing the pentacle and Mondra, and the outer circle. Once she'd made a complete circuit within the other two, she stepped back through the outer ring. Everything was complete and in place. It was time to end things.

CHAPTER 34
SEPARATE WAYS

The effect of the exorcism powder was mild at first. The red mist spread its tentacles across the floor like a wispy octopus. When it contacted the powder, it curled in on itself. A screech, barely audible but there all the same, rose above Mondra's ceaseless chanting. It sounded like the mist was alive. For all anyone knew, it was.

Mondra was a powerful witch, and with the augmentation supplied by Mercy, anything was possible now. The once-invisible magic practiced by witches for centuries had now come into contact with one who'd returned from the other side. It had happened in rare instances throughout the centuries. Things would be different now.

Thankfully, Mercy's touch had worked both ways. Mondra's powerful dark magic was being put to the test against Henry, Joanne, and Wanda's white magic. Wanda smiled. Three against one—she liked those odds.

The red mist further receded, and for the first time since she'd begun her spell, Mondra faltered. She brought her head level and gazed around the room with those glowing ruby eyes, unfocused but searching out the source of the drain in power. It was all Wanda needed to set things in motion.

"Henry, now!"

Henry moved without hesitation. He grabbed Biltmore around the chest in a reverse bear hug and tried pulling him backward. The man wouldn't budge. Darren didn't squirm, didn't even seem to notice what Henry was trying to do. He stared blankly at the Reiki table, with eyes half-open and vacant. Drool glistened from the corners of his gaping mouth. Henry looked to Wanda for help.

"Keep at him, Henry. He's the weakest link in the circle!" Wanda shouted.

Henry wondered what it would take to remove the strongest link from the circle and glanced over at Joanne standing at the ready behind Mondra. He pulled Darren backward again; this time he felt movement. He took a deep breath, lifted the man in the air, then leaned backward and let his own body weight do the job for him. It worked. Darren's hands came free from Archie's and Mercy's at the same time. Both men crashed to the floor.

Henry sprang up, ready for a fight that never came. He watched as the professor spasmed on the floor, twitching and moaning in pain. To Henry, the pain seemed more psychological than physical. He watched in wonder and could only imagine what Biltmore's eyes had seen. If their physical condition were any sign, he'd seen something close to hell. Where there had been white in those eyes before, there was now bright red blood. The irises held color no more, looking like craters on the surface of some distant red planet.

Mondra twisted her head to the left, seeming to sense more than see what Henry had done—unfocused, like a blind person tilting her head at hearing a sound in an empty room. That she couldn't actually see what was going on around her showed how deep into the spell she was. It was a weakness now. Having broken the circle, the others had to act fast, but also in sequence.

Byron grabbed Archie under the arms. He'd seen how Henry had struggled with Darren and was bracing himself for the same. When he pulled Archie backward, however, he came loose with almost no struggle at all. The only indication of any resistance were the red and ragged scratches on the back of his hand where Mondra had dug her nails in, trying to claim him back from Byron.

Blood bloomed in the tracks she'd left. When the droplets hit the exorcism powder on the floor, they sizzled, sending plumes of steam into the red mist. There was no question of the mist being something alive as it screamed and recoiled from the white steam. Screams filled the room everywhere now. Terrified voices of men and women and creatures seemed to fill every space—voices coming from places no one wanted to think about for too long.

Byron threw Archie's arm over his own shoulders, holding it there with his right arm and bracing Archie around the waist with his left. He guided him away from Mondra's circle and to a beanbag chair in the corner. When he placed Archie gently into the chair, Byron felt relief wash over himself. It was short-lived. When he stood, he looked into Archie's face and what he saw scared the shit out of him.

Archie wasn't so much as looking *at* Byron as he was *through* him. Byron waved a hand in front of his brother-in-law's eyes and got the same empty stare. What Archie was seeing, Byron hadn't a clue, but Archie seemed to *talk* to it all the same. And what scared Byron the most were the sounds coming from Archie's mouth. Whispered sounds. None of them actual words, just gibberish. He feared for his brother-in-law's sanity.

Byron whirled around, coming back from his terror and remembering Wanda's instructions. "Raul, now!"

Raul was terrified and staring into Mondra's eyes. He was slowly being drawn into their dark-red embrace. He knew those eyes, but he didn't know how. The terror he felt ebbed gently into wonder and then shifted ever so slightly to desire. No, not exactly desire, but a memory of it. He saw water; he smelled gasoline, perfume, and wood.

Byron stepped in front of him, cutting Raul's connection with Mondra's eyes. Raul shook his head, clearing the cobwebs.

"What was that all about?" he asked the chief.

"I don't know, buddy. But you need to do what I asked you to do. Are you okay?"

Raul took a deep breath and blew it out, nodding. "Okay, Chief."

He stepped around Byron and moved to the side of Mercy furthest from Mondra. Mercy was still elevated a few inches from the floor. Raul had to tilt his head slightly upward in order to do what came next. He looked again at Byron, as if asking, 'Are you sure?' Byron raised both hands from his waist in a 'get on with it' gesture. Raul turned back to Mercy, kissing her gently on the cheek.

Both Mercy and Mondra reacted to that kiss.

Mercy said, "Daddy?"

And then, maybe a half second later, Mondra spat, "You!"

Raul stepped back from Mercy in confusion.

"Why is she calling me 'Daddy,' Chief?"

Byron closed his eyes and swallowed hard. When he opened them, Raul saw sympathy and apology written all over the chief's face.

"I couldn't tell you until now. She's your daughter, Raul. Wanda and I just found out when we were digging up info on Mondra in the cruiser."

"How is that possible?" Raul was lost.

"Well, I can think of a few ways, Raul," the chief said, smirking, "but now's not exactly the time."

Byron pointed to Mondra.

The red witch was frantic now. Raul's kiss had ripped apart the black magic's hold on everyone within the circle. The red mist swirled faster and faster. The exorcism powder Wanda laid in the circle bubbled first, then slowly absorbed the mist, turning it black as it fell to the floor as ash. Thirty seconds later, the mist disappeared.

Mercy's eyes cleared, and her irises regained their color. Her feet returned to the floor.

Mondra was losing control, and the spell wasn't finished. She was so close! Archie's essence was almost completely within Zachary now. Inanis was almost removed from the child and absorbed into her being, but she didn't have enough strength left to complete both of her objectives.

That kiss! It had ruined everything! How in the hell had they found him? After all these years, how did they know? She didn't recognize him. It was so long ago, that night in the boathouse. The night she'd chosen her path of self-satisfaction at all costs. A cost which had included putting the child within her up for adoption. She never knew what became of her baby, nor did she care, until the day she needed to find her. The day at the quarry. Nothing was going to stand in the way of the things she wanted. Nothing! But now the situation was desperate. She had to choose. Delilah's mother was behind her and ready to pounce. She could feel it.

In that moment, the choice crystallized in her mind. She tightened her grip on Mercy's hand, but it was weak. Sensing the time running out, Mondra released Archie and Zachary from the spell and focused on capturing the demon within Delilah. She used the remaining borrowed strength from Mercy and pulled Inanis from Delilah. The baby coughed uncontrollably and cried.

Joanne could wait no longer. She leaped at Mondra's back, grabbed two fists full of her dress, and flung her backwards and away from the Reiki table. Mondra screamed in frustration, landing on her behind and skidding across the polished black floor and through Wanda's beaded door, finally slamming into the wall of the hallway Mercy had hidden in earlier. She landed with her back against the wall, dazed and clinging to consciousness.

Jo and Henry ran to the Reiki table at the same time. Jo plucked Delilah from the carrier, held her close, and stroked her head, trying to calm her. Henry put his arms around both of them and let out a long sigh of relief.

Wanda knelt over Archie. He was still babbling nonsense. His eyes still had a faraway look. The lights were on, but if anyone was home, he was probably hiding in the basement.

Wanda feared her best friend would never be the same. And if she didn't do something quickly, the damage would probably be irreversible.

"Where's Villitz?" Wanda shouted.

THE RED WITCH

Byron glanced quickly around the room. "I don't know! Haven't seen him since she started that spell and he took off."

"We need him if we're going to bring Archie back."

Raul and Byron fanned out and searched every corner of the Emporium's safe room. Villitz was gone.

CHAPTER 35
MESSAGE IN A BOTTLE

Penny watched from the ether as Zachary sneaked into the church. She returned to her body and rose silently from the floor in Mondra's bedroom. She crept to the doorway and peeked around its frame. Villitz had come back. He seemed more real to her now. More solid. The hood was down and the back of his head was to her. His raven-black hair gleamed in the soft candlelight. She watched as he scuttled about the room, holding a satchel in his left hand and dropping random items into it with his right. Penny stepped into the room.

"We thought you might come back," she said.

Zachary whirled around. "You."

Penny nodded. "Leaving town?"

"Yes, we are," he said.

She tilted her head, "We? I don't see a *we*."

A crooked grin crossed his face. "We can't exactly stay around here, now. Can we?"

"You keep saying we, not I."

"I think you know who I mean," said Zachary.

Penny did. And was prepared for it. She pulled a flask from behind her back. It was pewter, about the size of a liter bottle of vodka. Wanda had brought it with her from the Emporium. She didn't think there would be a need for it, but you never knew. Good old Wanda, never leaving anything to chance.

Wanda had told them all she agreed with Byron that Inanis might indeed be back. And she also agreed he had clung to Delilah's soul as she lay dying on the Emporium's floor.

Inanis had used the flask to trap the soul of a body he'd taken possession of on the battlefield during the Crusades. Once opened by Wanda, the soul had fled to its delayed reward, and the flesh inhabited by Inanis had rapidly decayed, exposing the "immortality" he'd claimed to his followers for the fraud it was.

Henry had branded the demon with its own name, which was engraved on the flask's side, sending the dark spirit to the void where it would disappear forever—a nonentity. At least, that's what Henry had assumed at the time. The flask still held its magical properties; it could still house a soul.

Zachary took his eyes from Penny's. "What's that?"

Now Penny held his gaze with her own crooked grin. "I think you know what it is."

He did. He remembered it from well over three hundred years ago. Part of the soul it had once contained was the reason he was still around. Zachary dropped the satchel and ran through the door leading out to the courtyard. Now that he had almost completely "become," he couldn't just flip into the astral plane at will.

He'd slipped out of the Emporium during the commotion and collapse of Mondra's spell. He was incomplete. Archie was not fully part of him yet. He figured it was better to get out of there with a large portion of the soul he believed belonged to him than to take a chance on being captured. Or worse. He could always claim the rest from whatever nursing home they would end up putting Archie in. Part of Zachary felt bad for him, but it was a small part. And, he figured, Archie wouldn't really be dead—more like a conscious part of him he'd be able to control. It would be a nuisance, but it was a small price to pay.

All this ran through his mind as he pounded up the sloped staircase leading away from the chambers secreted within the church. He would miss this place. It was home for over three hundred years. But Salem could no longer be called home. The League of the Moon would never stop looking for him.

The storm still raged outside. Rain pounded down through the canopy of the thirteen trees lining the flagstone walkway. Zachary splashed and careened across the dim yellow light reflecting from the stones. They reminded him of teeth.

He was running full speed toward the portal when he chanced a look behind him. Penny hadn't followed him. That struck him as curious, but he realized it too late as he ran straight into the portal at the end of the flagstone path. The portal he had fashioned to track the members of the League of the Moon. It now glowed gold instead of the pale blue of before. It now held him suspended in midair, helpless, like a fly in a spider's web. Penny's portal.

Zachary struggled to release himself as he glimpsed Penny casually strolling toward him through the rain. The flask was in her left hand, and she tapped it against her thigh as she walked. Rage consumed him as she got closer, and he bombarded her with empty threats. He held no cards here, nothing to barter with, and he knew it. Penny would end him now.

Earlier tonight, he'd thought it would be the child's mother, for she had become more powerful than he could have imagined. He thought he'd known better than Inanis—that he wouldn't make the same kinds of mistakes as his master. And as he thought about it, he realized it was the same overconfidence his master had engaged in, only in a different form. He watched, helpless, as Penny approached to collect for that mistake.

"You and Mondra should have left my brother alone."

"Your brother has *my* soul, not his own!" Zachary screamed.

Penny shook her head. "No, Zachary. You made the deal with Inanis. You should have died back then. You should have let go. You're not any part of Archie's soul now, just a splinter kept alive by stealing the life essence of others. Just like Inanis. No one is meant to live forever. And no one does... well, at least not in one body. We do go on. But there are exceptions to every rule. You and your master broke those rules. What may happen to you after this?" She shrugged. "I don't know. And I really don't give a shit. You'll get what you deserve. Of that much, I'm certain."

Penny opened the flask. Its top glowed a dim orange-red. She tipped the flask in Zachary's direction, walking toward him. Penny took one careful step after the other until it began.

Blue, iridescent orbs rose slowly from every part of Zachary's body, painting the flagstones the color of ice and turning each raindrop surrounding it into an ice-blue dagger. The orbs fled Zachary in an ever-increasing torrent like some bizarre fireworks show for two. Zachary screamed in protest and cursed the members of the League of the Moon by name. He hurled threats and insults at Penny. She yawned. The hooded entity's body became lighter—not brighter—but, Penny noticed, less "there." It was almost gone now. Then, the little glowing blue balls slowed until she watched the last orb containing her brother's essence disappear into the flask. And the last of Zachary Villitz disappeared from the portal.

Penny heard a small, meaty splat when it vanished. She went to the spot where the portal had been. There was just enough light for her to make out the object. It was a little round thing, about the size of a pea. Penny recognized it from her college days. She'd been an excellent student with a photo-retentive memory. It was a pineal gland. She couldn't be sure, but to her, it looked like this one had seen better days. It looked used up. She put it in her coat pocket, stepped through the doorway they'd all come through earlier in the night, walked through the church under the watchful gaze of Jesus, and out the front door.

CHAPTER 36
KISSES FROM A STRANGER

Wanda was worried. Her best friend in the world was running out of time and babbling nonsense. Archie's head rested in her lap and she stroked his forehead, trying to keep him calm. Though his eyes appeared locked with Wanda's, his stare still seemed a thousand miles away.

Mercy was being helped up from the floor by Raul. When Joanne had flung Mondra away from the circle and into the hallway, Mercy had collapsed. Whatever Mondra had done to complete the spell had taken something from her. Something big. Mercy was pale, sweating, and weak. Raul bent and swept his right arm toward her knees and put his left behind her back. He carried her to the Reiki table and laid her on top of it. She coughed out a ragged, "Thank you," then closed her eyes.

Byron had the joyous job of collecting Mondra from the hall. He swept the beads hanging in the doorway aside and stepped through. She wasn't there. A squeaking sound came from his left. He pulled the flashlight from his belt and shone it the length of the hall. Its beam cut through the darkness, reflecting swirling galaxies of dust, and finally landed on the door leading to the front of the store. It was open, swinging slowly back and forth—a giant and menacing finger inviting him forward.

Byron swallowed hard. He felt his pulse quicken and heard the blood rushing through his eardrums. *This is the part where the audience always yells, 'Don't go in there,'* he thought. But this wasn't the movies. He'd faced this situation a thousand times before in his long career on the Salem police force, he reasoned. No need to be afraid. But he was. He wished he could turn the clock back on the last twenty-four hours. Wished with all his heart he hadn't seen the things he'd seen tonight. But he had. And he knew through that door was one pissed off dark witch. With a goddamned demon inside her to boot!

"Fuck me," he whispered.

He moved forward, one leaden footstep at a time, keeping the flashlight locked on the swaying door and straining to hear anything over the pounding blood in his ears. As he reached the doorway, he heard movement in the room beyond. He killed the flashlight. No sense giving away his position. Byron didn't think Mondra was armed, but he wasn't taking any chances. As for weapons of the magical variety, there wasn't a hell of a lot he could do about that.

He knelt and crept up to the counter, using the old-fashioned cash register as cover. Once there, he peeked over the top of the counter and scanned the room. She stood motionless in front of the store's exit, a dark silhouette against the blueish, LED-lit rain falling behind her and tapping the door's glass. Other than her breathing, it was the only sound.

Byron couldn't tell if she was facing in his direction or facing the street. As if reading his mind, her eyes snapped opened. The area around Mondra was instantly bathed in crimson light, and the snakelike pupils locked on Byron's eyes. The effect was immediate, and Byron rose from behind the counter, slowly walked through the swinging counter doors, and moved through the darkness toward her. She was beautiful, and he wanted her.

In a distant part of his mind, a part now fighting a losing battle, he thought of Penny—beautiful, sweet, caring Penny. He felt a trickle of fear when he realized he couldn't remember what she looked like. In the next moment, the fear disappeared, and he couldn't remember her name, or why he'd been afraid. The closer he got to the red witch, the more he wanted her. With every step, a little more of who he used to be slid from his mind, and a little more of what he wanted, what he *had to have*, consumed him.

He stood in front of her, gazing into eyes that seemed to have their own gravity. She reached out her hand and he took it into his. Smiling, she pulled him toward her—he did not resist. *Could not* resist. Mondra reached out her other hand, running the backs of her blackened nails against the side of his neck with a feather's touch, then extending her fingers and riding them up and through the hair on the back of his head. She pulled him in, brushing her lips against his, darting her tongue across his lips, then pulling back. He responded in kind, then took it to another level, unable to stop himself.

Penny stood in the rain, watching. Byron seemed to be in a trance. The man she'd been married to for over two decades had his arms wrapped around a tall redhead with his hands in places they didn't belong. She knew what the situation was and jealousy was the furthest thing from her mind. Tucking the flask tight against her side, she sprinted from her spot at the store's front door and made for the parking lot, bursting through the safe room's door.

Her eyes fell upon Archie and Wanda. She rushed to them, handed the flask to Wanda, and said, "You know what to do."

Wanda was about to say something to Penny when she saw the look in her eyes. "What's the matter, honey?"

"Mondra has Byron. I saw them wrapped together at the front of the store."

In her concern for Archie, Wanda had mostly forgotten about Mondra. "Oh no! You need to get in there right now. Inanis is inside her. He'll kill him!"

Penny turned three shades whiter and stood motionless with shock. Wanda picked up on it and was ready. "Jo, take Penny with you to the front, Mondra has Byron!"

Jo looked up from the Reiki table, then wasted no time. "Take care of her," she said as she handed Delilah to Henry.

He nodded and said, "Go."

Jo didn't wait for Penny to follow her out of the room and through the beaded door. She took off at a sprint. Penny quickly recovered and was on Jo's heels. They ran past the Reiki table where Mercy lay weakened but still conscious.

Raul held his daughter's hand. He saw her eyes following Jo and Penny as they sprinted past her. "Help me up, please," Mercy said.

He looked at her, a dubious expression on his face.

"I'm okay. I have to go in there. Something terrible is about to happen, and I might be able to stop it."

Instinct took over and Raul helped her from the table. He knew the chief had gone after the crazy redhead, but he still had little understanding of what was going on here, so he didn't argue with Mercy.

Wanda watched from across the room. There was nothing she could say to help Mercy. She knew what the girl was about to do, and silently invoked Hecate, hoping the powerful goddess of the crossroads between life and death would not be needed. Better to ask and not need than the other way around. Wanda watched silently as Raul supported Mercy and they both made their way to the back door of the safe room and into the rainy parking lot.

Joanne slowed as she came to the doorway at the end of the hall. Much like Byron had done earlier, Jo reasoned that to burst into the room and announce yourself would be quite the fool's move. And, much like Byron had earlier, she crouched and used the old-fashioned cash register for cover. Penny was right behind her and following Joanne's lead.

Mondra pulled her lips from Byron's. He went to say something, and she covered his mouth with her left hand. Mondra, and the guest within her, both sensed something. She raised her head and swept the room with glowing ruby eyes like some hideous lighthouse from hell. The eyes settled on the area of the cash register and she sensed a presence. Whoever hid there had the aura of a warrior, and the spirit within Mondra was drawn to the possibility of violence. In fact, he craved it.

Jo felt the old, familiar feeling in her mind. Inanis was reaching out to her, trying to read her. It was how he rolled. Icy fingers probed through her thoughts, calling to her. Calling to David, because it recognized her soul. It knew her from long ago, when Joanne was the hunter David—husband to Madeleine during the witch trials, now, in this incarnation, wife to Henry Trank.

David had tried to kill Inanis, known as Dobson Molonos in those days. It hadn't ended well for David. The encounter left a mark on Inanis, however. He'd been impressed with David's ferocity. And the presence he sensed behind the counter could only be that of David. "Come out, David. Or do you prefer Joanne, now?"

Jo stood up behind the counter. Penny remained where she was, realizing instantly her advantage. The demon had only identified Joanne. She would bide her time and make a move when the chance presented itself.

"You can call me the fucking Easter Bunny, for all I care," said Jo.

He laughed, and it sounded like Mondra's laugh. But there was a lower, more guttural and menacing tone underneath. Jo recognized the evil wrapped within the narcissistic witch's tone. "I'll let him live, maybe," said Inanis.

Jo raised an eyebrow. "That's funny. I was just thinking the same thing about you." She took a step forward, testing who was really in control—Mondra or Inanis. The answer came quickly. He spun Byron around, grabbing a fistful of the chief's hair with Mondra's left hand, and yanking his head back to expose the neck. With Mondra's right hand, he pressed her sharp, black fingernails into Byron's jugular vein. Jo stopped.

"Kill this shit stain, Jo," Byron said.

Inanis bellowed laughter. "Look who's back!"

Byron looked a little dazed, and a lot ashamed.

Jo took another step forward.

Inanis put pressure on the jugular. Blood seeped from around Mondra's fingernail. In the darkness, it was a single, black trail winding its way from under Byron's chin, down his neck, and spreading across the collar of his khaki uniform shirt. Jo stopped again.

"One more step, witch, and I open him up."

Jo was well aware Penny had stayed behind. And she'd tested Inanis by moving forward as much as she could, distracting him so Penny could move silently into a position to attack.

The Emporium's counter ran across the back of the store and continued the length of both sides of the room. Penny had first started moving to the right-hand side, then felt a cool rush of air cross her face. She took it as a sign to move in the opposite direction and now crouched behind the counter on the left side of the store and to Mondra's right. The red witch's back was to Penny, and she gave thanks to whoever was looking out for her.

MERCY STOOD A LITTLE STRAIGHTER NOW. The cool rain had somewhat rejuvenated her, but she was still far from all the way back. Raul had held out an elbow for her when they exited the shop's back door and Mercy had looped her right arm through it, holding on to his forearm with her left. They turned the corner and went left out of the parking lot, walked along the store's side, and stopped where the outer wall ended and met Essex Street.

"What are you gonna do now?" asked Raul.

"I need to see what's going on in there," said Mercy. She removed her arms from Raul, crouched down, and crept toward the front of the store. When she got close enough to peek through the window was exactly when things went from bad to worse.

CHAPTER 37
NOT SO INSTANT KARMA

Wanda opened the flask and held it in front of Archie. For the first time in what seemed like forever, life started to return to her best friend's eyes. Glowing blue orbs gently flowed from the flask's mouth and entered Archie's body through the middle of his forehead and slightly above his wiry white eyebrows. They settled lightly on his skin and then melted their way in, like buttery beads of life. The color returned to his face, and he croaked out Wanda's name.

"Shh, honey. Give it a minute. You just came back from God knows where."

He nodded weakly. Archie closed his eyes and took a few deep breaths. A few seconds passed and Wanda could see the pulse in his neck slowing as the body got used to the soul being back home. Then his eyes shot open. "We have to get to Mercy!"

"Mercy just left here with Raul. They went out the back door, which was strange, but I'm sure Mercy knows what she's doing. It would have been nice if she could have recovered a little first, but—"

"No! You don't understand. That wasn't Mercy who just left here!"

"What do you mean?" Wanda asked, icicles of dread forming in her chest.

"Mondra has played everyone for a fool! I saw it all! Zachary was nothing more than a gateway."

"We already know all this—"

"All of this is about Mercy! It'll take too long to explain. Henry, can you help me up?"

Henry was listening to their conversation from the Reiki table, on which he had just laid Delilah in her carrier. She was fast asleep now. He took the carrier from the table as gently as he could, rushed over to his father's side, put the carrier on the floor next to Wanda, and helped Archie to his feet.

"You okay to watch her, Wanda?"

"Of course, sweetie," she said, then turned her face up to Archie. "Are you sure you can handle this right now?"

"I don't have a choice. None of us have a choice," said Archie.

Henry asked, "If that wasn't Mercy who just left here with Raul, then where is she?"

Archie pointed to the only other human being left in the room. Darren Biltmore lay sprawled on the floor. Eyes closed, breath shallow, and moaning quietly.

Wanda held the flask out to Henry. The same flask he'd used to brand Inanis and send him to the void almost a year ago. This time, Henry thought, he's not coming back.

Archie and Henry rushed over to Biltmore. Each grabbed

an arm and dragged him through the beaded door and toward the front of the store.

~

MERCY RECOVERED QUICKLY, Raul thought. It was only a few minutes ago she seemed barely alive. Now, she looked like a cat ready to pounce.

He looked over her shoulder as motion inside the store caught his eye. It was all the distraction she needed. Mercy whirled on Raul and kicked him square in the jaw. Raul stood for a moment, a dazed look on his face, then his legs wobbled and he went down in a heap on the rainy sidewalk.

At the same time Mercy was dispatching Raul, the demon living inside Mondra reacted to that motion caught out of the corner of its eye.

From outside the shop, Mercy saw the cop's wife fly at Mondra, running full force into her and knocking the redhead sideways and into the shop's front door. The frame rattled, glass shattered, and rain blew in sideways in furious sheets through the broken door's window.

Byron was flung into the far corner of the room. He crashed into the counter, knocking over a glass display stand containing gems and crystals. The dazzling display of colored minerals flew in a million different directions, twinkling in the light from the streets. The chief was a crumpled heap in the corner.

Joanne seized the moment. As Inanis, now seemingly in complete control of Mondra's body, was regaining his balance and homing in on Penny, Joanne remembered her lesson from earlier tonight, when her baby had been taken from her. There would be no green fire like before. She hadn't learned to control her new powers enough to trust them yet. It was time to make things up close and personal.

Jo was in motion the moment Penny made her move. At the same time Inanis reached to grab Penny by the throat and gouge her eyes out with Mondra's nails, Jo barreled into the demon-possessed witch. The remains of the door exploded into shards as both Jo and Inanis crashed through it and onto the street outside—an echo of what David had done to this same evil spirit over three hundred years ago.

The two landed at the feet of Mercy. Relief swept over Joanne at the sight of the girl. With the power Mercy had, combined with the newfound powers Jo retained from the girl's touch, the demon wouldn't be a problem. Joanne stood quickly, and said, "Let's finish this bast—"

The last words never left her mouth as Mercy delivered a wicked backhand to the left side of Jo's face, spinning her head hard to the right and staggering her backward and off balance. When Jo regained her footing, she stood with her hands at her sides, too stunned for words. The look of confusion and hurt on her face made Mondra smile through Mercy's face.

"What was it you said to me earlier tonight? Oh, that's right—you said I would regret ever crossing paths with you. Then I said, 'Finished?' And you said, 'I'm just getting started, red.' Still feel the same way? You cocky bitch!"

That confused Jo, but only for a second. "Mondra?" She whispered the question.

Mercy's face smiled, but there was nothing "Mercy" about it.

Now, two displaced and angry souls inched forward on Jo. It was the most scared Joanne had ever been in her life, but she didn't show it. *If this is how I'm supposed to die,* she thought, *then I'm taking at least one of them with me.*

As Jo thought this, Henry crept through the wrecked entrance to Wanda's Wicca'd Emporium. Inanis and Mondra had their backs to him, and Joanne never let on she saw him, never so much as tipped an eye in his direction.

Henry weaved through broken glass. He was now within three feet of the demon's back. He reached out with his left hand and grabbed hold of the demon's right arm, spinning Mondra's body around. The red eyes inhabiting Mondra's skull flamed with anger, then shriveled in fear at the sight of the flask in Henry's hand. Its name glowed brightly on the flask's front.

Joanne needed only a second's distraction to pounce on Mercy. She grabbed her left arm, pulled it behind her back, then yanked up hard, causing the witch within Mercy to scream in pain. Jo said, simply, "I told you you'd regret it."

Henry and Jo spun them around, forcing them back inside the Emporium. Mondra's eyes fell on Biltmore lying on the floor in front of her. She struggled fiercely from within Mercy's body to escape Jo's grasp. Jo rewarded her with a fierce tug of the arm upward, and she yelped in pain.

"Ahh, the Queen of Lies returns," said Archie. "Mercy was supposed to die that day at the quarry, wasn't she? And she did, but not long enough for you to take over."

Mondra stared out through Mercy's face. Anger and hatred radiated from every fiber of her being. Archie thought nothing in the world could look more unnatural. Mercy was kind, sweet, and sincere—almost to a fault. Mondra being inside her was an affront. It was time to set things back the way they belonged.

"So angry." Archie shook his head in mock disappointment. "You played it almost perfect, I'll give you that. And if Penny hadn't been at the church to stop Zachary, who knows?" He shrugged. "Oh, you would have tracked old Zachary down, eventually. I just can't believe you would do what you did to your own daughter!" He seemed to give that some thought. "Nah, scratch that. I can. You are a narcissist's narcissist if I've ever seen one."

"Spare me the high-and-mighty speech, Archie. You're no better than me."

He held up his hands. "Nothing is ever your fault. I get it, Mondra. But what I don't get is why go to all the trouble? Why bring everyone here to do what you did? Why not just do it at the church?" Archie cupped his right elbow in his left hand and chewed a thumbnail, his brow furrowed in thought. He was asking more for himself than Mondra.

Henry said, "I know why."

"Do tell," said Archie.

"The pentacle in the safe room. When Inanis died and latched on to my mother, it happened in there. He left this world from there! It's the only safe place on earth he could return through, because the soul he latched on to also passed from that portal. Spiritually, they were fused together there."

Archie raised an eyebrow. "Yes. That makes sense—for him. But what about me? And Mercy for that—" Archie stopped. He closed his eyes and nodded. When he opened them, he said, "*Everything* happening tonight took place there!" He snapped his fingers, then pointed at Henry. "The night I introduced Mondra to Wanda, we sat and had dinner —or at least tried to—in the center of the room. On the pentacle."

Henry asked, "What happened?"

Archie told him about the events of that night. And of the threat Mondra had made to Wanda.

The last piece of the puzzle was Mercy. Archie said, "Mondra touched Mercy inside the pentacle tonight—and that was on purpose."

Archie turned to Mondra again, "Why Mercy? Why try to take her body as yours?"

Mondra smiled from deep within Mercy, and sang a creepy rendition of a line from the movie *Don't Say a Word*. "I'll never tell."

Wanda appeared almost out of thin air at Archie's side. No one heard her approach, and everyone seemed shocked to see her there. She locked eyes with Mercy. "I know the reason you stole Mercy's body tonight. And I know it was *you* who pushed her from the quarry ledge. The voice she heard from the other side was *yours*."

No one said a word. Everyone but Mondra seemed confused.

Wanda continued, "When Mercy didn't die, and you couldn't capture her soul, you had to find another way. Since you're not nearly powerful enough on your own to perform the spell, someone had to be used to house Mercy's soul, to keep her powers within the loop. That's why you started a relationship with Dr. Biltmore—insurance if Zachary ever figured out how you were using him, which he did. Darren is in the pain he is because two souls—his and Mercy's—inhabit the same body."

"But what about Zachary?" Archie asked.

"Zachary doesn't remember her, Archie." Wanda faced the witch. "You've been rejected by the same soul twice. The love spell you put on Archie is the same spell you tried to put on Zachary in 1692." Wanda shot her a disgusted look and continued, "Zachary doesn't *remember* who you are, and you know that. But *Zachary* remembers who made him what he is. He remembers Inanis is his master, but recalls nothing of his life before Inanis *changed* him, so he reveres him. He wants nothing more than to serve him, and he was more than willing to house a part of Inanis within his newly formed body. You took advantage of that. In a way, I feel sorry for Zachary. He's been nothing more than a zombie for over three hundred years. And Mondra, knowing who he used to be, knew what powers Katherine Andersen was blessed with. That's why she's been after Mercy all this time."

Mondra, her secrets laid bare, seethed within Mercy's body. Jo tightened her grip. Henry held Inanis in place with the threat of the flask. Delilah snoozed on the counter at the back of the room.

Wanda said, "I knew you were a self-centered narcissist the day I met you, but I never thought you'd possess the delusions of grandeur that you do. You want to rival Hecate. You want to challenge her in the three realms."

Archie whistled low. "Yes! I see it now! Hecate is the triple goddess. The guardian of the three realms."

Wanda nodded and smiled. "The Heavens, Earth, and the Underworld. And by taking control of Mercy's soul, she had the heavens, because Mercy has glimpsed heaven. Archie, you would have been under her spell again *and* given her the Earth aspect. Incorporating Inanis would have sealed the final realm—the Underworld. Everything she would have needed to wage war with Hecate. Now that's narcissism on steroids."

"There's still something I don't get," said Archie.

"What's that?" Wanda asked.

"How did Mondra know Mercy would come back with the power she possesses now? It's fairly obvious she tried to kill her that day at the quarry, but she never planned on her being able to come back. How could she?"

"That's where Zachary comes in. He travels the astral plane at will. He was supposed to capture Mercy's soul if and when she died that day. They never counted on the EMTs being able to bring her back so quickly. Thank God for modern medicine. Now remember—Henry, Jo, and I have all touched Mercy at one point and felt we knew her."

Archie nodded.

"Mercy was supposed to become part of the League of the Moon back in 1692," said Wanda, "but in the early morning hours on the day of her initiation, Henry Wandell—my last incarnation—was executed, so the initiation never happened. It's why I had no idea Mercy, much like Henry, would need protection in *this* incarnation. Now, follow me here. We already know you were Zachary, Archie. That leaves Mercy. Who was Mercy? It turns out she was a widower named Katherine Andersen, who just so happened to speak to David earlier that day, as Henry reminded me a week or so after the events of last Halloween. Since she is the only one left who was of any concern to Inanis on that day, it only makes sense she's the last of the League of the Moon unaccounted for.

"What was so special about Katherine?" asked Archie.

"Two very important things. Zachary and Katherine were lovers, and Katherine was a housekeeper for Dobson Molonos, aka Inanis. Katherine, as we know now, was also a potent witch, blessed by Hecate herself with the power of augmentation on the condition she spy on Inanis.

"When David came to Katherine's home on All Hallows

Eve, she told him of the trunk where Inanis kept his most prized secret—the flask. Once Inanis returned home that night and saw it was missing, he went to Madeleine and David's home to arrest them. On finding neither of them at home, his followers torched the place. Madeleine fled to the forest, where she was caught and killed. David came upon his burning home and followed Madeleine's tracks into the woods. He confronted Inanis and was killed. Later, just before dawn, Inanis and his followers raided the home of Katherine Andersen. They tortured a confession out of her and hanged her in the town common later that day. Zachary was beaten within an inch of his life, then spared by Inanis once he agreed to do his bidding—which was nothing more than an insurance policy should anything happen to the soul within the flask. Inanis flayed his soul, leaving only enough to keep him alive by consuming the third eye essence of other beings. That's what the pineal gland business was all about."

"We have to set this right, and it has to be right now," said Archie.

Wanda nodded. "Already a step ahead of you."

"Wow, Katherine Andersen! You gave birth to the soul who'd bring you down," Jo said. "Karma's a bitch, ain't it?"

CHAPTER 38
EXITS

Wanda pulled a small bag from her robes. It was made of black velvet with a gold rope sash running through its top. The rope was pulled from both ends to seal the bag shut. On its face was embroidered a pentacle in a gold ring. It looked exactly like the pentacle on the floor in her safe room, save for ash smeared across its front.

Shortly after Henry and Archie had dragged Biltmore from the room, Wanda pieced together everything. Given that Archie had located Mercy within Biltmore, it could *only* be Mondra inside Mercy now. Wanda reasoned the ash from the exorcism powder could reverse the effects of Mondra's spell. Its existence was all the evidence she needed.

A typical Mojo Bag is filled with herbs, minerals, or other items with magical properties, usually adding up to an odd number. The person the bag is intended to help writes instructions, prayers, or a name on a piece of paper, then puts it in the bag. Intentions are whispered into the bag for the desired outcome, then the bag is sealed and carried by the person hoping to attract whatever they desired. But Wanda found a new use for it.

She'd filled the bag with the ash, held it over a smoldering stick of dragon's blood incense, and then dropped a piece of paper in the bag (the third ingredient) with one simple word written in Romanian on the paper—*Inversa*—meaning reverse. She opened the bag and dabbed her left index finger into it—Wanda believed magic always needed to be done with the left hand (the magic hand) when possible—and bent over Darren Biltmore. She drew a pentacle on his forehead and his body shuddered.

She looked next at Henry. "Keep that flask as close as you can to Mondra's body, if Inanis so much as flinches, bury that flask right between his eyes."

Henry nodded and held the flask as close as he could to the redhead. The demon's eyes held his with nothing but pure hatred. But it knew better than to move. Wanda walked over and traced another pentacle on its forehead, dead center where the pineal gland rested a few short inches away.

She next turned toward Mercy. "Jo, hold her tight," said Wanda.

Joanne kept Mercy's left arm pinned behind her back, then swung her free arm across Mercy's chest, reinforcing the hold. The witch within Mercy struggled to get free, but was no match for Joanne, who had six inches, thirty pounds, and a shitload of pent-up anger on her.

Wanda waited patiently until the strength ebbed from Mercy's body, and defeat finally leaked its way out from eyes that didn't belong. Wanda drew the final pentacle in the same spot as the other two. She stepped backward and away from Mercy until she was equally distant from all three pentacles she'd drawn.

The white witch then closed her eyes, lifted her arms to the heavens, and said, "As above"—then lowered her arms until they were parallel with the floor—"and on earth"—and finally let her arms drop so her fingertips pointed directly at the floor—"and like below, goddess show these three the way to go." She opened her eyes. "Inversa!"

The results startled her. After hearing Joanne's green fire story, she shouldn't have been surprised, but to see the magic she'd always practiced visibly manifest in this world left her breathless. Mercy had brought something miraculous across the veil, and Wanda only hoped others wouldn't pervert it.

Directly in front of Wanda, a ball of light formed. It cycled from red, to green, to blue, and back to red. The orb was extremely bright, and the colors pulsed in rapid succession, painting the entire room and the street outside. Tendrils of electricity shot from the ball and connected dead center with the pentacles Wanda had drawn. Once the tendrils connected, the ball in the middle became a muddy brown as the colors blended together, and then each tendril turned its own individual color as souls returned to their rightful homes.

Mondra's body connected to red, Biltmore's to a faint and shaky blue, and Mercy's to green. All three shuddered violently for a short time, then became still.

Joanne held on to Mercy as she went limp. Biltmore's eyes closed and he became still, appearing to be asleep. Mondra fell to one side, only to be scooped up into Henry's waiting arms. He laid her on the floor.

The Emporium was silent. Everyone watched the

bodies... waiting. Rain fell through the gaping hole in the wrecked front door. The air crackled with the electricity of anticipation.

There was a stirring in the shop's corner. In all the excitement, everyone had forgotten about Byron and Penny. The chief leaned on his wife, and they walked over to stand next to Joanne. Byron really had taken a liking to Jo, and with all this magical hoo-hah going on, he felt safest next to her. Jo sensed this, and she smiled to herself.

Mondra was the first to awaken. Everyone watched her with a wary eye. Byron wanted to make sure there wouldn't be a problem with her. He moved her way, then Penny grabbed his arm.

"I'm okay, baby," Byron said.

"Are you sure, By? You were out cold for a long time." Penny looked worried.

He bent down and kissed her cheek, smiling. "I'm sure."

Penny let him go. He had just started across the room when he felt a hand whack him on the ass. "Go get her, sugar lips!"

He whipped around. Jo was smiling at him and Penny was biting the heel of her hand, trying not to laugh. Byron looked to Henry for help. Henry smiled and shook his head. "Welcome to my world, Chief."

Byron was grateful the room was still somewhat dark as he felt the blood rush to his face. He made his way over to Mondra, flipped her on her stomach, and cuffed her.

"You fucking peasants!" Mondra said through gritted teeth, "I'll make every one of you pay for this—"

Byron put his heel gently but firmly on the back of her head and pushed her face into the floor. She wriggled wildly, her body a declaration of outrage. When she realized, after a fair amount of time, Byron wasn't about to let her up, she calmed.

"Listen here, lady. I don't know what you think you are, but in my eyes, you're a common fuckin' kidnapper. You might wanna shut that ever-lovin' trap of yours right now. It might go easier on you when you're in front of the judge," Byron snapped. "You copy?"

Mondra said nothing. Byron looked over at Jo and Penny. Joanne gave him a nod and a smile that showed she was impressed. Penny gave him the same face, extending her arms and clapping quietly.

Mercy was the next to awaken. Wanda rushed over and knelt down to help her up.

"Why does my head feel like it's been bounced around in a clothes dryer?" asked Mercy.

Wanda said, "Well, it's been bounced around. But not exactly in a dryer."

"Huh?"

"Never mind that now, honey. Are you okay to stand?"

"I'll give it a try, Ms. Hein—Wanda."

Wanda smiled, and a tear leaked from her left eye. Mercy was back. All the way back. The poor girl had been through hell.

Henry asked, "What about him?" And nodded at the floor in Darren Biltmore's direction.

Archie said, "That's where Inanis is. You know what to do, Henry."

Henry nodded. He took the flask from his back pocket and knelt over Biltmore, shaking him awake. Biltmore looked up at Henry, then frantically around the room, trying to understand why he was on the floor, in the dark, surrounded by strangers. He caught Archie's eye.

"Love? What the hell is going on here?" Biltmore demanded.

Archie frowned. "You don't remember any of what happened?" He didn't believe the guy, but if he was lying, he was sure putting on an Academy Award performance.

"He won't remember anything," said Mondra. Byron had removed his boot heel from the back of her head. And she'd remained uncharacteristically quiet for the time being.

"Why's that?" Wanda asked.

"The love spell was obliterated. He won't remember a thing, which was how I intended it to be from the start," said Mondra. "I mean, look at the guy. You think I wanna be stuck with that?"

Wanda just shook her head in disgust.

Henry asked, "Archie, What about Inanis?"

Archie nodded, indicating he wanted Henry to hit Biltmore with the flask. It would stun Darren for a bit, but it couldn't be helped.

Henry leaned down and grabbed the back of Darren's head, then brought the flask forward, pressing it to the man's forehead. He grabbed Henry's arm, trying to push it away. Henry held firm.

"What the fuck are you doing to me?" Biltmore demanded.

"Just hold still. We're trying to save your life," said Henry.

"Save my life? From what? Get this fucking thing off of me!"

Henry held on for a while longer. Biltmore complained and struggled. Archie and Wanda exchanged worried glances.

"He's not there, Archie!" Wanda said.

"Where the hell could he be?" Archie asked.

A flutter of panic seized Joanne. "The baby! No, no, no! Not again!" She took off for the back of the store, near the register. Everyone in the room followed, leaving Mondra and Biltmore behind and forgotten, for the moment. Joanne reached the carrier first. Delilah was safe and sound, snoozing away. Jo let out a heaving sigh of relief, and Henry hugged her.

As the League of the Moon stood around the child, the sound of an engine starting reached their ears. It came from behind the store. They heard tires squeal on the rain-slicked asphalt, and followed the noise of the roaring engine as it made its way toward Essex Street from the right-hand side of the store. And then watched as headlights painted the bushes on the opposite side of the street.

Brakes squealed. A car skidded to a stop in front of the store. It was Raul's cruiser. Raul was in the front seat, staring straight ahead. Aaron Hendricks kicked open the back door, and Mondra, still cuffed behind the back, bent low and bolted for it, diving in and scrambling to a seated position. Hendricks leaned over her and pulled the door shut, then kissed her. It wasn't a peck on the cheek, either. Raul turned his head toward the store, smiling. His eyes glowed bright red. Then they were gone.

CHAPTER 39
THE END ... OF THE BEGINNING

Tuesday morning dawned bright and sunny. The rain had stopped in the wee hours of the morning and the members of the League of the Moon had all gone their separate ways after what turned out to be a good news, bad news kind of night.

Delilah was safe, happy, healthy, sleeping, and demon free. But now there were three psychos on the loose, and it wouldn't be long before they would have to deal with them again.

Henry and Joanne exited the elevator, turned the corner, and ran into Mrs. Greenblatt.

"You two look like you've been Jell-O wrestlin' with a grizzly bear! And what the hell are you doin' cartin' around that little one at five a.m.?"

Henry smiled at her. He couldn't really be mad. It was just her awkward way of showing him and Joanne she cared.

"It's a long story, Mrs. G.," Henry said.

"Oh, I'll bet. Nothin' good happens after eleven at night. Nothing!"

Joanne turned the key in the lock, signaling to Henry it was time to go in. He was grateful for that, and relieved Jo didn't turn around and engage Mrs. Greenblatt. He was pretty sure she would have ripped Mrs. G. a new one. Henry was definitely the calmer one in the marriage.

Once inside, Joanne fell face first onto the couch and was snoring less than two minutes later. Henry laughed, took Delilah into her room, and laid her in the crib. She hadn't opened her eyes once since he'd taken her from the Reiki table inside Wanda's Wicca'd Emporium. He thanked his higher power for that, crawled into bed, and didn't open his eyes until 3:13 p.m. later that day. And *that* was only because his iPhone chirped.

He sat up, rubbed his eyes until he could see straight, and saw the text on his screen. Byron wanted to meet up later today at the Cracked Cauldron.

ARCHIE WASN'T AS fortunate as his son and daughter-in-law. He had classes today. He told Annie he would be late and to shift things around if she could. Annie was nothing if not great at her job. She'd rearranged Archie's entire schedule and made it so things wouldn't get rolling until after 11:30 a.m.

He arrived at the U at 10:25 a.m., said good morning to Annie, and took his muffin and coffee into his office. No sooner had he sat down when the phone on his desk rang. He picked up the receiver.

"DB on line two, Arch. You want me to blow him off?"

Archie closed his eyes and pinched the bridge of his nose. He sighed. "No, Annie, it's okay. Put him through."

Click.

"What can I do for you, Darren?"

"I, um—what the hell happened to me last night, Archie?"

Archie? DB had *never* called him by his first name. Ever.

"Well, do you remember anything? Anything at all, Darren?"

There was silence on the other end of the line. Archie was wondering if Biltmore had hung up when he finally said, "I remember waking up on the floor of that store. That guy tried to plant something in my forehead—"

"That was my son, Henry. He was actually trying to save your life. I know that's hard to believe, but it's true."

"I know," said Biltmore.

"You do?" Archie asked, surprised.

"Yeah. Bits and pieces of the last few days are coming back. I know that crazy redhead did something to me. And I remember something happening in a room with a shiny black floor, but what I remember most was the dreams from last night. You know, I don't really believe in all that spiritual stuff you talk about. At least, I didn't—"

Archie sat up in his chair. He'd had a lot of problems with DB over the years, but he wasn't about to shit all over a man who seemed to be on the edge of an epiphany. "What's changed, Darren? What was in your dreams?"

"Memories. They weren't my own. They were all over the place. Different people, different times. Hideous things. Some from the witch trials, some from a time before that. Some from now. Violent shit. It scared the hell out of me. Anyway, enough of that stuff. That's not exactly why I called."

Archie's heart fell. He thought Darren was close to

changing his stripes. Maybe on the verge of accepting something larger than himself. At Biltmore's change in tone, he was prepared for another speech on how the man wanted to rescind his funding, or how he thought Archie's class was a joke. What he got instead floored him.

"I'm not exactly sure what happened to me. But I know you are. And I realize now the stuff I've said about your class before was off the mark. I think we can help each other out. I want to combine our budgets. I want to bring quantum physics together with parapsychology. What do you think?"

Archie stared at the statue of Hecate on his desk, smiling.

JOANNE WAS CLEANING the floor behind the counter of the Cracked Cauldron coffee bar. It was seven o'clock in the evening and twilight was drawing its silvery curtain down over Salem. The shop had been closed since six. Henry sat across the counter from her, nursing an iced coffee. Delilah cooed in the carrier, sitting atop the counter in front of him. They were waiting for Byron and Penny.

The bell over the door dinged and, right on time, Byron and Penny walked in. Penny hugged Henry, Byron shook his hand. Joanne hopped over the counter, smiled, and gave Penny a fierce hug. She turned to Byron. He smiled, gave her a big hug, and said, "Sugar lips, huh?"

They all laughed.

Henry said, "Let's go in the back. Jo already has coffee set up for us."

Penny and Byron went to the end of the counter and through the beaded doorway. Byron leaned back through the beads and looked at Joanne as he held a strand of beads in one hand. "Seriously? Isn't one beaded doorway in Salem enough?"

Jo smiled and shrugged. "What can I say? I'm into the retro thing."

Byron shook his head, then winked at her. Penny yanked him back through the beads.

When they were seated, Byron spoke first. "They found the cruiser abandoned out west off of Route 2 in Athol. Someone reported a crimson Dodge Challenger stolen from one of the streets near a place called Lake Ellis."

"Athol? That's what—like a hundred miles from here?" asked Jo.

"'Bout seventy, give or take," said Byron.

Henry asked, "What the hell's out that way?"

Byron said, "Beats the shit outta me. I know there's a tool factory out there. What else?" He shrugged. "I'm not sure. I wanted to meet here tonight because I wanna make sure we're all on the same page about this."

Jo gave him a serious look. "*Are* we on the same page about this?"

Byron looked her in the eyes, then looked down at his hands. What he was about to say was hard for him. But say it he must. "You know, I thought you all were nuts. I thought Wanda was crazy as a loon. And the stuff Henry was tellin' me the other night—I thought it could all be explained logically, and that *Henry* was maybe losin' his marbles. I'm a cop. It's how I was trained to think. Evidence is king. Well, I saw the evidence last night. Shit, I'm exhibit A now. What that thing was able to make me do..." He trailed off.

Henry said, "I get it, Chief. Like I said before, I *was* where you *were*. So don't sweat it."

Byron nodded, relieved. He said, "Penny thinks there's a

way to find them. And we talked it over at the house. It's a good idea. It'll work."

Jo asked, "What's your idea?"

Penny reached into her shirt pocket and pulled out a Ziploc bag. She laid it on the table in front of Henry and Joanne.

"What is it?" Henry asked.

"When I took out Zachary, this fell on the ground. I almost didn't see it at first, but it made a little splat when it landed. It's the only thing left of him. It's his pineal gland."

Jo stared at it, then looked up at Penny. "So? What can we do with *that*?"

Penny smiled. "You *do* realize where this thing has been and who it's been around, right?"

WANDA WAS in the back room of the Emporium. The workers had left for the day after fixing the front door and replacing the glass stand Byron had been hurled into and broken. The store was closed for the day, and she sat at the center of the safe room in her beanbag chair. An identical black leather beanbag chair sat empty across from her and a cup of chamomile tea steamed on the floor at its side.

Mercy had finished replacing the items in the repaired case at the front of the store, wished the construction workers a good night, and strolled into the safe room, taking her seat across from Wanda.

"Mmm," said Mercy as she closed her eyes and sipped.

"Indeed," said Wanda.

"Oh, there was some mail up front for you. Mostly the usual stuff—lights, gas, stock invoices. But there was this weird envelope on top. It just has your name on it, and there's a red wax seal on the back holding it shut." She handed the pile of mail to Wanda.

Wanda put the regular mail aside, placed her tea on the floor beside her, and examined the strange envelope.

Mercy was right, just her name. No imprint on the seal and nothing remarkable at all aside from the seal itself. Wanda opened the letter and began reading...

Dear Ms. Heinze,

My name is Armand Moreland. We know someone in your coven has used overt magical power on the streets of Salem. In a world filled with cameras at every corner, this is unacceptable. How this occurred is of great concern to us. Should it happen again, there will be consequences. We are watching.

The Council of the Realms.

Mercy saw the look on Wanda's face. "What's the matter, Wanda?"

She handed the note to Mercy. When Mercy finished reading, she placed the note on the floor next to her beanbag chair. Wanda watched her reaction. It was not what she expected.

She held Wanda's gaze. A serious look crossed her face. Mercy said, "We need to talk."

FROM THE AUTHOR

Thanks for reading *The Red Witch*: League of the Moon Book 2. I hope you had as much fun reading it as I had writing it.

Full disclosure: I thought I would release this book in the late spring to early summer of 2021. The world had other ideas. I don't have to mention the big one. We all know about that and, for sure, no one wants to hear more about it.

Then, as I was just starting to really pound out the chapters, my landlord dropped the bomb on us; he was selling the house. We had twenty-plus years of living stored in the cellar and our apartment, so there went that summer!

We spent our weekends looking all over Massachusetts and New Hampshire for a house we could afford. Finally, at the end of October, we found one and spent the next month getting ready for the move.

By December 2020, we were in, but there was a *lot* of work to be done. I wrote whenever I had a spare moment. I wrote in the car. I wrote after work. I wrote on the weekend... you get the idea. And then there were the characters—old *and* new—who decided they were going to do things I never intended them to do. In particular, Mondra just kept moving in a direction I never intended, but that's how it goes sometimes.

I don't outline my stories and I don't plan my characters or their actions. They literally just walk on stage in my head and start doing shit! They get on my nerves sometimes, but somehow it seems to work out in the end. I wouldn't have it any other way.

Again, thank you so much for reading my book.

Happy reading!

Rob.

Next in the League of the Moon Series

vinci-books.com/bloodmagic

A terrifying dream. A cryptic message. A mysterious death.

As the haunting echoes of a nightmare fade, Henry tries to shake them off. But nothing in Salem is ever that simple.

Turn the page for a free preview...

PREVIEW OF BLOOD, MAGIC & MERCY

CHAPTER 1 — PREPARING THE STAGE

The area was ready. He'd chosen it long ago—before they'd named it. Few knew its history. The name of the area, in historical terms, had existed for less than the blink of an eye. In mortal terms, it was almost a hundred years old. The irony of the name was timeless.

What would take place here, a few short days from now, was inevitable; he'd made certain.

Even when you could see the future, you never really knew for sure. You made your best guesses and planned accordingly. The future *was* predictable—to a point. Still, people reacted in ways you couldn't predict.

He'd always seen well beyond time's horizon, but it was like seeing a vast forest from far away. A huge green blob that loomed in the distance. Individual trees emerged only when the distance was closed. It had taken almost nine hundred years for the first trees to separate from the pack—

the first hint of their soul grouping coalescing. Souls he'd need to get the job done.

Everything went according to plan. Right until two days ago. When someone who wasn't supposed to know what was happening stuck his nose in where it didn't belong. He'd have to watch him now. Guide him. Arranging it so those who knew and loved him played their parts. There was much to do and scant time to do it.

The Red Witch looked out from the bell tower's opening. She couldn't see him, of course, but he ducked back into the forest all the same.

As he eased into the tree line, he backed himself against the enormous trunk of a maple. He noticed the missing arms of the crucifixes atop the twin spires at the front of the church, and wondered why they were missing. Then dismissed it as simple vandalism.

It would begin tonight. The guardian would be the first sacrifice. But not the last.

vinci-books.com/bloodmagic

About the Author

Robert Sanborn lives in north central Massachusetts with his wife, Diana, their sweet-natured dog, Coco, the Brussels Griffon, their psychotic black cat Luna, the Devon Rex, Jason, the extremely talkative African-Grey Parrot, Angus, the cranky Quaker Parrot, Artemis, the cute-as-hell Java Finch, and two Parakeets named Sweetie and Sunny. He spends a lot on pet food.

Oh, yeah. And a Crested Gecko Lizard named Gretel. Sheesh!

He is a survivor of Hodgkin's Lymphoma, diagnosed in 1993.

He has been clean and sober since September 24, 1991.

His first book, *In Your Dreams*, was written and published in July, 2020, during the event which shall not be named, and between making deliveries to health care facilities as part of his day job. Not nerve-racking at all.